Chorus Endings

David Warwick

Chorus Endings

You live your life forward…
Understand it backwards

Matador
9 Priory Business Park,
Wistow Road, Kibworth Beauchamp,
Leicestershire. LE8 0RX
Tel: 0116 279 2299
Email: books@troubador.co.uk
Web: www.troubador.co.uk/matador
Twitter: @matadorbooks

ISBN 978 1785892 035

British Library Cataloguing in Publication Data.
A catalogue record for this book is available from the British Library.

Printed and bound by CPI Group (UK) Ltd, Croydon, CR0 4YY
Typeset in 11pt Minion Pro by Troubador Publishing Ltd, Leicester, UK

Matador is an imprint of Troubador Publishing Ltd

To: Andrew, Eve, Peter, Richard, Susi and Vee;
the friends of West Dean Writer's Circle.

Just when we're safest, there's a sunset-touch,
A fancy from a flower-bell, someone's death,
A chorus-ending from Euripides,
And that's enough for fifty hopes and fears...
The grand Perhaps

Robert Browning
Bishop Blougram's Apology

This curious stock in the Meon Valley is supposed to have descended from the Jutes... Everybody thinks them rather curious, both in looks and manner, quite different from us true-blue Hampshire.

Sydney R. Jones, England South, London, Studio Publications, 1948, p. 128

Prologue

Liverpool, 1941

They came early that night. Sweeping in over the balloons tethered in a protective curtain around the city. Heinkels for the most part, some 400 of them. First, the high altitude Pathfinders, laying a carpet of flares and incendiaries to illuminate the target area. Behind and beneath them, the main force. Altitude 7000 feet, within the range of anti-aircraft fire now. Harried by the fighters, some swinging off-course towards a decoy Liverpool, in flames apparently, to the west. The rest delivering their payload - bombs, parachute mines, further incendiaries - ninety tons of high explosives on shipping, factories and warehouses in the estuary below. The residential areas of Birkenhead and Wallasey also. Three hundred and fifty bombs, he read later, sixty mines, 270 incendiary groupings. Six hundred and thirty-one dead, a similar number badly injured; over 500 houses destroyed.

The men clearing the debris alongside him said nothing, but he felt their resentment. It had been like that from the outset; each having a genuine reason for being there: firemen, ambulance drivers, those who had failed their medical or were prevented on one ground or another from taking a pro-active part in the war. He alone having to be drafted in. 'Conchie' they called him, not bothering to learn his real name, nor his reason for refusing to enlist, few of them searching further than cowardice for an explanation. All might have been well if his objections had been on religious grounds. Some all-embracing theory regarding the brotherhood of man might have won them round. But talk of the inviolability of individual conscience, the 'establishment's war' (had he really said that to the Board?) would have meant as little to them as it was beginning to mean to him. Fine at a distance, to refute the folly by withdrawing from it. Different entirely when viewed up-close, frame by frame; living the actuality rather than thinking the concept.

A threadbare exegesis; it was the individual tragedies that returned to haunt him. The woman who'd flung her baby from a topmost window; the severed hand he'd found among the rubble; blackened nursery rhyme paper; Three Blind Mice and Ride-a-Cock-Horse peeling off the wall; a splintered cot spilling out among the wreckage in the street below. The Anderson shelter, together with a family, their neighbours and the vegetable patch they'd been tending, all of it blown apart. Above all, the man he'd found in his kitchen a few days earlier.

A noise in the early hours had brought him downstairs to find the stranger crouched beside the fridge, its contents scattered over the floor, milk dripping from one of the upper shelves. A dishevelled figure, hair matted with sweat, speech slurred but well-spoken. Very frightened, with hands shaking as he raised them to shield his eyes from the torchlight; the ill-fitting suit stained and ripped in places; his fingernails black with grime. To be pitied rather than feared. Above all, needing to be fed.

As they ate he'd taken stock of the situation. The intruder meant him no harm. Fortunate that. Wiry and emaciated the man might have been, but tall; still able to handle himself, and there were few left in the building he could call upon for help. At least age would have been on his side in a struggle, by twenty years or more if appearance was anything to go by. It was not, his visitor – it transpired – being six months his junior. An officer, lately from the war zone, first separated from his regiment then caught up in the general retreat. Quite obviously a deserter. Or an enemy interloper, the kind they'd been warned about. Not that he'd challenged the man, nor had there been need to do so. Once he'd slept, had a bath, changed into the only clean clothing that fitted – some spare fire-fighting uniform kept at readiness in the wardrobe – he'd been only too willing to talk, in a stumbling manner, incoherent at times, yet eager to share his misfortunes with a total stranger. As if by doing so he could be rid of them.

It was always assumed he'd be a soldier, the intruder told him; taken for granted, for as long as he could remember. A tradition that ran in the family and, lest he forget, there were albums filled with faded photos, framed prints of men in uniform, medals displayed in velvet cases, to remind him of the fact. The prospect had not daunted him. Nor had the training: marching and counter-marching, lectures on leadership and battlefield strategy, long nights of simulated warfare between mock battalions out there on Salisbury Plain. Nothing, though, had prepared him for the gut-wrenching terror he felt the first moment they'd set foot abroad, increasing as they advanced into enemy territory, paralysing him completely the moment they came under fire.

Up to then he'd coped, given orders in a confident manner, had been able to set an outward example at least. Now, with the eyes of his men upon him, eagerly awaiting some response, he froze, unable to think or to act. The sergeant it was who stepped forward, had hurried them under cover, summoning up the counter-attack. Who'd brought him tea in a tin mug, spoke affectionately, assured him these were symptoms common to all subalterns. Unexpected and completely at variance with the man's raucous barrack-room manner. Surprising also, the NCO unfastening the medallion from around his neck and handing it over. St Christopher carrying the Christ-child to safety over a raging torrent, given to him by his mother before she died. He'd refused at first, but the sergeant was adamant and, from that moment, had become a father-figure; keeping the young officer always in his sight, providing medication that saw him through the worst of the bombardments, helping him avoid the action whenever possible as, with communications down, they fell back from position after position, continuously under fire, taking heavy casualties as they went. Remember the St Christopher, the sergeant had told him; the words inscribed on the reverse: *Vade Mecum – Constant Companion*. They'd come through this together.

But they hadn't. The end came at dusk one evening, holed up in woodlands, pinned down by sniper fire; he ridden with guilt, the men battle-weary and fractious, becoming increasingly suspicious. The sergeant merely smiled, passed the mess can across, took a shot through the neck, lay spluttering at his feet. No paralysis on this occasion. Revulsion rather. And fear. Pure, primitive, undiluted. Propelling him up and out of the bunker. Zig-zagging through a hail of bullets. Abandoning helmet and rifle, before collapsing down into a ravine. Screaming all the way.

Just how he made it back to England was far from clear. Part bluff, part bribery; a good knowledge of French, some German and the assistance of collaborators en route. Ingenuity and a large helping of luck also. Followed by life continuously on the run, living hand-to-mouth, forever frightened, suspicious of all those around him. But staying well clear of home territory. No one had witnessed his flight; better his family knew nothing of it. 'Lost in action' they'd have been told. '"Some corner of a foreign field that is for ever England"'. The stranger smiled ruefully and, by way of proof, pushed the medallion across the table to where Conchie sat sipping the last of his tea. Hardly conclusive, such items were obtainable anywhere. Picked up from the battlefield even, accounting for the chain, which had snapped. Spies, so they said, came in many guises, nuns on bicycles being the running joke.

Playing for time, he'd promised to think matters over, do nothing till a full recovery had been made, hoping that by then, spy or no spy, the man would surely have made his escape.

In the meantime, he must return to work. A metal helmet, purloined from the stores, would offer some protection should the worst happen. The stranger, huddled down in a corner, comatose almost, convinced that it would. He caught himself envying the man. Freed, at a stroke, to remake his life. Loss of face, position, the regard of others, family even, a small price to pay for independence; jettisoning forever the restrictions of what, for Conchie, had become a jaded domesticity. The moment passed. He said nothing, merely fetched the helmet from the cupboard, strapped his watch to the other man's wrist, promising that, whatever happened, he'd be back within the hour. And he'd get the medallion's chain repaired so it could be worn around the neck once more.

The Heinkels beat him to it. Some 400 of them. Diverted to a decoy Liverpool west of the city – starfish they called it – they'd flattened Wallasey. Shipping, factories and warehouses. The residential area also. Six hundred and thirty-one dead, the stranger among them. Watch and helmet smashed, remnants of the uniform he'd borrowed melded to a body burnt beyond recognition. A fate that both men might have suffered but for that five-minute delay in dismissing the squad; the moments spent, a few yards only from the doorstep, unbuttoning his tunic in search of the keys, remembering he'd lent them to the deserter. The flash projecting his shadow, instantaneous and enormous, onto the wall opposite; the blast, felt rather than heard, spinning him round. In time to catch the fireball rolling, phoenix-like skywards. Grasped by some invisible hand, flung backwards into the smouldering bushes. Coming to – ten minutes, ten hours later? – to hear familiar voices. 'Conchie,' they were saying, 'it's Conchie's house.' He struggled to get upright, tried to call out but no sound came. 'Still in there. What's left of him.' A scrabbling among the wreckage. He fell back exhausted.

Later still: a spattering of rain, men heaving bricks, masonry, charred rafters aside. The body found. Comments, reaching him from a great distance, a chasm, so it seemed. 'Not such a bad chap.' 'Kept himself to himself.' 'Stoic.' 'Pity we didn't get to know him better.' He heard them called away, shuffling off through the debris. 'Wrong-headed, that's all.' And they were gone. His strength returned. Raising himself painfully up, he peered through the foliage. The house had been wrecked, one crenulated wall upright, the others reduced to rubble. Plaster, bricks, broken glass strewn everywhere; two pieces of charred wood tied together to form a rough cross. Marking the spot where they'd found the body? The stranger – his houseguest – the interloper, of course. And Conchie gone with him. Remembered with greater affection by his colleagues than ever he'd earned during his time among them.

Two deaths for the price of one. He dozed, stirred, slept once more, then woke to birdsong and the realisation as to precisely what this meant. Overnight, his dream had become a reality. Anonymity; the freedom to go where he liked, do as he wished. So why did he feel responsible for what had happened? There'd hardly been time to get to know the man; he'd neither invited him into the house, nor scheduled the raid that had killed him. And the guilt. As if he'd conjured up the whole episode. Willed that particular plane to drop that specific bomb on that precise building at exactly that moment. Achieving the independence that now was his. Not that he'd get far in his condition, on the remnant of last week's wages. Gingerly he felt in his pockets. Two ten-shilling notes, four half-crowns, a handful of copper. And the medallion. Cheap, mass-produced, hardly worth the chain on which it now hung, pirouetting; catching the morning sun as it did so.

A magic charm when all was said and done. Lent a certain cachet by the church, but no more efficacious than a clover leaf, rabbit's foot, or lucky birthstone. Constant Companion, yet dispensed with so readily by the sergeant, who'd been killed in action a few days later. The mother dead, too, no sooner than she'd parted with it. As was the deserter, lying out there among the ruins. Whilst he, with the St Christopher safe in his pocket, had survived. He'd never been superstitious, but the medallion's pedigree spoke for itself. From around him came the sounds of the old world awakening. *Vade Mecum*: literal translation, *Go with me*. A stronger chain would be required, that much was certain. And to put as much mileage as possible between himself and the man they'd called Conchie.

Part One

Every Story Tells a Picture

Chapter One

Fiddlers Three

You live your life forward; understand it backwards – that's what they tell me. And I'd go along with it. It's one thing to have witnessed betrayal and espionage, treachery and insanity, attempted murder even, when not yet into your 'teens. Quite another for them to have passed you by. There'd been clues of course, and I might have spotted them – if I'd paid a little more attention to what was going on around me. Had I not watched without seeing; heard rather than merely listening to what I was told. And who knows, I might even have remained ignorant to this day, but for ten minutes of a television programme, caught almost by accident, some thirty years down the line.Which is as good a starting-point as any…

…Harrogate, 1985: an autumn evening mid-way through my university career; Helen just beginning her own as a librarian. No longer my student, not yet my wife – Mrs Rayner, that is. 'Partners' I suppose you'd call us these days. The 'living-in' sin was how her mother described it.

The scene's a domestic one. Myself out in the kitchen preparing after-dinner drinks; Helen curled up on the sofa watching a variation of the *Antiques Roadshow* recorded earlier in the week. Members of the public bringing treasured possessions to be valued by a team of specialists. These seem to have been chosen at random, with no clue as to what's coming next. Otherwise I'd have been in there glued to the set from the beginning.

There's a shout from the front room: 'Quick, Peter, it's that hero of yours. The one you keep going on about. And they've got some of his pictures.'

No name required; the tone of voice, that 'going on about', spoke volumes. The picture I recognised the moment I saw it: *Fiddlers Three.* I'd been there when it was painted – though 'picture's' hardly the word to describe it, nor 'painting' the technique employed. Magnificent to the eyes of a nine-year-old, but what had any of us known about art? Nor, till then, did I realise he had any sort of a following. The critics, the few of them who knew of his existence, had been dismissive, but a small band of aficionados appeared to have taken him to their heart.

I took the zapper and reversed the tape. *Fiddlers Three* disappeared into a shopping trolley; the waiting queue shuffled backwards towards the exit, then forward again in real time as I pushed the button and the sequence recommenced. 'My word,' Frank Murgatroyd, the resident expert, known throughout the business as 'Murgo', is saying in that excited, avuncular manner that's made him a household name on our side of the screen; the darling of chat-show hosts and impressionists on his. 'It's years since I've seen one of these.'

He beams knowingly at a nervous-looking member of the public, a middle-aged woman of medium height, dressed – as are most of those around her – in a loose-fitting summer outfit, liberally decorated with flowers of indeterminate origin, a large straw hat clamped to the back of her head. But it's Murgo the camera loves. Focusing in on him it pans lazily downwards, lingering over buff shirt, orange bow tie, mottled green tweed jacket, bulbous leather buttons; resting on the familiar scarlet carnation pinned to lapel, taking in corduroy trousers with stout red braces, before finally resting upon the item in question: a picture of sorts, glazed, roughly A4 size, in a fragile wooden frame. He turns it this way and that before placing it on the table. The camera sweeps in once more, blurs, then swims into focus. We discover that it's not really a picture but some kind of parchment, creamy yellowish in colour with lettering, bold black and cursive, uncoiling with confident ease beneath a gold and vermillion heading. The capital letters are wreathed in ivy or trails of vine leaves whilst, clinging on to each with tiny claws and grimacing menacingly, are a series of tiny multi-coloured creatures, some bearded, others horned, one in particular cloven hoofed, shaggy-thighed, merrily blowing into pan pipes.

'A Saintley, by God,' exclaims Murgo enthusiastically. 'In good condition, too.' And, receiving no response: 'Before your time, I expect. Not many of them around these days. But each of them unique. Quite a collector's item, in fact. A bit of a one-off himself, too, James Saintley. Lived down in Hampshire – Bereden I believe.'

A mistake all of us made, so Jimmy claimed. Across the years, I hear his plaintive correction: *Not Bereden, lad. It's Beredene. Pronounced 'beer' as in the stuff you drink, then 'dean', the minor church official. Part of your heritage, Peter, don't you forget it!* He might as well have saved his breath. For as long as I'd lived it had been Bereden, pronounced *Bher-a-den,* and, as far as I know, it still is.

'...bit of a man of mystery he was, a hermit really. Took himself off to the woods; there was still quite a bit of it left in those days. That would be, let's see, the late 40s, early 50s? Appearing as if from nowhere, so it seems, then just as suddenly vanishing without trace. Lived off the land, communed with nature I suppose you'd say. Fancied himself as a poet as well. Mystical stuff: water maidens, woodland sprites, myth, folklore, legends about the Brits, Goths and Saxons, you know the sort of thing I mean. Had this strange theory about the appearance of his poems as well; the way they were set out. This had to be just right, nothing else would do...'

Presentation and content; form and intent. They're one, Peter. Can't you see that? What a story or poem looks like is part of what it has to say.

'... had these weird ideas about nature, but the man was a genius when it came to craftsmanship. Well, you can see that for yourself. Sketching, artwork, papermaking, calligraphy – you name it, he had the skills, so that each one of his poems were completely original from start to finish. He not only composed them, but made the paper on which they appeared, produced the ink from local plants and leaves, illustrated each one by hand, wrote them out longhand or chose an appropriate style of print, if requested would carve frames for them. Each one unique, a one-off production. And if we look carefully, we should be able to find his trademark. Yes, see there, at the bottom of the page? The bell. No one knows why, but it was the symbol he chose for each one of his works. He sold them, door to door, you know, like any other travelling salesman. Not many of them have survived, but those that have are worth quite a few bob I'd say. Let's have a closer look.'

The camera closes in once more on the object in Frank's hands, his commentary continuing unabated.

'One of his early works, I'd say. The script is beautiful and just look at the colouring, as bright now as the day he painted it. And those figures in the margin, enchanting aren't they? It's the story of the village draper. I managed to read it earlier; all of us did! Anyway, the fellow was also a violinist in the local band. He happens to be in Italy, don't ask me why, but notice the vine leaves draped around the lettering. Once there he meets up with the great Paganini, who prides himself on being the fastest fiddler in the world. Our friend thinks he can do better and issues a challenge, but Paganini is too proud to compete with such a bumpkin in public. Privately, though, he agrees that, if the man is brave enough to meet him in the woods that night, the matter can soon be settled.

'So off he goes, deeper and deeper into the woods. See, between each line the forest beasties are following his every step...'

Every story tells a picture, Peter. Every story tells a picture.

'... finally, he meets Paganini in a clearing and the contest begins. Faster and faster they play, furious and more furiously, becoming so engrossed in their music that neither of them notices they've been joined by a third figure. There he is, look, the one with horns sitting astride the 'H', tail draped to one side, leering evilly down at them. We can all guess who he is...'

... It's the bishop, darling, and don't pretend otherwise. Poetry, art, call it what you will, this time Jimmy's gone too far...

'... He produces a scarlet violin of his own and joins the duet. The tempo increases, the music gets wilder and wilder, woodland creatures of all kinds creep out from behind the script; see there and there. Soon they're dancing round the trio until Paganini, exhausted, sinks to the ground. Our village hero has not noticed, though. Thinks it's the maestro himself beside him and continues at a furious pace. His violin starts to smoulder, but still he plays on. It begins to smoke but still he continues. And then, see there at the bottom, just when he thinks he can last no longer, a roar of anger rips through the forest. Old Nick flings his violin aside and vanishes in a puff of smoke. But still the draper plays on until Paganini revives, begs him to stop, and they return home, the violinist back to Bereden, unaware that he's outplayed the devil himself.

'Well, that's the story.' The camera swings and pans round taking in two dozen or so onlookers, zooms in on individual faces, intent on Frank's every word. 'Worth £700 or so. But somewhat out of fashion, I'm afraid. Not much call for such oldie-worldie stuff these days...'

When the folk are dispersed, Peter, their landmarks uprooted, boundaries forgotten; who then will be left to tell their tales? What then?

'... But you've got another tucked away somewhere, I believe. Quite like the London buses, isn't it? Wait for years without seeing one, then they all start arriving at once. This one rather different, though. And unless I'm much mistaken...'

The camera swings down and focuses on the picture itself: circular in shape, a solid block of text at the centre surrounded on all sides by a series of figures. Quite obviously Romans, the one to the right, richly attired in a toga, accepts what looks like a petition from the elderly serf. Below this a high-born lady, arms outstretched, seeks to detain him as he strides out into the street. On the left, figures crowd round him, daggers drawn, and the toga is soaked in blood. More stylised than the artwork we've just seen, unmistakably from the same hand, and – like Murgo – I recognise it immediately. Part of a series; I'd come across reproductions in magazines, even caught sight of one in an art shop window – but that had been some time ago, in Canada, I think, and when I returned later the premises was closed with my flight due out in a few hours' time.

But there's a commotion on the settee beside me. Helen, who's been riffling through the *Radio Times*, signalling her indifference to 'Saintley' and all his works, has my arm in a vice-like grip. I freeze Murgo in mid-sentence.

'My God!' She's craning forward now, pointing at the screen. 'It's our *Shakespeare*. Or one just like it. On the wall in Daddy's study. Mother hated it.'

The relationship between her parents had not been good; ended in tragedy, in fact. I had the bare outline only, but enough to be concerned that the sudden appearance of this new picture might bring it all back to her. I made to switch the programme off, but Helen shook her head and we continued to watch.

'I thought so. Hardly mistake them, once you know what you're looking for.' Murgo is holding out the picture at arm's length. 'The *Shakesphere* series, hence the shape. He took extracts from the plays – Hamlet's soliloquy, Romeo's wooing of Juliet, Mark Anthony's speech over Caesar's body, which is the one we've got here – and placed the words *Friends, Romans, countrymen* in the middle, see? And arranged the characters involved around the outside. There's the rebels plotting Caesar's downfall, the man himself being warned by the soothsayer about not going to the Senate on the Ides of March, his wife begging him to stay home, and there he is getting his come-uppance when he did so. Bit of a gimmick putting them into round-shaped frames like that, giving them a catchy title. Proved popular though. He made quite a few bob out of it, till the novelty wore off. People began reframing them in more conventional fashion using mounts with circular holes cut in the middle. I've even come across individual characters cut out and framed separately.

'And the value, I hear you ask.' Floral Lady denies all such mercenary considerations, but she fades into the background as the camera sweeps in to catch the celebrated 'Murgo moment'. 'Fair condition, frame slightly damaged in the corner here,' magnifying glass pulled from inside pocket, 'complete with bell logo,' polishing the lens with a scarlet handkerchief, 'still in its circular frame. Genuine, not that there's much future in faking a Saintley. Around the £800 plus mark, I'd say. Might make an extra seventy/eighty if you pick the right auction.'

Floral Lady seems delighted, but not her picture, she explains. Brought along on behalf of a friend rather, someone who'd never part with it. And no, she has no idea as to its source. Some discussion follows as to the value of Jimmy's work on today's market. Not well known, apparently; never had an exhibition of his own, but some galleries included the occasional Saintley among their collections, stored away in their vaults for the most part, and one or two specialists might just be interested. By then the time allotted to Floral Lady comes to an end and the camera moves on to another group.

At which point I switch off the set and turn to Helen, intrigued by the coincidence.

'Daddy's was *As You Like It*,' she tells me. 'Jacques' "Seven Ages of Man" speech, with each of them, infant through to dotard, grouped round the text itself. Smuggled into the house, mother hated it that much. More to the point, what's all this about "Saintley"?' She's returned her magazine to the rack and swivels round to face me. 'God knows you've gone on enough about the man, but it's only now I get to hear his name. Or that he was a talented painter. We might have spotted the connection long ago, but for your holding back.'

Holding back! When only a moment ago she'd complained about the way I'd "gone on" about "that man". Helen was no admirer of Saintley: his ideas, way of life, ethics, penchant for Browning – the one poet she couldn't stomach. His stories especially. The antithesis of values she'd been brought up to respect, attributing my reminiscences to the ramblings of someone "in his anecdotage". She always joked about the disparity in our ages – her twenty-five years to my forty-five. Light-hearted banter, begging the obvious response: that she was too young to appreciate the subtlety of such tales. Or I'd rib her about jealousy. His getting in first; my being that close to someone outside the family before she came on the scene. Not that there was anything disreputable about it; the man was always surrounded by children. Get any closer and he'd clam up – push you away metaphorically – but to the prurient all things are impure.

'Saintley wasn't his real name,' I said. 'Just the critics' version of a nick-name we gave him. Making fun of his detachment, the kind of life he lived, the elevated ideas he had about art. Words framed by pictures, pictures framed by words, alphabets decorated with flowers, numbers hidden among trees… any combination, you name it.'

'I can see that – *now*. No wonder he wasn't better known if all his supporters were as reticent as you seem to be about his work.' Helen busied herself clearing up the glasses. 'A man of mystery, according to Murgo. Appearing from nowhere then vanishing just as suddenly as he arrived. Which is just about the most interesting part of the story, so how come I've not heard about it before?'

'Because there's nothing more to tell. I grew up, got a job, and – well – we just lost touch.'

'Lost touch! After you'd been so close? Weren't you just the tiniest bit curious as to what became of him?'

Of course I was. But I'd moved on, made new friends by the time I reached secondary school. After which ties with that part of the world had become severed; there was the writing, and my work took me out of the country a lot of the time. Besides which, given his antipathy to over-familiarity, I had a lurking suspicion that even if I'd known of his whereabouts a reunion might not be all that welcome. It might even destroy illusions I'd built up over the years. I took the tray and followed her into the kitchen.

'And that's it? All you know about how he ended his days, his "disappearance without trace"? There's got to be more to tell.' Our glasses joined plates and cutlery deposited in the sink from a previous meal. 'Your friend had real talent, I can see that, but he must have told you a little about himself. Who he was, where he came from? Most of all, just what was it made him value his privacy so highly?'

'Not really.' I fetched a towel and dried the plates as she handed them to me. 'He left all that to the likes of Murgo and the rest. Naïve of him really, not realising that the more he shut them out the more convinced they were he'd something to hide. Same as it was with officialdom in any shape or form: council, church, school, police, charity and welfare even. Nor could any of us fathom just why this should be.'

I held the last of the glasses up to the light. Squeaky clean;

my reflection caught, squat and distorted, in the curvature. Just how much, I wondered, had we really got to know about the man? Aloof and unassuming, I told her. A recluse one might say; close in some respects, distant in others. Accessible when it suited him; unreachable when it didn't. Kindness itself when it came to children, whatever his mood, yet unwilling to give of himself completely to anyone. True, there were parts I omitted – the 'unreliable narrator' as Helen would have put it. But then, which one of us isn't?

On several occasions over the next few months I was to change my mind as to the kind of person he was, just what his intentions might have been. But at that juncture, fairly early on in our relationship and unaware of the revelations that were to follow, I suppose I was merely playing for time.

Chapter Two

Figures in a Landscape

We called him Saint Jimmy, or Jimmy the Saint, and he'd been with us for as long as I can remember. As much part of my childhood as the village itself: its gravelled square, the grey spire of St Matthias, the wooded backdrop beyond. Flint-studded Amberstone Hall concealed within a hollow in the hills, the tanneries, cowpat pasture, frogspawn shallows. The growl of distant tractors, clash of metal on anvil. Waking in my teens to a dense wall of birdsong; earlier still, the drone of aircraft, incoming and hostile, each night.

Others were less kind, picking up on the name and converting it to 'Saintley'. Hinting at sanctimoniousness, delusions of grandeur; linking it to the hermit-like existence he led, or the poetry he wrote. Adding that 'e' to his name to make him appear more childish; missing out completely on the significance of his logo: the bell.

There were six of them altogether – bells I mean. 'All tolled' according to Jimmy, who was infamous for his puns. They made a complete peal and at some point in the past had acquired their own epithets: *Sideman, Curate, Parson, Bishop, Cardinal* and *Saint,* each just a little bit larger than the other, deeper and more sonorous in tone. *Sideman* was rung by Danny Earl, local handyman, a wizard with all things electric and a ham radio buff; *Curate* was the responsibility of Thomas Carter, the local fishmonger, who sang baritone in the church choir. Alfred Thomas hauled on *Parson's* rope when not pulling pints for the regulars down at The Jugged Hare; Joe Wickbourne – farrier *par excellence* and a genius when it came to mending anything made of metal – took charge of *Cardinal,* which left *Bishop* and *Saint* in the hands of Jimmy and the Squire respectively.

Yes, we still had a Squire back in the late 40s, as they do to this day. Not one of those titles I see advertised, or knocked down at auction, along with miniscule portions of real estate on Mars or the moon; the Amberstones had been up at the Hall for five centuries or more. I call them 'Squires' – it was how they liked to be known – but they were rather grander than that. The lineage took in generals and admirals, freebooters and privateers – military men all of them, serving their country with great distinction down the years, and suitably rewarded for doing so. Their portraits lined the corridors, escutcheon and musketry gracing the walls. We'd play hide-and-seek among suits of armour, race uncontrollably up and down the stairs when the place was thrown open for parties, at Christmas, Harvest-time or in celebration of one or other of the Amberstone birthdays. The family still occupied the pew reserved for them at St Matthias each Sunday, much kudos continuing to be attached to the shops they patronised. Cottages they owned about the village were let out on generous terms and always kept in good repair. Their role had, in fact, become almost entirely a social one by the time I came on the scene, disappearing entirely in the 1960s. Since then the Hall has been taken over by a charitable trust, but an Amberstone remains, much respected for his business acumen, with a young daughter destined one day to take over what remains of the heritage.

It was his father, Sir Desmond, who headed up the family in my day. I remember him as an irascible, tweedy man; his wife,

Dame Alice, a tall, anxious-looking woman, viewed from a distance on the sideline as hostess at children's parties or sitting on the front row at village concerts; situations in which it must have been only too natural to be anxious. No love lost between the Squire and Jimmy, you might have thought: the one a formidable upholder of privilege and the status quo, once Lord Lieutenant of the county; the other a rugged individualist, distrusting authority in any guise. But this was not the case, just the opposite in fact. Nobody knew quite how it had come about, but here was Jimmy living on Amberstone land, free of charge so it was rumoured, and how – other than with the Squire's support – could he have hoped to have made a living? Certainly not through the poems he hawked from door-to-door. Nor those pictures. Of some value certainly, but not to everyone's taste; nor did any of them seem to get sold.

Strange, the way Sir Desmond treated him: in the friendliest manner, forever taking his part; defending him against all the accusations that came his way – and there were to be plenty of these. Perhaps they'd met somewhere before? A distant relative maybe? Possibly the Squire owed him a favour, or did Jimmy have some claim on the Amberstone estate? Even more far-fetched was the gossip he was a spy. Not that the Russians could have had the slightest interest in anything down here in rural Bereden. Except, maybe, for Sir Desmond himself, who'd served in intelligence during the war and, it was said, still had connections with MI5. How else could someone like Jimmy, who'd appeared from nowhere, have obtained the relevant papers – identity card, ration book, etc. – allowing him to live rent-free out there in the forest? How, but for such patronage, could he have afforded the materials, paint, brushes and canvas to produce pictures such as *Fiddlers Three*? And there lay the solution, a large part of it at least. Sir Desmond had lost the elder of his two boys during the war, as competent an artist as he was an airman to judge from his battlefront sketches; mentioned several times in dispatches for conspicuous bravery; buried abroad with full military honours. All this I discovered growing up in and around Bereden and it was Sir Desmond who, by introducing Jimmy to the bell-ringing team, had been responsible for the name we gave him, the one later purloined and bowdlerised by Frank Murgatroyd and his cronies: Jimmy the Saint.

A bell-ringer he might have been, but Jimmy was better known – among us children at least – for his stories. Of which he had an inexhaustible supply, forever startling us with obscure aspects of the village life unknown even to our parents; never actually repeating himself, but for ever introducing some fresh variation or other to the more popular of such yarns.

He was most often to be found up at St Matthias beside the war memorial; a small wiry figure, back pressed hard up against warm grey stone whilst round about him we'd jostle one another for pride of place. 'Tale, treasure or travel?' he'd ask when we were settled, and turmoil would ensue as the merits of each were noisily contested. Jimmy would sit there amongst the clamour, hands resting on knees, fingering his beard – short, dark, ashen-fringed, frayed as the corduroy trousers he wore – that or the medallion that hung around his neck in a theatrical manner. The stance signalled he was in the process of contemplation; divining through acclamation or show of waving hands just what form that afternoon's entertainment should take.

His timing was impeccable; the routine never-changing. He'd wait till the clamour reached fever-pitch before raising his hand. Silence would fall. If it was to be a 'treasure' he'd make a great show of searching his person, the loosely-woven mud-coloured pullover, his faded tartan-patterned shirt, turning out trouser pockets, running fingers through the grass at his feet, throwing us his discarded jacket for inspection. Then, at the precise moment when our interest was wavering, he'd find his prop – the 'treasure' for which, supposedly, he'd been searching. This would be nothing special. A strangely shaped pebble, maybe. A tiny eggshell: creamy, mottled or sky-blue. Sometimes a coin would emerge from the deeper recesses of his clothing, at others an orange-coloured fungus or loosely-splayed fir cone. On one occasion the tiniest of bird nests gingerly withdrawn from a bag he'd been carrying; on another the chalky skeleton of some tiny woodland creature was discovered wrapped within his handkerchief. We'd crane forward to get a better look, and Jimmy would begin his commentary. How the object had been found, how it got there: if from the natural world, speculation on the type of species, its colouration, habitat or life-cycle; if man-made its origin, construction, variety of purposes to which it could be put.

'Treasures' such as these were interesting enough, but his 'tales' generally proved more popular, whilst the more adventurous among us simultaneously clamoured for 'travel'. There was, in fact, little difference between the content of these two categories, each of them crammed with anecdote and drama, centring around some memorable character or critical incident in the village's past. Jimmy's response depended on his frame of mind. Most frequently he opted for a straight 'tale', in which case we'd push forward for a ringside seat, making ourselves as comfortable as we could. Sometimes, though, his response was more dramatic. 'Travel it is!' he would exclaim. Leaping to his feet, he would grab the hands of those closest to him and, without another word, sweep them out of the churchyard, into the woods, across the fields, or down one the many tracks that in those days served us as roads, the rest of us tagging excitedly behind.

So, a visit to the remains of the toll gate that had once stood on the old Bereden/Winchester road might focus on the tricks played by travellers to avoid paying their dues, or the adventures of the highwaymen who used to meet here, their names, exploits and particular mode of thievery being modified to suit the prevailing mood. Here it was that 'Chirper' Edwards, the town crier – so called because of his high-pitched squeaky voice – would announce the latest scandal from London, disseminating it morning and evening having first proclaimed, 'If each before his doorstep sweeps, the village shall be clean!', and Harry, the toll keeper – just as eager to dig the dirt – met his maker. Anxious to impart each minute detail of the latest public hanging, he volunteered to give a practical demonstration but, no sooner had he placed his head in the noose, than the village band passed by, marching tunefully to rehearsal. His audience flocked to the window, leaving Harry swinging in his booth.

An expedition to Scapegoat Heath would be enlivened with tales of how the inhabitants would creep out each night, moving the boundary stones that marked the extent of their property. A trip to the railway station at the outskirts of the village reminded Jimmy not only of how the line first came to be built, in order to bring Hampshire strawberries – which he maintained were the best in the world – to Queen Victoria's tea table, but how various disasters, through fire, storm, explosion, incompetence or fog, had narrowly been averted. He would explain the workings of what was left of the old signalling tower that stood on the edge of the wood, one of fourteen between Portsmouth and London. The network, so he told us, pre-dated electronic modes of communication, which it excelled through transmitting a message from coast to capital in under four minutes. The process consisted of hoisting a series of coloured balls by day and lights by night, but was sometimes misused – as on the occasion when one of the operators attempted to send a message to his sweetheart in Deptford, only to have his assurances of undying love and eternal devotion arrive on the admiral's desk!

Between the woods and Harry's toll-booth lay the village square, beneath which – according to Jimmy – were a series of underground passages, and we spent hours trying to trace them.

The haunt of smugglers, so he said, bringing contraband from across the Channel, or treasure pillaged from the holds of foreign galleons. Not to be confused with 'owlers', who took goods *out* of the country rather than being employed in the import business. Regardless of nomenclature, if apprehended each shared the same fate: to swing in chains from Portsmouth Hard, meat for crabs till three tides had passed over them.

The contraband trade, whether into or out of the country, had been funded by a long line of village squires, the most infamous of them being 'No Good' Naughton whose interests lay chiefly in the 'liquid assets'. No Good had a special underground extension to the system constructed, emerging in the shrubbery behind the Amberstone Hall but, being in a constant state of inebriation, never could quite remember its precise location. Until one fateful night when, in the act of relieving himself, he'd actually stumbled upon it, falling headlong down, dislodging the roof props and blocking any way back to the coast. Neither able to retreat nor climb back up, he was never seen again. Still, there was a good supply of rum down there, so Jimmy assured us, and if ever we were out in the woods and listened very carefully, we might still hear footsteps wandering to and fro, his bawdy songs echoing from the depths of the earth.

A similar fate befell No Good's foolhardy yet foppish son, Freddy, who had an assignation with his lady-love on the other side of the forest. No more than a woodland really, lying in the valley between St Matthias and Amberstone Hall, but that's the way we liked to think of it, inhabited from time immemorial – according to Jimmy – with all manner of creatures. The devil-screecher, for example, whose razor-sharp beak was only matched by the tenacity of her memory. One might escape unharmed if straying beneath her nest, but sooner or later, this year or next, she or her partner would have vengeance, seeking you out and sweeping down with a blood-curdling shriek when least expected. Or the grampus, a bulbous, blunt-headed sea creature that had found its way into our part of the world, waiting to pounce on those who strayed nearby. Worst of all these mythological creatures was the cockatrice. With the wings of an eagle, the tail of a dragon and the head of a cockerel, it emerged from a duck's egg hatched by a toad and, like the gorgon of old, turned mortals to stone with a glance. His sweetheart had presented Freddy with a mirror, assuming he'd have sense enough to realise that, seeing its own reflection, the cockatrice would be the one to suffer. But the foolish man used it to arrange his wig, affix beauty spots to his cheek and generally preen himself, and so failed to hear the creature's approach. 'Saved them making a statue,' Jimmy told us. 'Just carted him up to the Hall and stood him in the garden among the fountains.'

* * *

Stories such as these must have been passed down from generation to generation, in pub, playground, market square or corner shop, or over garden fence. No one questioned their accuracy. To do so would be to miss the point; they served a deeper purpose. Nor is it quite certain just how a stranger like Jimmy came by them, but the Squire relished tales of his disreputable ancestry and you can see how, as children, we adored them. And how Helen, carefully brought up in a Catholic household, would have had her doubts.

Chapter Three

A Tale of Two Childhoods

Peter's right, I never cared for Jimmy's stories. The violence must have had something to do with it. All those spectral figures: screech owls, cockatrices, and the like. Highwaymen hanging from gibbets; the unpleasantness of Harry garrotted to death as the band marches by; generations of smugglers – or 'owlers', I never remember which it is – devoured by crabs as the tide comes in. Anecdotes, he'd assure me, never intended to be taken seriously. Maybe, but I drew the line when it came to religion. Jimmy inflicting his views, or lack of them, on children that young.

We'd met back at the University, myself the self-assured, high-minded post-graduate student, answering to the name of Helena, and Peter, a modest, middle-ranking member of the Social Science Faculty, lively enough in seminars or the lecture theatre but single-minded and almost totally lacking in ambition. 'Headstrong Helen' it became following frequent clashes in discussion or tutorial groups, spilling out beyond the classroom into teasing of a more intimate nature. Me chiding him, like as not, over the difference in our ages, with Peter taking up the jealousy theme. How I coveted the hours he spent together with that man – innocent though they were – before my time.

'Jealousy' is putting it too strongly. I never begrudged Peter his friendship with Jimmy. Envied, rather, the freedom he'd been granted. To roam the countryside at will, his backdoor the gateway to an adventure playground. The home guard drilling out on Scapegoat Heath, American troops lined up along the roadway awaiting D-Day. Clambering with his chums over papier-mâché gun emplacements set up as decoys for enemy bombers. In and out of air raid shelters, building magpie collections of shrapnel, used shells, camouflage. Blackout curtains converted to skull-and-cross-bones flags, ARP helmets padded out with newspaper, long-handled shovels intended for piling sand onto incendiary bombs transformed into lances for knightly tournaments. Waking some mornings to find the countryside strewn with metallic strips, black on one side, silver on the other, cut to correspond to the frequency of our radar stations and blinding them as a consequence. *Chaff*, they called it, or *window*. *Dragons' teeth* – concrete tank-traps, pyramidal in shape, about the size of modern traffic cones; *pill boxes* – circular, heavily reinforced rifle or machine-gun emplacements; *stirrup pumps* – primitive, portable fire extinguishers. A whole new vocabulary for someone born fifteen years into the peace.

No such playmates in our household; just the companions foisted on me by mother. Not the 'common' children from whom I might catch rough habits, to say nothing of swear words, colds or head lice. Young ladies rather, those I met in school or at church; taking tea at their houses, with only the chosen-few receiving return invitations. All such outings would be vetted before setting out and on my return: what had we done? What had I said? Did I remember to say 'please' and 'thank you'? Not to take a second cake, no matter how tempting this seemed? Never satisfied, it seemed, till she'd discovered some misdemeanour. All of which I could have stood had her motives been altruistic: to make me a better person, ensure that I got a good start in life. Not a bit of it. Mother's sole concern was how she herself would emerge from such encounters. It was the same with the cleaning lady. A good half hour before her arrival would be spent going round the house, brushing carpets, washing crockery, tidying the living room. A charade repeated whenever visitors were expected. Followed by her perennial greeting on their arrival: to 'take us as you find us'.

I found consolation in Daddy's study, tucked away at the top of the house. A sanctuary reserved for lesson preparation and the marking of sixth-form essays. We'd retreat there, the two of us, when I was bored or fretful, or bad weather prevented me playing outside. Perfect for the kind of entertainment he'd devise. Hide-and-seek, in and out around the kneehole desk, searching for sweeties secreted between the bookshelves, the rediscovery of the Noah's Ark he'd played with as a child. Best of all, the stories he'd tell. By the time I went to school I had each one of them off by heart. Real stories; longer, more detailed, having a beginning, a middle and an end. Not set in the self-same village, as Jimmy's had been, but far-flung locations: Russia, the lush forests of Africa, a volcanic island, market places of the mysterious East.

'Where animals talk, events happen in threes. People with fanciful names live in turreted castles or thatched cottages and declaim rather than speaking to one another.' That had been Peter's response, back at the University, sounding off to a bevy of admirers, female mostly, hanging on his every word. 'Folk tales,' I'd insist, contriving to be on the opposite side of any argument, 'formulaic for a purpose, peopled with archetypes.' Citing *The Golden Bough,* Campbell's *Hero with a Thousand Faces,* with Jung's collective unconscious, the seven basic plots of literature thrown in for good measure. Foreplay I suppose you'd call it. The way to this man's heart was through the intellect.

Serendipitous, then, the cathedral requiring a sociologist of repute for a series of evening sessions just as my studies concluded.

Uncle Henry: (the current incumbent, my mother's brother): Must be a Catholic.
Myself: Academic credentials more important.
Uncle Henry: High church at least. And familiar with the terminology.
Myself: But grasp of the subject essential. (Uncle Henry's sermons, self-published, had received a drubbing from the critics.) I know just the man!

Providential, you might say, Uncle Henry leaving me to check out Peter's qualifications and credentials; pure luck, being loaned out to assist with his research. But 'never leave coincidence to chance', a dictum remembered from one of his lectures.

Which is how I came to be sitting so intimately beside him, watching that particular television programme some eighteen months further down the line. With mother pointedly avoiding our unmarried status, and finding endless opportunities to do so; Uncle Henry hinting at my absence from confession. The year, 1985; October I seem to remember, an evening of 'mists and mellow fruitfulness'.

Peter had told me something of Jimmy's paintings. Lurid, comic-book stuff, I imagined. Thrown off for the amusement of the children, just as his stories had been. Nothing, then, had prepared me for the wonder of *Fiddlers Three.* Imaginative, colourful, perceptive; technically brilliant, with subtle touches of wit captured in each of the brushstrokes. A *tour de force*, as Murgo himself had been forced to admit. Strange, though, Daddy's *As You Like It* print turning out to be one of Jimmy's pictures. How I'd lived with it throughout my childhood, giving no thought to the artist whilst Peter, having spent so much time in the man's company, apparently knew so little about him. 'Never claimed to be anything other than himself' was all he'd say. Later, it's true, there were minor details regarding the Amberstones, parties up at the Hall, and that bell. Till, caught off-guard by my sudden interest, embarrassed by the inadequacy of his own response, he disappeared into the attic in search of the family 'archive'.

This was no more than a battered old suitcase, held together with a frayed leather belt, crammed with the last remnants of his schooldays: reports, exercise books, certificates, holiday snaps, letters from his parents and the like. I was all for pitching in immediately, reading the contents at random in the hope of making some chance discovery. But no. They had to be sorted out carefully, then, and only then, fed to me. One at a time, in the correct order.

First to emerge was a small leaflet, *Notes on St Matthias* by the Rev. Stephen Archer. A brief paragraph had been marked for special attention:

Nearby a studded doorway, dating from Norman times, leads down to the crypt (not open to the public) containing the tombs of the Amberstone family. The nave is dominated by the rich rococo memorial to Sir Ignatius Amberstone (1789 – 1880), disparaged by Posner but adored by Betjeman. Of particular note is the depiction of the church band, one of his life-long interests, including several instruments which have subsequently passed into obscurity. Sir Ignatius' ear trumpet, originally held in the right hand, has now been removed to Winchester County Museum.

'Bassoon, trombone, ophicleide, serpent, hauyboy, comopean,' Peter was reciting in sing-song fashion. 'Drilled into us down at the village school, the instruments, I mean. Each one handed down from generation to generation. The Squire's pride and joy – in the early days, that is, before the deafness set in.'

'Hence the ear-trumpet?'

'The genuine article, still there in my day. Until the church was broken into and it got carted off. For safety's sake, so they said, though no one's seen it from that day to this. Lucky for us, Jimmy was on hand to fill in the gaps.'

'I might have known. Go on!'

'It was sitting in the Squirarchal pew all those years alongside the bull-horn that did for his hearing. He must have left the trumpet at home on the day they appointed a new rector, Tobias Jones, a dyed-in-the-wool socialist. First the Squire knew about it was when he wanted a pathway from Amberstone Hall down to the church, with a special doorway in the east transept where the band led the hymn-singing. Tobias wouldn't hear of it. Told Ignatius straight: this was God's House, with one entrance only for rich and poor alike. As for the band, nothing but an organ would do for the worship of the Almighty. And Tobias knew exactly where it should be placed.'

'Let me guess.' I made a great show of massaging my scalp, furrowing my eyebrows. 'Would that have been the East Transept?'

'Heaven help us.' Peter brought the forefinger of each hand together in the form of a cross. 'The girl's a witch!' Playing along as we often did in private.

'Neither Ignatius nor Tobias would give way,' he continued, 'and the stalemate continued for years. Then, quite suddenly, the rector died. To Ignatius' relief, till the will was read, specifying precisely where and how he was to be buried. Nothing elaborate, just a single granite block – must have weighed a ton – let into the wall alongside the pulpit where he'd preached so often. Which just happened to be...'

'... the East Transept...'

'... And, humble as he was, Tobias required no more than his name and a single Scriptural text. Worn down completely by the time Jimmy took us there on one of his 'travels'. John X I.'

Peter was looking expectantly across at me. 'Thought that would have been one of the first things they drummed into your head back at the convent.'

He reached down my copy of the Bible, found the right place:

He who does not enter the fold by the door but climbs in by another way, that man is a thief and a robber.

'Convenient,' I said, 'the inscription worn away.'

'O ye of little faith! Well, here's something I can vouch for personally.' Peter produced the next piece of archival evidence, one of the brass-rubbings he'd made as a child, traced in shiny black crayons on a large sheet of what I believe is called sugar paper:

☆

The Hon. Vernon Amberstone
Eldest son of Sir Desmond and Lady Alice Amberstone
Killed in action, France, January 1941

☆

Some Corner of a Foreign Field that is
For Ever England

The outcome of another of Jimmy's 'travels', apparently, referred to by the Rev. Archer on the second page of his leaflet:

> *The commemorative tablet to Hon. Vernon Amberstone in the south transept was the cause of some controversy, the father, Sir Desmond Amberstone, having commissioned the design from his protégé, a local artist, known for his antipathy to the church. He it was who – against the wishes of the rector, Rev. Theobald Draper – chose the lines from Brooke's poem, rather than a Biblical quotation. There were those who felt that the ultra-modern lettering, believed to have been created by the artist himself, was out of keeping in such a setting. The family, however, approved, Dame Alice being particularly taken with the text, and the work went ahead.*

No matter how he felt about the church, nor what I thought about the man, Jimmy had excelled himself. Gaunt capitals, elongated vowels, trailing word-endings – capturing a mother's anguish for a lost son to perfection.

'Not Dame Alice's choice.' Peter was re-examining the script. 'The Rev. Archer, whoever he was, got that part wrong. Given her way it would have been the tag-line from some movie.'

'For a memorial plaque? You must be joking.'

Peter shook his head. 'The old girl was crazy about the flicks as we called them. She'd have them delivered to the Hall in enormous tin cans, silent ones mostly. Used to invite us there sometimes at Christmas, to watch Charlie Chaplin or a Laurel and Hardy, with iced buns and ginger beer served during the interval. Quite civilised after Saturday mornings rushing up and down the aisle at the Odeon, standing on our seats screaming at Flash Gordon, hissing at the Ming the Merciless. Anyway she got it into her head that nothing but a quote from her favourite film would do for Vernon's memorial. The Squire, never the most sensitive of souls, hit the roof; nor would the rector, usually a meek-and-mild character, hear of it. Eventually it took a visit from the Bishop before she changed her mind and Jimmy stepped in with those *For Ever England* lines.'

'Makes a change from Browning.'

'And the very last poem you'd have expected from him. A great one for the apt quotation – something the both of you have in common – but nothing past the Victorian Age. Had us children guessing just what it was the old lady had in mind. Ollie Hardy's "Another fine mess you've got me into" was our best bet, or Bugs Bunny's "What's up, doc?'

'Mae West's "Come up and see me some time"?' I suggested, still not quite certain how seriously to take him.

Peter was looking at me admiringly. 'You, Helen, are *wasted* in the library,' was all he said.

'She died not a few months later, as much from grief as old-age.' He was searching for another document among the archive. 'But if it's the calligraphy rather than punch-lines you're interested in, here's something rather more informative. Or thinks that it is!' He found what he wanted and passed it across.

The Encyclopaedic History of British Art was a compendious volume, its contents arranged in four columns across a hundred or so yellowing pages. Illustrated here and there with the occasional blurred photograph or sepia print and published in weekly episodes within *The Daily Guardian,* 1962, it provided all the reader might wish to know about the great and the good: Abell, William (1446-70) to

Zucchi, Antonio (1728-95). Dog-eared through continual use in A-level revision, but falling open under 'S':

> *Saintley, James (c. 1940s): little factual evidence – not even his real name – is available concerning this multi-talented artist, craftsman and poet, active in the Hampshire village of Bereden in the immediate post-war period. The sobriquet by which he is known derives partly in response to his hermitic mode of existence, partly an ironic comment on his critical attitude to all things religious.*
>
> *Saintley attempted to marry content to form in a number of ways, encompassing various kinds of painting, pottery, sculpture, wood carving, and was a calligraphist of the first order. Here, he produced his own pigments, going back for inspiration to the illuminated manuscripts of mediaeval Europe and working wherever possible with materials that were immediately to hand. He also drew heavily on local history and folklore, his interpretation of which owed more to the imagination than accuracy. This, together with his eccentricity, a delight in the surprise approach, of shock tactics, often detracted from Saintley's real merits.*
>
> *Stylistic influences are William Morris and Eric Gill, although Gillray and Hogarth might also be cited, but most obviously William Blake. Here, the combination of technique and content, freedom of expression, mysticism, disdain for current art forms and anti-clerical attitude are too close to be coincidental. Little of Saintley's work is extant, and what there is in private hands. Some interest remains concerning both the contents and the fate of his final work, Mappa Mundi, said to epitomise all he found distasteful regarding both religion and authority.*
>
> *GL*

Peter was unimpressed. 'I'd forgotten how little there was.' He shrugged dismissively. 'And how inaccurate. Not surprising the writer can't bring himself to give his full name. Probably one of Murgo's pseudonyms!'

'That's hardly fair. For all you've told me Jimmy could be a figment of the imagination. Or some elaborate hoax.'

'And most of it rubbish. "Saintley"? I'd never heard him called that in my life – not till the experts took notice. "Limited success"? It was popularity that put paid to the *Shakesphere* series. He sold the copyright for a pittance then hated the publicity that followed. "Produced his own pigments"? Made a pig's ear out of them more like. As for "*Mappa Mundi*" – most likely something "GL" dreamt up to fill out the article.'

'Slag him off as much as you like,' I said, 'at least the man's prepared to share his ideas. The part about Blake especially – "too close for coincidence". Anyone can see that – if *Fiddlers Three*'s anything to go by.'

'Never in a hundred years.' Peter laughed but, catching my expression, changed his tone. 'Sorry, I didn't mean to be flippant. Sure, Jimmy recognised Blake's talent – once it was drawn to his attention. Loved what he was trying to do and the way he was doing it. Detested the poetry, though. Just as he hated the man's piety. Same applies to Hogarth, Gilray and the rest. He respected their work right enough, once it had been pointed out to him, but I honestly don't think he paid them much attention once he began the doodling.'

'Doodling?'

'That's what he called it. To begin with. And, for all the Squire's support, it might well have gone no further. Jimmy would never have been sure enough of himself, given no thought to putting brush to canvas. Might well have remained content just telling us stories, writing those dreadful poems. And it's a dead certainty he'd never have appeared on that television programme. But for the Quintock factor.'

Chapter Four

Tea Bomb Epiphany

'It was long before either of us were born that Enid Quintock arrived in the village. A student-teacher in those days, straight from a northern manse having lost her fiancé in the early years of the war. 1914, 1915 it must have been.'

Helen had rooted through her own archive, what there was of it, and produced some photographs together with a few of her old school reports – putting my own to shame – and we were comparing notes.

'Hard to imagine,' I said. 'No more than eighteen, plunged suddenly from a city having all the amenities into a backwoods like ours. Caged, day after day in a one-room remnant of Victorian times with a dragon of a headmistress. Just the two of them, continuously at it, coaching pupils of all ages in the three Rs, with Enid taking the flak for everything that went wrong.'

A stern task-master that first boss, she used to tell us, but workmanlike and efficient. Unlike her successor who simply couldn't cope. Before long the woman had drifted into a different dimension, or 'took off with the fairies' as the villagers put it. At which point Enid had come into her own. It had taken twenty or more years for her to become accepted within the village, but now she was appointed headmistress and set about dragging the establishment from the nineteenth into the twentieth century.

One of her first acts had been to institute a collection of footwear of all shapes and sizes to replace boots sodden during particularly long walks to school and, right from the beginning, the punctiliousness of her register failed to note the absence of certain pupils at strawberry-picking or harvest time. Before long the fume-belching 'tortoise' stove was ousted from the central hall, she'd bullied the authorities into replacing the outside toilets with main drainage, taken personal oversight of regular medical inspections (red cards signalling the presence of nits, green ones the 'all clear') and, as Bereden increased in size, saw to it that separate classrooms were erected and new teachers appointed. Which was how matters stood in the mid-forties when I became one of her pupils.

Jimmy's arrival in the village preceded my own by a few years only and it was not for some time that I got to know him, apart from reputation that is. Miss Quintock was aware of all such encounters, but as far as I knew they'd never met. Little, however, slipped our teacher's attention so that his assistance with our homework came as no surprise. 'Consultation' he liked to call it and, to be fair, he never actually supplied answers to the problems we'd been set, merely pointed us in the right direction through a series of questions and manipulating the responses we gave.

'An excuse for making it up as you go along if you ask me.' Helen could not restrain herself. 'We had one of those once; not bothering to do her own homework, let alone set anything for us to get our teeth into. Far easier to get us to look it up or write 'project work' in her lesson plans and leave it at that.'

The basis of most MA or PhD research, I might have said – it was an issue we'd crossed swords over on a number of occasions – but made no comment. Truth of the matter was that Jimmy's interventions were not always that helpful. No doubt about his competence in art or composition, but his grasp of mathematics and science was sorely inadequate, whilst the slant he gave to subjects such as history and the Scriptures was invariably at odds with those supplied by our teachers. 'Tell that woodland friend of yours that Jane Seymour was the third, not the fifth of Henry's wives,' Miss Quintock wrote in our exercise books, or 'an extra two marks, compliments HoB (*the Hermit of Bereden*)', if pleased with the result. To which Jimmy would respond with an appropriate yet respectful message for 'her up at the school'. Nor was our teacher unaware of Jimmy's prowess as a storyteller, constantly encouraging him to come and visit us for such purposes – invitations that he always refused.

The breakthrough came whilst visiting Jimmy one afternoon shortly after the beginning of the autumn term. His home, universally known as Third Class Cottage, stood on Squire Amberstone's land, leased out to him – so it was said – for peppercorn rent, and was reached down a pathway leading into the forest. Or what we called 'forest'; it was no more than woodland really. Nor was the name of Jimmy's residence anything to do with the quality of the building or its state of repair. It was, in fact, two railway carriages placed side by side, most of the internal divisions removed, topped over with a corrugated iron roof that creaked noisily in any strong gust of wind. It stood some distance from the railway station and no one could remember just how or why the carriages had been brought there.

'Wonder that any rolling stock survived along that line if half of Jimmy's stories concerning disasters and derailments were to be believed.' I reached across for something to write on, found one of the 'student-centred' dissertations I'd been marking, and sketched out a ground plan on the back cover.

The interior consisted chiefly of a single room with a mahogany roll-top desk on which rested his ancient Smith-Corona typewriter, a matching bookcase placed to one side of it and a low divan-type bed at the other. On the wall above hung a single, neatly framed picture depicting what appeared to be seventeenth-century noblemen setting out for war. Between desk and bookcase stood a stripped pine table with drawers for cutlery, alongside which was a cupboard where Jimmy kept his provisions. There were two doors at the back of the room: one, painted yellow, which led into a small, very basic kitchen, with a primitive stove and porcelain sink; the other, coloured blue, behind which was an even more basic earth closet. The modern open coal fire, from which the interior received its warmth, was a more recent concession to comfort, as was a commodious radio, perpetually tuned to the Third Programme and a cuckoo clock that never succeeded in announcing the correct time. Windows were set into the walls on all sides, most of them later additions but two, dating from the early days of steam locomotion, announced this to be a *Third Class* carriage – hence the cottage's name.

Here we – 'Chunky' Richards, Tim McPhail, Charlie Dowse, Andrew Boydell and myself – would retreat on an evening as summer drew to an end. Harsh white gaslight hissed continuously from gauze mantles set into the ceiling, a softer glow from oil lamps illuminating the darker recesses of the room. Logs we'd help drag in some five weeks earlier burnt in the fireplace as, huddled round it, we'd toast chunks of bread on sharpened sticks, sipping tea – sweet, dark and very hot – from chipped mugs. Rationing had not yet come to an end; commodities we now take for granted were in short supply, so each of us was expected to make some contribution to the feast. This might be bread, apples or margarine, but usually it consisted of a spoonful of sugar purloined from pantry or kitchen, mixed together with a small quantity of tea and if possible an equal amount of condensed milk, all screwed within a scrap of newspaper. Should any of us be unable to supply the required ingredients Jimmy would make up the deficit, adding the defaulter's name to a ledger kept pinned on one of the walls – the first and most practical of our introductions to the world of accountancy. I don't ever remember such debts being called in but, as I say, rumour had it that – whatever the reason – Sir Desmond made certain Jimmy did not go short. On arrival, these 'tea bombs' were tossed in a pan of boiling water, twenty minutes or so later the sodden mass of yesterday's bylines and editorials being swept from the surface and deposited on Jimmy's compost heap. What remained was a rich mahogany-coloured brew.

Helen wrinkled her nose in the way I find so attractive. 'Finest brew in all my tea-drinking years,' I assured her.

This particular year – the late forties as I say – we'd experienced an Indian summer, warm enough for us to sprawl in a rough circle on the small lawn outside the cottage. Charlie Dowse's younger brother, Saul, had joined the group. The six-year-old had only just started at the big school and, much to our disgust, had trailed along behind us at break-times throughout the week, demanding to be included in all games and discussion. Now, they trudged together down the pathway, Charlie sheepishly dragging Saul, red-eyed and tearful, by the hand. The child was ordered to sit still and say nothing whilst his elders got on with that day's business which, I seem to remember, involved the conversion of poles into furlongs, pecks into bushels, or one of the computations set out on the back cover of our exercise books. Jimmy was sympathetic but, problems such as these being beyond his forté, turned his attention to the youngest member of our group. Surely he wasn't old enough to be set homework? He was? Well, anything would be of more interest than all this agricultural nonsense. Could the rest of us have a look? Saul removed his thumb from his mouth, almost ripping his satchel apart in his eagerness to comply. The rest of us hooted with derision as Jimmy stooped to take the copybook from him, and fate took a hand.

Set out down the page were a series of sentences printed in

the most elegant and flowing of copperplate script with gaps between them for the pupils' own efforts. These would have been culled from any of the thousand or so uplifting works considered to be part of our literary heritage, with teachers encouraged to use them according to the occasion or season of the year. It was typical of Miss Quintock to have neglected such advice, although – looking back – it might well have been our earliest intimation that all was not right with her. Jimmy's reactions could also be seen as predictive but, as he himself often remarked, hindsight makes prophets of us all. Be this as it may, had our teacher not set especially irksome arithmetic homework for that evening, had not those particular lines by that particular poet been chosen, had not Jimmy been particularly susceptible to them…

He stooped, picked up the book, and read:

Oh to be in England
now that April's there.

Quite entranced, he disappeared indoors and reappeared with one of the Browning volumes from his bookcase. Taking up a dramatic posture yet without consulting it, he dumbfounded us by declaiming:

Whoever wakes in England
Sees, some morning, unaware,
That the lowest boughs and the brushwood sheaf
Round the elm-tree bole are in tiny leaf,
While the chaffinch sings on orchard bough
In England – now!

And entered into an enthusiastic and impromptu appreciation of the poem.

He explained its title, *Home Thoughts from Abroad*, who wrote it and how this came about, dwelling in some detail – as only Jimmy could – on the plight of this exile some hundreds of miles away, in the baking heat at siesta time under cloudless Mediterranean skies. How had he come to be there? Was he a traveller? Had he been banished from the kingdom? Perhaps this was a holiday? A business trip? A long-term incarceration? Whatever the case, this man (or was it a woman?) recalls the sights and sounds of an English springtime, and here Jimmy drew heavily upon imagery from the rest of the poem, instructing us to 'read it for yourselves later.' In his mind's eye our wayfarer sees not the *gaudy melon-flowers* which surround him now, but the pear-tree blossom of home tumbling onto morning dew, wild flowers among the hedgerows, fields of golden buttercups. Once more he hears the birdsong of England: chaffinches ('chucks, your grandparents would have called them'), whitethroats ('furzechicks'), swallows ('they must have had a name for them, too') and the thrush, who:

> *– sings each song twice over,*
> *Lest you think he never could recapture*
> *The first fine careless rapture.*

Helen seemed less pleased. 'Exile my hat! Written on one of his expeditions to Italy. All the man had to do was to pack his bags and catch the next boat home!' Browning could do no good in her book.

More to the point, regardless of what she, Murgo, 'GL,' or any of the experts might say, this incident marked the true beginning of the Saintley saga – its epiphany if you like…

'He might even have been thinking of Bereden,' said Jimmy. 'A little bindweed, that's all it needs.' He retrieved the workbook from young Saul, rummaged through one of the drawers and, before anyone could stop him, had produced the stub of a pencil, licked the end, and began sketching the tendrils spreading across the lower part of the page. With a few deft strokes they reached out for the bottom line of text, caught hold of the letter 'A', and swarmed to its apex before searching round for further purchase.

'The bindweed. Over at Frogspawn Shallows. Remember?' he repeated, admiring his handiwork at arm's length but puzzled by the less than enthusiastic reception it was receiving. We remembered right enough. We also recalled Miss Quintock's strictures regarding the copybooks. There were hardly enough of these to go round, so each was clearly inscribed with the recipient's name, on the front cover, alongside the Ministry of Education crest. The property of 'HM Government', she'd told us, along with dire warnings as to the consequences should any one of them be lost, damaged or defaced. And, fair minded though she was, our teacher was not a person with whom one trifled. She might just about have accepted an inexplicable loss ('Must have slipped out of me satchel, Miss'), damage even ('Door must have been left open and Rover not on his lead'), but there was no possible excuse for defacement. The word in itself held a grim foreboding, and the copybook had definitely, and quite deliberately, been defaced. Nor could there be any query concerning ownership; Miss Quintock's own hand proclaimed it to be the property of one *Saul Dowse.*

Jimmy, always sensitive to what was taking place around him, was immediately sympathetic but, as usual, less attuned to the long-term results of his actions. Explain as we might, he would not be persuaded as to the seriousness of the situation. We felt torn between conflicting loyalties. Somehow, in a way we could not put into words, we had betrayed a trust placed in us. Yet, at the same time, we wished desperately to protect Jimmy from the nemesis of 'HM Government': a looming presence, having neither shape nor form, yet spoken of by our teachers with bated breath as holding all their futures in thrall. For Saul there was the added terror of Miss Quintock. He did not know her as we did; had accepted without question the exaggerations and half-truths ritualistically extended to new pupils. Words could not express his despair, but a pungent stream trickled down his leg to form a pool on the lino. And, by the time we had cleared this up, tried to comfort him, assured Jimmy that all would be well, the clock had cuckooed nine, meaning it was now six o'clock and time to rush home.

As we rushed, our resolve failed. Next morning it had dwindled still further and, by the time our homework was due, it had all but failed. Too late now to retract the untruths we had told about our teacher, the child would only think we were trying to comfort him; nor did we have the nerve to approach Jimmy, so proud of his artwork, rewarded by Saul in such an embarrassing fashion ('the lad will grow up to be a critic, just see if he don't'). After much debate we had agreed that confession was the best policy and that this should be done together as a group. The only chance we had, though, was at the end of the day but were terrified lest Miss Quintock, HMG, or both of them together might launch a pre-emptive strike.

Meanwhile, word of the misdemeanour had spread throughout the school and speculation was rife as to what the consequences might be. We half expected PC Granger (the 'Lone Granger', we called him), to appear in the playground on his bicycle ('Wild Silver'), remove his cycle clips, lumber up onto the stage during morning assembly and call upon the culprits to come clean, just as he'd done after the apples were filched from Sir Desmond's orchard. Or would Miss Quintock sweep down from the platform to harangue all of us indiscriminately at close quarters, which was her invariable response to infringements of school rules? But hymn, prayer and announcements passed off without incident, as did the longest day any of us could remember. Till, finally, with Saul mentally rehearsing and re-rehearsing his confession, we filed out of our classrooms.

Miss Quintock's 'office' was no more than a cupboard really, partitioned off from one side of the classroom. Hardly room for the six of us as, with eyes averted and much shuffling of feet, we listened to Luke's proffering of the defiled homework, his tearful apologia. She took it from him, studied the offending artwork for a time, contemplated us over the top of her glasses – and laughed:

'Quite the best use of a copybook I've ever seen!'

'But don't you dare tell anyone I said so,' she added, holding it up to the light for closer examination.

'So delicate and lifelike.' She seemed to be speaking to herself. 'The plant might almost be growing there, taken root on the page. Carefully observed, yet completely uninhibited. And this took him just a few minutes, did you say?'

We affirmed that this was the case, Miss Quintock drawing the whole story out of us, her current levity in the matter a mystery to us all.

'Just leave HMG to me,' she told us. 'He's not really the ogre you imagine him to be. You'll find that out soon enough, and I'm sure he'd approve of the additions that Third Class friend of yours has made to the book, every bit as much as Mr Browning would.'

Could the poet be one of HMG's spies, we wondered? And the reference to Jimmy's cottage astounded us; teachers were not supposed to have access to any such information. Nevertheless we were eager now to be away; to bring him the good news. But Miss Quintock was not done with us yet.

'Of course,' she said, 'there's a penalty to be paid. You can't tamper with official copybooks and get away with it completely. Tell the woodland hermit that the price HMG exacts for his wrongdoing is to finish what he's begun. There was a thrush in the poem, if I remember, and an orchard? Don't you think they deserve a place on the page? And what about the whitethroat? Tell that arboreal artist to put them in, together with anything else he sees fit, and report back to us all when it's done. Then, and only then, he might just be fully forgiven.'

Relieved of the penalty that had been hanging over us all day, we were out of the room in an instant, rushing down into the forest, banging at the yellow door, interrupting one another in our eagerness to pass on the good news. Jimmy feigned indifference, but we could tell he was flattered by her message, making a number of excuses – that he did not have the expertise or the equipment, he was busy, could not see the point of it – before agreeing to one, at least, of her requests.

'Alright,' he said at last, 'I suppose it could just about be managed if all of us put our heads together. As for public presentations, best leave that to the experts!'

'And that,' I told Helen, 'was how Chunky, Charlie, Tim, Andrew, myself – and Saul, of course – became co-creators of the first of the "Saintleys".'

Chapter Five

The Quintock Factor

Jimmy always maintained that *Home Thoughts* was a joint effort, and I suppose it was – to begin with especially.

We'd gather at Third Class Cottage each evening after school, steaming mugs of tea set to one side as we pored over the *Complete Works of Browning*, opened at the appropriate page. Saul was given the honour of reading the poem, which he did in his best 'morning assembly' voice, Jimmy instructing us to stop him each time the poet mentioned particular flora or fauna by name. One point would be awarded for each correct interruption, one deducted for any error, with bonus marks added for accurate descriptions of each of the items selected. We did well in the naming of the various birds, were less successful over those of the plants, with generic terms – 'orchard', 'spray', 'dower', 'brushwood', 'dewdrops', etc. – leading to especially fierce controversy. One of us would be appointed as scribe, charged with keeping a record of proceedings so that, after a number of such preliminary sessions, the chief components of Jimmy's picture had been decided upon.

Throughout this dialogue he was lightly penciling in the detail we supplied, continuously modifying earlier images, eliminating them altogether, or shifting them, like chess pieces, from one position to another. This must have continued for the best part of a week, after which he brought the consultative part of the process to an end, thanked us for our assistance and sent us home with strict instructions to leave him 'alone with his genius'.

None of us knew just how long it would take him to complete *Home Thoughts*, nor did we have much notion as to what the outcome would be. Each of us had our own ideas and, as the days went by and Third Class Cottage remained a no-go area, the tension mounted. Arguments broke out in the playground; even Miss Quintock seemed unusually irritable, and the most loyal among us began to wonder whether Jimmy would fail to deliver. Then, one morning just after the milk break, we caught sight of him, making his nervous way across the school playground, a large brown paper parcel tucked under his arm. Tim, who was nearest the window, nudged his neighbour, who leant across the desk to get a better view, attracting the attention of those directly behind him and bringing Miss Quintock bustling down the aisle. By now Jimmy was making his exit having deposited his parcel in the porch but, with a swift flanking movement, she cut off his retreat, took him by the arm and manhandled him into her office.

The silence of thirty straining ears fell over the classroom whilst Andy climbed up onto his desk to peer into the window set high in the partition dividing it from the main part of the school, from where he provided a running commentary:

He'd given her the parcel… She was unwrapping it… Carefully untying knots in the string which held it together… Rolling this into a ball… Folding up the paper for future use… Yes, it was our picture… She was holding it at arm's length… And smiling… Pointing towards the classroom… Jimmy edging out of the door, trying to make his escape… She was giving him a 'talking to'… he was shaking his head… She'd taken him by the arm, and…

Andy scrambled down from the desk and all of us studiously resumed our reading, as Miss Quintock hauled a reluctant Jimmy into the classroom with all the finesse of a warder dragging his prisoner into the dock.

'We have an important and long overdue visitor, who's brought us a present,' she announced. 'All stand!'

The 'present' was indeed *Home Thoughts*, but there was something strange about it. Something that from where the five of us sat at the back of the class we couldn't quite make out. It seemed so much larger than we remembered, the lettering that much bolder and more exact. Then it dawned on us. What we were looking at was far more than random copy-book decorations.

Oh to be in England
now that April's there...

...had been the starting point right enough, but Jimmy had taken our suggestions, weaving them into the text itself so that words and images had come together to form a single unified composition. This was dominated by the poet's pear tree, which now formed a decorative framework for the 'picture' as a whole. Its trunk had been placed over to the left, with gnarled roots running lengthways across the bottom, between brushwood and buttercups beaded with *hoary dew,* as the poet had put it. The upper branches, interwoven here and there into the actual letters of the text, curved down to sprinkle blossom, creating a lacy backdrop, the first rays of sunlight slanting through the initial 'O'. Meanwhile, there was the thrush, singing his heart out at the top of the letter 'A' of *April*, whilst the whitethroat had just snatched a *tiny leaf* from Browning's *elm tree's bole* to reinforce her nest, snug in the hollow of the letter 'b' (*be*). Unidentified birds – chaffinches presumably – had chosen other letters as their perch; sleek swallows swept in and out between the lines. And there, stretched out at the bottom of the picture, leaning up against the tree, knees drawn up before him, slept the unmistakable figure of Jimmy himself. Grasped in one of his hands was a large brush. This rested on his chest, large dollops of paint dripping from it onto his shirt. The other was carelessly flung out, overturning the pot and spilling its contents onto the grass beside him.

An unwilling Jimmy was sat down on the dais at the front of the class and invited to tell us – cross-examined rather – about his picture: its composition, the kind of pens and pencils he'd used, where the charcoal came from, how long it had taken him, etc., etc. Jimmy's answers were monosyllabic, punctuated with the occasional grunt of assent, an embarrassed nodding or shaking of his head. Gradually, though, he regained something like his old composure. It was then that Miss Quintock remarked on the similarity between *Home Thoughts* and other artists who'd worked in this style; reminded us of the illustrated manuscripts of medieval times; how we'd learnt about the *Bayeux Tapestry* in our history lessons, suddenly cutting across his mumbled self-deprecation to recall the work of Blake.

Jimmy looked blank. 'William Blake,' she said. 'Your style is so like his. Surely you're familiar with his work? I'm sure the children can help you:

Tyger, tyger, burning bright
In the forests of the night
What immortal hand or eye
Could frame thy fearful symmetry?

Didn't we have that in morning assembly only last month?'

And, leaving the class to admire his handiwork, she fetched 'the book' from her office: *Songs of Innocence and Experience*, brought out so often in English lessons and frequently replacing the Bible at prayer time.

Helen had learnt many of the poems off by heart, but I knew the book only by its cover – orange coloured with faded gold lettering and a tasseled silk marker; it held a special place in Miss Quintock's affection. Others she would willingly lend out or pass around the class, inviting the closest of perusals. But not the Blake. She might share its contents with us; extracts would appear on the blackboard, individual verses set for us to learn by heart but, once this was done, it would be locked away again in her desk. No one, not monitor, parent, inspector, nor – for all we knew – HM Government itself had access to that book, so why had she produced it now? Had Blake also written his *Home Thoughts*? We didn't think so. Nor could we remember any other poem remotely resembling it.

All such queries faded as Miss Quintock opened the book, and we caught the full impact of the poet's intentions, recognising instantly the similarity between his approach and Jimmy's. Here were verses squeezed between foliage running down the side of each page. 'The School Boy', 'Little Girl Lost', or 'Earth's Answer' according to Helen.

Angelic figures disported themselves amid burgeoning tendrils, just as the birds had in Jimmy's picture. 'That would have been Blake's "Infant Joy". Or the dancers in "Blossom Nursing Song"', she pronounced.

One I remembered particularly had figures in solemn procession arranged top and bottom of the page.

'"Holy Thursday" maybe.'

Similarities such as these were to become obvious to anyone who cared to make them. The love of nature. The innate mysticism, an indignation at the wrongs visited by mankind one upon the other. Above all, the determination to speak out against such matters in the only way either of them were able. How could he *not* have known about Blake, critics such as GL ask, forgetting how out of fashion his poetry was at that particular time.

They needed to have been there, that afternoon in the classroom where it all began. To have witnessed first-hand Jimmy's surprise. Frustration, envy, resentment – these would have been my own reactions. Picture Captain Scott arriving at the South Pole only to discover that Amundsen had beaten him to it; imagine Armstrong landing on the moon, discovering a Russian flag already in place.

'Or Tennyson's frustration on a visit to the theatre. Proud of his description of waterfalls as *veils of thinnest lawn* only to find this was precisely how they'd always done it on the stage?' Never short of a literary allusion, my Helen.

Jimmy was not slow to recognise a kindred spirit, though. He was full of questions – the man, his life, the poetry, his artwork, the reception he'd received – with Miss Quintock only too willing to oblige, visiting the county library and returning with two further volumes. Ordering books on Hogarth, William Morris and the like, together with manuals on painting in general and calligraphy in particular. Searching about for paper more suitable for his work, extracting a promise that on no account would he make further use of HMG copybooks. Also to emerge was a side to her character that none of us had suspected: she'd arrive at school each day weighed down by the most lavishly illustrated tomes, hoarded over the years and which – from the way she spoke – must have fuelled imaginary journeys through Florence in the company of the Medicis, to Rome with Leonardo. Jimmy seemed to know far more about this style of painting, theoretically at least. Somewhere, at some point in the past, someone must have had a hand in his artistic education, but he told us neither who it was nor how this had come about.

Being aware that he was not the first to work in this field seemed to give him confidence, as if looking to his predecessor for posthumous support. He was invited to come back and tell us more about his work, demurred, but relented in the face of popular demand and, sure enough, presented himself punctually at the school gate the following week. Meanwhile, we had prepared for his visit. Miss Quintock recalled some *Book of Kells* artwork sent to her by the education authority and rooted it out from the cupboard. Charlie reminded us how the strip cartoons in comics such as *Dandy, Beano,* or *Hotspur* combined words and pictures in much the same way as Jimmy had done and, working in groups, we produced our own adaptations of proverbs or mottos presented in what Frank Murgatroyd would no doubt call the 'Saintley style'.

Jimmy was delighted. Forgetting his initial reserve, he moved from table to table, finding something positive to say about each one of them; insisting they were displayed around the walls of the classroom. From that point on he became a regular visitor to the school, never interfering with our lessons unless specifically asked to do so, but helping to tidy up at the end of the day, walking home with us afterwards or talking over the nature of future projects with our teacher.

She it was that encouraged the earliest of his experimental artwork. There had been the early treatment of a Kipling poem. This one I could quote from memory: *Boots: Boots – boots – boots – movin' up and down again,* with the words consisting of different kinds of footwear: boots, shoes, plimsolls, slippers. Jimmy smuggling the motto for the month, *Many Hands Make Light Work,* from behind the teacher's desk and producing his own version, consisting entirely of fingers and thumbs.

And it must have been about this time he grasped the potential of the approach, not merely as a way of combining words and pictures in a novel and pleasing manner, but of producing something having far sharper an edge. Again with Enid Quintock's support, co-conspirator even. Not that any of us realised it at the time. But the evidence was there, in a folder lying beneath *The Encyclopedic History of British Art* that I now retrieved from the archive.

Chapter Six

The Postbag Papers

The folder Peter handed up from the archive was buff coloured and A4 in size. The type we still used on a daily basis down at the library. Much older, though, with the rusty imprints of paper clips, stigmata-like, at each of its corners. Inside, a series of pages, about four of them all told, had been skilfully removed from a thinly lined exercise book. A one-inch margin ran down the left hand side of the sheets, each filled with neat copperplate writing – Enid Quintock's, recognisable from reports elsewhere in the folder; the title – *Jimmy's Postbag; Christmas, 1949* – boldly underlined in red, heading up the first page.

Peter sketched in the background.

With Christmas over, she'd asked her pupils to bring in cards they'd been sent. These were of all shapes and sizes and made a fine display across one side of the classroom. Jimmy, whose knowledge of folklore and custom had provided a completely new dimension to the festivities, seemed delighted. Nevertheless something seemed to be troubling him, and it took Miss Quintock the whole lesson to discover just what this was. Not, as they feared, the sending of Christmas cards. His was a far broader quarrel: the marketing of seasonal goodwill for commercial purposes no less. How they traded on the children's sentimentality; worse still, the exploitation of human frailty.

Few of the pupils understood. The oldest could have been no more than ten. And he might have given up the struggle had not Miss Quintock intervened. They were seen plotting together in her room, Jimmy adding a number of flourishes to what he'd drawn. His pencil commandeered by the teacher. A cancelling out, or an addition. Striding out to fetch a card from the display. Heads together, conspiratorial chuckles as they considered the outcome. Then, a few days later, Jimmy arrived with the final outcome: a dozen or so cards that became known as the *Christmas Postbag.* Each consisted of a single sheet of paper folded in two, having a picture on the cover – no more than a sketch really – with a short message inside. Text, image and size matched to perfection, capturing the essence in a few brief strokes. The pictures had long since disappeared, Peter having only a vague memory of what they looked like, but Miss Quintock had evidently decided to keep a personal copy of the words. For use in one of her lessons, so he'd thought long ago when adding them to the archive, confirmation, now, of the key part she'd played in the development of the 'Saintley' talent.

*

The first had been produced on a large hard card with roughly trimmed edges; the text, Jimmy's imposing version of what we would now call Times Roman Bold:

> *Now, see here, Dickie, this is the most important card you've got and you're lucky to have it. None of your 70 or 80 gram rubbish here. Just feel the weight of the vellum; look at those distinguished uncut edges, the elegant embossed print. Real quality! As for size – a good ten inches by six, enough to see off even the most pretentious of rivals. And what about the full colour art picture, eh? Not part of the card itself but ever so lightly glued to it. Shows I've got taste, you see. Turner it was last year. Stubbs this. 'Horses', I told my secretary, 'and make sure they're famous. Don't pay less than £2 per card and be certain that it shows!'*
>
> *None of your illegible scrawl, either. Not likely! My name is printed inside; there, below the greetings, proving what an exceedingly important*

and busy person I am, and how very, very fortunate you are to know me. So, you need to give my card pride of place, centre of the mantelpiece, putting all others to shame. None of this sneaking back and slipping someone else's in its place as soon as my back's turned. Caught you out doing that the other year, didn't I!

The next had originally been written in old-fashioned Marion Richardson script. Shaky and uneven, but neater by far than any of Miss Quintock's pupils had achieved.

Don't you just love this little card your old Nan's picked out, special like, just for you, my dear. My, what a time I had choosing it.

Went to the sweetie shop on the corner, I did. You remember where we used to spend our coupons after my Tom, that's your Dad, got left behind in France. They're so nice there. Janet's taken over completely from her mum now – but my, the trouble she's had with her back – well, she pulls out shelf after shelf of they cards and tells me the price of each, and at last we settle for this one.

The little red puppy dog. Jumping out of the stocking on Christmas morning, licking the little girl's face. Like Cindy used to do. You remember. Course, we can't keep our doggies here at Sunnyvale no more. Not since that new matron arrived.

And there's this dear little poem inside:

'"This puppy wakes on Christmas Day
To greet his mistress new.
He says "quick, come out to play
All the long day through!"'

Now isn't that lovely? And look, underneath I've written, ever so careful like, without any of they blots or scratching out: 'to my dear little Richard from his ever loving Nan'.

Where was I? Oh yes. Would you believe it, when I comes to buy the stamp, they put the cost up again, and when I looks in my purse there's not enough money there. Danged, though, if I can get the hang of these flibbertigibbet coins! Well, I says, that settles it – the bus can go hang. I'll take the card and walk the four mile home. Then Janet says all of a sudden like, 'my, someone's left a stamp on this envelope!' And so they had. Funny, that, it being there at the bottom of the shelf and all.

So here's my little card, as usual, and I hope as how it won't get lost like last year's did; so, when you brings us over on New Year's Day it be there with all the others.

The last card had, apparently, been written in childish scroll. Precisely the kind they'd assisted younger brothers and sisters to prepare in the weeks before Christmas:

Hey, what about me! I'm over here! Pushed down behind the Oxfam camels. Between Santa Claus riding an Esso tanker and the Giles family. The snowman in white chalk on untidy blue sugar paper. That's the one. He's got a beetroot for a nose and pieces of coal for eyes and I couldn't quite fit him all in. Took me all afternoon with the Children's Hour colouring kit, it did. Got paint all over the carpet; it's on your wallpaper now. Then Mum put her hand over mine whilst I held the pen and we sort of pushed it around the page. Writing came out. 'To my Daddy' she said it wrote. But why do you think she was crying?

* * *

So different from my previous image of Jimmy. Miss Quintock too. A strong influence on the 'rustic woodsman's' future development, steering him in less facile, more productive directions. Playing a significant part in Peter's childhood as well. Just as Daddy had in mine. He'd have adored the *Postbag* – every bit as much as mother would have hated it. But there's no doubt which of them would have had the last word…

…the room across the landing from the study had been converted into a nursery. I'd lie there at night alongside my dolls telling them

Daddy's stories. Alert also for the sound of the study latch being closed, the squeak of his chair; sometimes an expression of disgust as he marked the results of a test or set of essays. Just occasionally I'd creep from my room and sit watching him at work. He'd pretend not to notice me. Say nothing. Then, when he'd finished, or heard mother locking up for the night, take my hand, tuck me back in bed. I always slept soundly after that.

Often enough, though, there'd be raised voices drifting up from the kitchen. I'd catch the occasional word, snatches of dialogue –

'... school like that... dumbing down for dunces... make something of yourself... deputy head by now... hold my head up... Daddy a bishop... should have listened... unless there's other things keeping you there.'

– not fully understanding what was said.

Later, approaching my early teens, I'd slip into the study to check up on a reference, complete some homework project, or scare myself rigid with the ghost stories – M. R. James, Algernon Blackwood, Walter de la Mare – secreted away among the English poets. To the accompaniment of heated discussions downstairs:

'...friends she's been keeping... language... common... cousin Lucy... respect... what she'll grow up to be...'

Crouched down, my back against the wall. Knees pulled up to chest:

'No, no, no, Donald. How can you even contemplate it? Grammar school... out of the question... teaching there's one thing... no daughter of mine... doesn't bear thinking about... spoil that girl badly enough as it is...'

A muffled response from Daddy:

'Don't talk nonsense... think they look up to you?... ruin her chances at Somerville... Henry's put in a good word for her... honestly think she'll thank you?'

Daddy, agitated now; words unintelligible, but the sentiment clear. Again over-ruled:

'... socialist clap-trap... not Henry's opinion... Parable of the Talent... cost worrying?... he's got a solution there, too...'

And so off to board at the convent; holidays spent overseas mostly, with new friends. Then university. Infrequent visits back home. Childhood's end.

Or so I thought...

* * *

The brilliance of *Fiddlers Three* and *Postbag Papers,* to say nothing of how *Home Thoughts* had originated. I don't know what the pupils made of the *Postbag;* I almost warmed to the man. But the stories still bothered me. There was something unsettling about them. Over and beyond the constant bloodletting, their overt masculinity, the continuous nick-naming. All the more upsetting for not knowing precisely what this could be. And why, I wondered, had Jimmy not developed the *Postbag* approach more fully? He'd the capacity for bringing a number of seemingly unconnected notions together. For pulling ideas from the air itself, so it seemed. Then why content himself with the embellishment of other people's work? Why adopt such a time-consuming approach? Painstakingly producing each and every letter afresh wherever and whenever it was needed. The printing press had been available since Caxton's time. So why not avail himself of it? And, having found his *métier,* with Miss Quintock's support added to that of Sir Desmond, why the hasty and unexpected exit from the village?

Chapter Seven

Inkwell and Hourglass

It was simpler for Helen to ask questions than it was for me to answer them. Jimmy's work is easy to describe, but difficult to define. As to its rationale, the motive force behind it, many explanations have been given. All but the most obvious. Which is that, just like the stories he told, it came with the territory; emerged directly from the situation in which all of us found ourselves.

The war was over, but this made little difference to our way of life. Rationing continued, there was a shortage of petrol and a nine-month waiting list for cars, for those who could afford them. Any colour you liked as long as it was black. Anderson shelters were put to more practical uses: as kennels, garden sheds, storing unwanted furniture, forcing mushrooms and the like.

'"Dig for Victory", "Make do and mend", "Is your journey really necessary?"' Helen, who'd been involved in a *Forty Years On* exhibition run by the library, had most of the slogans off pat. 'Parachutes transformed into ladies' undergarments, to say nothing of star of the local soccer team running down the pitch decked out in the front-room curtains.'

I'd agreed to share reminiscences of those days, as part of the programme, foolishly including my prowess as member of the junior eleven in shorts run up from blackout material.

'"Careless talk costs lives"', I said, quoting another wartime adage

Jimmy had commiserated with Miss Quintock over the frugality of post-war educational supplies. Paint, brushes, canvas, paper – the stock in trade of an artistic existence – were similarly unobtainable; to the Squire even, so it appeared. No wonder he turned to whatever came to hand: newspaper, wood, cardboard, discarded packaging, even the backs of pictures he'd previously painted. He'd no choice in the matter really, and it always seemed to me that the philosophical justification for such an approach came later, theory following on from practicality as an after-thought almost. Maybe I do him an injustice? All I know is what I picked up from chance remarks made in my presence. '

Authenticity' had been a word frequently on lips, meaning little to me at the time, nor – till now – when obliged to follow it through.

'Lauding the natural over man-made products,' I suggested. 'The reason for all those pebbles; the twigs, egg shells, leaf mould and the other "treasures" he'd produce from about his person?'

Helen agreed. 'Just like the thrush in *Home Thoughts*, never recapturing the "first fine moment of rapture"'.

'"Magpie moments" according to Miss Quintock. Ideas came easily to Jimmy and he'd flit from one of them to the other.'

The 'magic of the moment' that had been his name for it. To delay, as in the cutting of a block or the cranking of a press, was to dilute. Nothing less than 'actuality', the recapturing of direct experience, would suffice. And nowhere was this more evident than in his struggles with – and failure at – the mastery of colour.

Biros, just coming onto the market, were expensive, banished from Miss Quintock's classroom on grounds of social equality; for more practical reasons also, as being bad for our handwriting. Fountain pens being similarly forbidden on account of their messiness. We were expected to write, and write neatly, with those strange wooden stick pens with detachable nibs you see nowadays in museums. This entailed frequent dippings into white ceramic inkwells – currently selling for a fortune in antique shops – the 'ink' arriving as powder in large sacks at the beginning of each term. The responsibility of mixing the powder with tap water was assigned to the 'ink monitor': the boy or, far more likely, girl who'd demonstrated the greatest cleanliness during the preceding weeks.

'No easy task,' I remembered. 'Too much liquid and you'd get an anaemic greyish fluid, quite illegible; too little and there'd be ink blotches everywhere. Gave my younger brother Luke nightmares for weeks just thinking about it. Once the brew reached precisely the right consistency, the inkwells had to be filled from an old-fashioned watering can kept in the cupboard. By which time the monitor usually looked like an ancient Briton setting out to meet the Romans and had forfeited their place in the "cleanliness" league for months to come.'

Jimmy had been fascinated by the whole process, but it earned him the first of many classroom scoldings. He'd reached down into one of the sacks and thoughtfully rubbed some of the powder between finger and thumb. A large quantity spilt on the floor and the teacher rounded on him, just as if he'd been one of her pupils. He slunk away with muttered apologies, but returned next day with a packet of powdered egg, left over – so he said – from his wartime provisions. Miss Quintock, somewhat ashamed of the way she had spoken to him in front of the class, was prevailed upon – and Jimmy was the only one who could have done this – to spare a small quantity of her precious blue powder. 'Sun and sky,' he told us, spilling both out onto a sheet of white paper, 'but what about the grass?' One of the girls remembered lettering of this colour that had decorated her birthday cake, and the class went on to debate other ingredients that might be used in lieu of paint, were it not for post-war austerity: mustard, flour, coffee – or ground acorn as it was in those days.

Matters might have ended there had not Miss Quintock brought out that precious book of hers and written some of Blake's lines on the blackboard. Some of the few I have learnt by heart:

To see a World in a Grain of Sand,
And a Heaven in a Wild Flower,
Hold Infinity in the palm of your hand,
And Eternity in an hour?

Helen recognised them immediately: 'Auguries of Innocence'.

'A good title,' I said, 'considering what happened next.'

One of the children, Charlie Dowse I think it was, came back from a seaside holiday clutching his souvenir – an hour-glass – to 'share' with the rest of the class during one of our 'Treasure Trove' mornings. Miss Quintock made a great show of demonstrating precisely how it worked, turning it upside down and allowing the sand to trickle through the narrow aperture between top and bottom. She told us about the importance of such instruments before the time of watches, how the glass was first blown then pinched at the centre and how only the finest sand could be used. Then next day, which coincided with one of Jimmy's visits, she brought in one of her own 'treasures': a glass phial containing a similar kind of sand of differing colours layered one on top of the other in a series of stripes. Jimmy sat all this time at the back of the class, but was unusually silent. Afterwards he disappeared without a word, nor was there any sign of him for ten days or so when he reappeared looking as if nothing untoward had happened and bringing another of his mysterious packages with him. Miss Quintock handed over a pair of scissors; Jimmy cut the string, stripped away the brown paper.

'By now we knew what to expect, a picture of course, and I don't know why, the subject-matter perhaps, maybe because we'd had no hand in the outcome, but it failed to grab our attention.

Just an ordinary sunset. You know the kind of thing: blue sky, blood-red orb sinking beyond a green horizon, leafy trees casting long shadows in the foreground, with a charcoal-grey pathway snaking its way between them. You can pick them up in junk shops, umpteen to the dozen.'

Helen grimaced. 'Sounds like Mother would have loved it.'

'Not if she kept it around the house for any length of time. Turned out he'd used the back of a wooden tray and sand rather than paint. God knows how he'd come by the ingredients to produce such varied colours, nor how he'd stuck these to the surface, except that it stank of fish, leaving a gritty trail behind, like dandruff, in its wake. Not even your father could have smuggled that picture into his study.'

Grains of Infinity had introduced Jimmy to the use of colour and, for the moment, only this would do. Nothing, though, must come between him and the creative experience. Previously he'd worked with pencil, chalk, charcoal, coal even. All elemental, straight from the soil, with nothing man-made about them. From now on he insisted that only pigments derived directly from the world of nature would do. Whether he genuinely believed the creation of such a palette added to the intrinsic merit of the work, enhanced his experience of the artist or that of those who viewed it was never made clear. Maybe it was just an idea picked up from one of our lessons on the mediaeval artists or one of the books Miss Quintock had lent him.

'Whatever the reason,' I continued, 'he had us out scouring the countryside for earth, mud, bricks, stones, the wings of butterflies, bodies of beetles, grinding them into powder, expecting to reproduce the azures, umbers and cochineals we'd seen in Renaissance paintings. Our parents were horrified; we'd arrive home in a filthy state, our clothes dirty and torn. By which time Jimmy had turned to botany and we were forbidden to help as he searched out plants and roots of all kind. First he tried mixing them with water – a complete failure till he brought it to the boil, which wasn't much better. Not till he had a breakthrough, culled from some radio programme, I think: the use of egg white. Tempera, I believe it's called.'

'That, along with salt and vinegar.' Helen nodded her confirmation.

This had the required effect, producing a variety of colours: blue from elderberries, yellow from parsley, green from carrots, orange from dock leaves and brown from hawthorn. Applying these to wood, paper or any of a variety of surfaces was quite another matter; either they failed to bond or, if they did, resulted in the palest, most anaemic of hues. These ingredients were, in any case, in short supply at the time, so unless he was to concentrate on miniatures, there was no future in the project. Especially when Miss Quintock returned from the Easter holidays and was horrified to discover what we were up to.

'You do realise some of your ingredients are toxic?'

'Toxic?' queried Jimmy.

'Poisonous!'

Which concluded Jimmy's efforts in that particular field – or back garden, pond or slag heap for that matter. He continued to use colour to great effect, but always from tubes, supplied no doubt by the Squire as and when they became available and over-painting his failures with fresh efforts. 'Palimpsests', he told us – a new word. Miss Quintock wrote it up on the blackboard and we copied it into our exercise books as she attempted to enlighten us. But later that week, leant back against the war memorial, Tim, Chunky, myself and the rest of our classmates sprawled out before him, Jimmy explained it to us in the way he knew best. A vivid story, full of incident; holding our attention, but which – like the *Postbag Papers* – I only fully appreciated in retrospect.

* * *

A traveller fancying himself as a connoisseur of fine art goes off to Russia. He visits all the galleries, admires the paintings and decides to do a bit of exploring – as much as his guide allows him to do. The 'Great Patriotic War' has just ended and, all over the country, religious images are being removed from the churches and destroyed. He ends up in a little village in the back of beyond and spends the night drinking vodka with the innkeeper, who lets him into a secret. Their own special treasure, the holy *Icon of Ekatesburg*, which has been venerated by the villagers down the centuries, was smuggled out of the local monastery just minutes before the government troops arrived. Only he and the abbot know where it is hidden. The traveller begs to be shown the icon; the innkeeper demurs at first, then agrees. They stumble out into the night, making their way through a blizzard and follow a treacherous pathway into the hills. At long last they reach a secret cave where, by the light of the flickering lantern, the visitor sees the most beautiful object he has ever encountered.

It must be added to his collection. How much is it worth, he asks? The innkeeper is horrified. This is not merely a picture, but a holy object, painted with devotion, imbued with the prayers of each successive generation. Down the years men and women have given their lives to defend it; the spirituality of the village itself resides within this icon. The traveller persists, offering the innkeeper a large sum of money. Think what could be done with such wealth, he says. The people could be clothed and fed. New houses could be built, the roads repaired; the inn itself is badly in need of renovation. The innkeeper hesitates. The traveller offers him twice, then three times the amount. Think of what might be done for the monastery. There could be a school, a new church devoted to Our Lady. At last, with the greatest reluctance and at five times the original sum, the innkeeper reluctantly gives way. But the greatest secrecy was needed, and how would it be possible to get such a distinctive item past customs and out of the country?

Back at the inn, they think long and hard over this until, at last, mine host has an idea. Young Igor Orlinksi fancies himself as an artist. Has turned his back on socialist realism and fills all the canvasses he can lay his hands on with the most outrageous daubs. Get him to paint one of his dreadful concoctions over the icon; he'd do it for next to nothing, and the customs men would probably pay good roubles to get it out of the country! But, protests the traveller, that would destroy the icon itself; not if Igor covers it with a thick coat of vanish first, the ingenious innkeeper replies.

So that is what they do. The money is paid over, Igor delightedly obliges with the gaudiest of abstracts and the picture passes without question through customs. Back home, the garish top colours and the varnish are carefully removed, revealing the *Madonna of Ekatasburg* in all her glory. The traveller is delighted with the success of his ruse and prepares to exhibit his new acquisition to the public. But first, for insurance purposes, he must get it valued. He hurries to the most respected of fine art specialists in London, who examine it carefully using the latest technology, then shake their heads. This is no masterpiece, they tell him. The wood on which it is painted is no more than ten years old, as are the materials that have been used. As for the brushstrokes: quite modern also. No iconographer would have approached his subject in this way. Far better to have invested his money in the new art which is coming out of Russia. Take these, for example. The work of Igor Orlinski. Anything by him fetches a five-figure sum these days, and so difficult to get hold of that their value must be increasing even as we speak…

Chapter Eight

The Indignant Page

It must have been three or four years after the first of Jimmy's classroom appearances that those of us in the top form moved on to the next stage in our education. At which point our paths began to diverge. Tim and I donned the maroon blazers, long grey trousers and segmented bi-coloured caps favoured by St Hugh's High, whilst Andrew, Chunky, Charlie and the rest were permitted the relaxed dress code adopted by the Joseph Freeman County Secondary School. To begin with we'd hurry home, both of us, eager to be rid of these objectionable garments before rushing out to join the others, just as we'd done since childhood. But things were never really the same.

We'd had our quarrels before. Over the sharing out of apples scrumped from the Squire's orchard, the swapping of cigarette cards, or the merits of one football club over another. Teasing, too. Charlie nicknamed 'Blinkers' because he wore glasses, Chunky for his girth and Tim on account of his sister's love-life. Squabbles that frequently ending in scraps; two small boys rolling in the dust egged on by a screaming ring of rival supporters, or pitched battles, one faction against the other. Allegiances were constantly changing within the group; alliances formed, then broken. But here was something quite different. Regardless of what had gone before, despite all efforts at concealment, parental ambition percolated insidiously downward. A line of demarcation had been drawn, between the 'freemaniacs' and 'humites' as we came to be known, corroding even the closest of relationships, inexorably dragging each of us from the orbit of former friendship.

We saw much less of Jimmy as well, Tim and I, taking up with Giles rather, younger brother of Vernon memorialised in the parish church.

'This him?' Helen, who'd been fishing around the documents, pulled a ragged photo from the pile. 'Tall gangly lad, so you said.' She held it up admiringly. 'Seems attractive enough to me. Dishy almost.'

'Son and heir to the Amberstone estate no less. "Gerundive" to us on account of his classical public school education. Superior even to St Hugh's. My parents couldn't have been more pleased.'

I retained close ties with Miss Quintock, though. My own brother, Howard, had just entered the village school and was to spend five more glorious years in her company.

'Or so we expected.'

What happened next reached me through a variety of sources: snatches of parental conversation, guarded and brought to a sudden halt when my presence became know; gossip overheard around the village and innuendo from teachers at St Hugh's – all of it caught but not fully understood. And, of course, there were the tales from the chalk-face that young Howard brought home with him. Her absent-mindedness, for example. Forgetting pupils' names or the homework she'd set. Repeating the same lesson twice on successive days, and once – unbelievably – forgetting to take the register. Then there was the time she attempted to write on the blackboard with a pencil and the occasion she'd cycled into school, ready to start teaching, on a Sunday. Stories were also circulating about her strange shopping habits: large quantities of breakfast cereals, ordering meat from the chemist, wine from the butcher – and, as everyone knew, she was strictly teetotal.

All of which had been going on for six months or so before matters came to a head, reaching me verbatim from Howard and his classmates.

Jimmy had arrived at the school, primed to discuss the continental migration of birds to our part of the world. But there'd been none of the usual greeting from Miss Quintock. At first she seemed startled, shook her head in disbelief, then smiled – in a way she'd never smiled before.

'Home, Reg?' she enquired. 'So soon. But how wonderful.' And, throwing down her papers, she clasped both his hands in hers. Some in the class giggled, others pivoted to get a better view; most remained rooted to their desks in horrified silence.

Jimmy, once he recovered from his initial surprise, was – by all accounts – splendid. Taking her gently by the arm he led her to the door. 'Class monitor,' he instructed, 'take over. And no nonsense from anyone. Margaret, you're a sensible girl. Go tell the Rev. Draper he's wanted here. Off with you now!' He made way to let the girl pass, but not before our teacher had flung her arms around his neck, nor swiftly enough for her to hear the words she whispered in his ear: 'Don't ask it of me, Reg. Not long now. I'll do anything you ask. You know that. But we must wait.'

After which the red-faced parson arrived to keep the class occupied for the rest of the morning. They paid him little attention, not with Jimmy sitting out there on the bench in the courtyard holding their teacher's hand and continuing to whisper to her. Not with the ambulance arriving, his guiding her into it, making his way back to the classroom to have a few hurried words with the rector before turning to the pupils, shrugging his shoulders and disappearing without a word. That afternoon the school was dismissed early. What we failed to realise at the time was that none of us – neither Howard nor myself, Tim, the Freemaniacs, nor the rest of her pupils – were to set eyes on Enid Quintock again.

From that moment things moved swiftly at the school. The following day a young man with a briefcase, pink, black-suited, HMG's own representative, so it was rumoured, appeared at the gates. Their headteacher was 'indisposed' he told the assembled pupils and it was unlikely that she would return. A new head would have to be appointed, but this had happened so suddenly that it might take some time to find someone capable of upholding 'the splendid traditions laid down over so many years.' In the meantime, all of them must work as hard as they could to help out in this moment of crisis.

The real problem, of course, was that Miss Quintock – rebel to the very end – had chosen the worst possible moment for her 'indisposition.' It was now mid-June and a mountain of preliminary procedures – committee meetings, advertising, selection panels and the like – had to be gone through if a fresh head was to be appointed for the beginning of the new academic year. And, no matter what the man from County Hall might say, our tiny school tucked away in rural Bereden was hardly the ideal posting for those aspiring to headship, however altruistic they might be. So that, over the next few months, Howard and his companions were to experience a succession of temporary appointments, varied as to enthusiasm, gender and effectiveness. Some had been reassigned from office jobs in Winchester, some on loan from other schools, a few drafted in from neighbouring counties. Occasionally also, there would be a flurry of excitement as candidates who had expressed interest in the position were brought to visit the school, sitting in on classes, asking awkward questions of both staff and pupils and poring over their teacher's meticulously kept records before departing – never to reappear.

Throughout this time Miss Quintock remained secreted away, quite comfortable but at the same establishment, some twenty or so miles from the village, where – ominously we felt

– her predecessor had ended her days. None of us really knew what was going on, nor was Jimmy forthcoming on the subject. He visited her regularly, and we pleaded to be taken with him. Always he declined, our parents adding their veto to his. It was too far for us to travel; she needed all the rest she could get; the hospital did not admit children. But the truth could not be withheld from us forever. Even if we did go, she was unlikely to recognise us; did not always know who she herself was. In fact, she was sinking fast. Then, as July turned to August, the older and more responsible among us were told to prepare for the worst.

It came one Sunday towards the end of the month. Harvest had been delayed that year, but now the heat shimmered off concrete, the melted tarmac sticking to our shoes as we waited for Jimmy's return from the hospital, Freemaniacs and Humites united on this occasion in our grief. I remember the constant beat of the threshers working late into the evening, chaff catching in eyes and throat, the growl of a tractor as it pulled into the square, delaying the arrival of Jimmy's bus by twenty minutes or so. And there he was, seated top deck, up front, as usual. We knew the worst the moment we spotted him. The way he came down those stairs, and were those tears in his eyes? No need for words. The merest shake of the head, a shrug of the shoulders, and he held out the book: blue with orange covers. *Songs of Innocence and Experience.* Enid Quintock would never have been parted from it whilst there was life in her body.

'It was her hold on reality,' he told us later, 'that book. Never out of her sight all these weeks, no matter who she thought she was or where her mind might have been. Quite lucid at the end, though. Insisted I take it. Smiled. You know the way she did. "I'll trade you Blake's vision for Browning's rationality", she says. "Any day!" And that was it.'

But it wasn't. Not quite. Blake remained tucked in alongside

Browning's *Complete Works* on the bookshelf right enough, and Jimmy continued the Quintock tradition of keeping it very much to himself. He would read to the children from it, allow them to look at the illustrations – in his presence and as long as it remained firmly in his hands – and never, no matter how urgently it was required, nor how respectable the individual, would he lend it out. There was the occasion, though, on one of my rare visits when I found it taken down from the bookshelf and Jimmy nowhere to be seen. Open at the title page, with some lines – from another of Blake's poems, 'Little Girl Lost', apparently – and an inscription written inside the front cover.

Children of the future age,
Reading this indignant page,
Know that in a former time,
Love, sweet love, was thought a crime.
Reg, Aldershot, 5th September, 1915.

* * *

Helen shook her head. 'Explains why you never got a look inside the covers. Anymore than Reg did, in a manner of speaking.' She laughed. 'Her fiancé presumably, and you've got to feel sorry for him. Off to the trenches, never to return, and no hint of home comforts. Leastways, not the kind he had in mind. You'd have thought she'd have shown some compassion.'

'Don't be too hard on her. Public morals were just as rigid in 1915 as they had been a hundred years earlier, or in Blake's time. And, don't forget, her father was a clergyman.'

'As far as I'm concerned the love-life makes her all the more intriguing.'

'But I thought you Catholics frowned on that sort of thing.'

Helen reached over and took my hand. 'Not all of us by a

long chalk. Would we ever have got together if I'd asked you to wait? Remember how shocked Uncle Henry was? And Mother? I thought she'd have apoplexy. What was it she called it?'

'The "living in" sin . How can I ever forget?'

Chapter Nine

Pied Piper of Bereden

Songs of Innocence and Experience – the perfect epithet. Miss Quintock's life distilled in five short words, her death as great a shock to Peter as Daddy's had been to me. And so much more dignified.

He'd failed to return from one of his conferences. Nor, for that matter, had he arrived, but tyre marks were found beside a lake well off the beaten track; the *Danger: Deep Water* signs ignored. A car had been hauled ashore, his body at the steering wheel; sandwiches, half-consumed, on the seat beside him. The receipt in Daddy's pocket was for ten red roses, to be delivered to Miss Alison Tate, Room 101 at the Greville Arms. With an accompanying note: 'See you tomorrow, as arranged, sweetheart, for the plenary session of your life. No "living in" sin here.' Daddy had dined out on it. Up and down the country; at and in between conferences; off and on, for the last three years. With the art mistress, no less. Uncle Henry had announced an ecclesiastical embargo but the tabloids had a field-day. At which point I arrived home, summoned from an expedition in the wilds of the Australian outback; too late for the funeral but confronted with a sanitised version of events.

I never really trusted anyone after that. Which probably explains my success, both academically and down at the library; my failure with the opposite sex. Till Peter came along. Older man meets guileless student; that's what they all thought, another take on the Innocence/ Experience theme. Well, hardly. Given his reserve, my own lack of restraint. It might well have affected my attitude towards Jimmy, though. I revisited the well-worn jealousy jibe: how the two of them had been friends before ever I came on the scene; my reaction to the stories he told. Childish fun, so Peter assured me; told for amusement only, to pass the time of day. But my suspicions went deeper than this. Instinctive almost in ways I never quite fathomed. Till he opened the 'archive', handed up the manila folder, and I took a renewed interest in Enid Quintock's 'hermit from the woods'. It was then I first heard Jimmy's version of pre-Norman history, the *Jutish Chronicles* as it came to be known, and realised just how much Peter had underestimated the man.

He'd moved on to St Hugh's by then, so it was from younger brother Howard and his companions that the latest of Jimmy's stories reached him.

The Jutes, so Jimmy had told them, were one of the tribes employed by the Britons as protection against the Picts and the Scots once the Romans left our shores. But they took a fancy to the land and decided to settle. Some in Northumbria, others in Mercia or Wessex; the Jutes along the Kentish coast. Most of them remained there, but the hardiest struck out westwards, hugging the coast till they reached Southampton Water. There they followed upstream before finally putting down their roots in the Meon Valley which together with Kent, and according to Jimmy, were the only parts of the country where their traces could be found.

Little distinguished these people from surrounding tribes. The way they cleared the forest, set up villages, tilled the land and bred livestock was all much the same. As was the damming of streams for fishing, the hunting of deer or wild boar in the woodlands, the trapping of hares, rabbits and other small animals, for food and clothing. The warriors listened to sagas commemorating battles won, toasted one another in the Mead Hall; the women wove loose flowing garments – as did all such people. Much the same as set out in most history books.

What set Jimmy's version apart was the way these people were governed. In a democratic fashion, so he insisted, based on communal meetings held in the Mead Hall, where all voices were heard. With land and possessions handed down in equal measure to every member of the family, women included.

'Unique they were, the Jutes,' he told the children sitting around him in the churchyard, hanging on his every word. 'Search the land over, you'll not find their like. And you've their blood running in your veins. Each and every one of you. Sets you apart, that does. Makes you special. Can't you just feel it in your bones?'

'Imparting his own slanted version of reality,' I protested. 'Not the world as it was but as he would have liked it to have been.' All compounded tenfold by his treatment of these people's religion.

The whole ridiculous rigmarole would commence in February or March with the children preparing simnel cakes for Easter. A signal for Jimmy to wade in with his own version: 'Solmonath', the time of sowing, when the Jutes would bake loaves and decorate them with runes. Then, as the church prepared for the greatest of the Christian festivals, an alternative version would be on offer down at Third Class Cottage telling of the goddess Eostere; decorated eggs rolled downhill to represent the turning of the sun in the sky and buns marked out with his symbols. Harvest time, with the church full of fruit and sheaves of corn, classroom walls covered with harvest-gathering pictures, was prefigured among the Jutes by the dramatic feast of Haligmonath; Christmas by their Yule when the houses would have been decorated with streamers, candles and greenery. Mistletoe would have been as much in evidence then as now. As were customs such as bringing in the yule log, setting up of a tree, the celebration of Twelfth Night, common to both cultures.

'Dressed up and paraded to appear more exciting than anything that Anglican church of yours has to offer, Peter, or my Catholic one, come to that.' I was seething by now.

Not content with this, Jimmy set about peopling this world

with a collection of stock characters, rivalling any of the Arthurian legends. Similar to Daddy's, longer than usual, more fully sustained, but told with the man's same ulterior motive.

First, there was Stoyan, son of Ceowulf, not yet in his teens yet charged with returning his father's sword – Eanfled – to the place where the warrior-king had fallen. Four companions are sent by Morgana of the Mists, the resident goddess, to assist with the search. There's Tonbert, the fisherman; Swidhelm, a wonderful cook who keeps the local tavern; Redwald, the blacksmith, immensely strong, who announces this a puny bunch for such a dangerous mission; and Alric, the nobleman, wondering what business he can possibly have with such low-born fellows. Saba, the falcon tethered to his wrist commiserates with him about such matters. But off they set as Morgana has instructed, crossing the emblem of a mighty stag carved in the hillside which forms the boundary of Jutish territory. Soon, though, their way is barred by a torrential river, too deep for safety, too broad to cross. Not to worry, Tonbert has experience of all things aquatic; he tests the rate of flow, condition of the bank, speed and direction of the prevailing wind; makes a number of rapid calculations and leads them to a point where they are able to cross.

Pushing forward they find themselves in an arid wilderness, where they seem likely to starve or die of thirst. This time it's Swidhelm with his culinary skills who springs to the rescue. The roots he grubs from the soil may seem inedible, as are the beetles he grinds to a pulp and water drained from cactus-like plants gathered from the wayside – delicious, though, when nothing else is available. But now they are lost, till Tonbert discovers a shard he just happened to have pulled from the river a few days back and for safe-keeping has placed in his knapsack. It's covered with runic symbols which none of them can decipher. Step forward the educated Alric, who tells them it's a message from Morgana, a primitive sat-nav in fact, indicating landmarks they need to follow. Off they set once more, to the north, eventually reaching a dense forest, impenetrable to anyone except the blacksmith who hacks his way forward and, yes, there's Saba acting as additional direction-finder from the sky above their heads.

Beyond the forest lies a wasteland with nothing but stumpy trees and rocky outcrops as far as the eye can see. But suddenly there's a subterranean rumble, one of the boulders rolls aside and Ceowulf stands before them. In a rousing speech he praises their fortitude, censuring Alric's high-mindedness at the beginning of their adventures and Redwald for believing that strength alone would carry them through. Along the way they'd met insurmountable dangers; individually they had the skills to overcome them, but it was only working together they had succeeded. A simple magic, more powerful than all the shamans' sorcery, not to be forgotten on their return. And no further need for weapons such as Eanfled. Taking the sword he kisses the hilt then plunges it into the nearest rockface. 'Here she shall remain,' he proclaims, 'sleeping through the ages lest called upon in time of greatest peril. 'Seek not otherwise to disturb her slumber.'

'Not the old *Sword in the Stone* routine?' I broke into the narrative. 'Mallory or Tennyson? T. H. White's *The Once and Future King*?'

Peter seemed unconcerned: 'I don't think Jimmy ever heard of that lot. To him it was always "The Sordid Stone." Ceowulf's rockface, a "cliff-hanger".'

The new 'magic' works wonders. Stoyan draws men of all quality into his counsel, nor are women excluded. Skill and experience count for more than hearsay or rhetoric. The frail and the elderly are cared for, the young brought up in the ways of their ancestors.

'A proto welfare state,' I protested, 'in which harmony prevails, everyone is educated to the full extent of their ability, prosperity evenly distributed?'

But there is a cloud on the horizon. The Saxons have been converted to a new religion, which they intend inflicting on all neighbouring tribes, by force of arms if necessary. Surrounded on all sides, his army hopelessly outnumbered, Stoyan remembers his father's sword, held fast in the rockface.

The five companions reconvene hurriedly to retrieve it. Stoyan heaves with all his might but Eanfled is stuck fast – a twist in the tale I'd not seen coming. Neither is Tonbert, the blacksmith – who has the strength of three such men – anymore successful. The people mock them both but Morgana puts in a timely appearance and reveals her master-plan. The 'sordid stone' was to be their talisman; victory assured in ways other than open battle. And the strategy they were to follow would be distinctive of the Jutish people from this time onwards.

'Shamans and broadswords, meadhalls and female inheritance, falconry and animism, equal rights for thane and peasant. Bit of a rag-bag, isn't it?'

'You're not enjoying it then?'

'Carry on, Scheherazade, I can't wait to hear what happens next.'

Part of the Saxon army has been drawn up along the open plains before the village, the other ordered to attack from the forests in the north. It is to this group a traitor appears, promising to lead them into the village by night. They find it deserted. Stoyan, coward that he is, must have surrendered his birthplace without a fight and fled into the forest. They're about to send out search parties when a trapdoor flies open and a hoard of Jutish warriors pour out from a secret passageway. Pandemonium breaks loose; men on both sides are hacked down till it's discovered this has not been a battle of Saxons versus Jutes, but two sides of the invading army fighting against one another. Just as one traitor had led the northern army into the village disguised as Jutes, so another had persuaded the southern troops to adopt the same ruse: dressing in enemy garb and following him along Stoyan's escape tunnel. Each had attacked what appeared to be their Jutish foes, the two 'traitors' disappearing in the midst of the fray to rejoin their companions deep in the forest.

Here Stoyan and his followers adopt totally new tactics. Routes are marked out by-passing the usual pathways, lookouts posted in true Robin Hood style up in the tree-tops. Secret caches of weapons are hidden, underground escape routes tunnelled in case their main encampment is over-run. Harried from all sides from the moment they enter the forest, the Saxons are driven into pits or caught up in scarcely visible nets like a haul of helpless fish. They're set upon by an unseen enemy that materialises silently from nowhere then disappears back into the mist – we've all of us seen the movie – or are picked off silently, one at a time, by snipers supplied with deadly armaments devised by Redwald, the 'blacksmith from hell'. Worst of all, close-quarter combat when they're cut down in an instant – James Bond style – by the dreaded Jutish secret weapon.

Tonbert it was who'd discovered the stream, Alric who recognised the moss-covered stones over which it flowed. Swidhelm had used oil from the fish that swam in it for his cooking, whilst Redwald knew the exact temperatures to which his forge should be heated. But it's Stoyan, guided by Morgana, who brings stone, water, oil and fire together, honing each Jutish blade to a sharpness and durability none had thought possible.

The new guerrilla tactics have brought success. In their rustic mead hall the bards immortalise their new hero, one to whom all future Jutes would aspire. Austere in dress as he is in speech. Scrupulous in judgement, expecting much of those who served him; implacable in resolution, ingenious beyond belief.

Spare of tongue yet sharp of wit

They sang;

Steadfast in kinship, slow to quit

– tagging him 'Jute of Jutes'.

Stoyan, the perfect role-model for the coming generation; tied in children's minds to a less than flattering image of the faith.

'Convenient,' I said, 'Jimmy landing on the Jutes. Just about enough known about them to establish their existence, but so little else that almost any claim could have the semblance of credibility. On a par with Robin Hood, Hereward the Wake or Arthur, but with a more sinister motive running through them.'

With Jimmy not the Uncle Remus figure they'd taken him to be. A Jean Brodie character rather. Svengali even? Better still – given the man's admiration of Browning – the Pied Piper of Bereden, leading its children astray.

Bias on my part, according to Peter, especially as I'd never met the man. Warning me about judging events in the light of personal experience, that 'if you want to find something badly enough, you're sure to succeed. Search hard enough for the proof and it will be there.' His students were at it all the time. Along with those who 'thought the earth was flat; the Americans had never landed on the moon; Hitler was alive and well and living in South America.'

'And, if you're *that* bothered,' he continued, 'how about the books you read as a child? The Arthur Ransomes, Enid Blytons, Malcolm Savilles? Weren't they every bit as culpable? Same as storytellers the world over. Behind the plots and sub-plots, the settings and the dialogue, their choice of heroes and heroines, there's always a message. Holding up some values to the exclusion of others; telling us that certain lifestyles are to be emulated, others rejected. Implanting notions of gender, class, compliance. And Jimmy was no exception. You might not approve of the slant he gave to his stories, but he had just as much right to his ideas as any of the others. It's the same with the history books. Nineteenth-century England, for example. Read about it in Macaulay, then Hobswan. Same events. Same characters. Same setting. But totally different stories. If Jimmy was guilty of manipulation, then so were they.'

'Except these were children – nine, ten years old at the most.' I'd heard all this before. 'It was their parents' choice, the stories they heard or had read to them. That's what legitimises their characters and plot-line, why we take such care down at the library.' All the fuss there'd been about golliwogs; the re-titling of Agatha Christie's

Ten Little Niggers. Why, after *Batman* programmes on television, we warned children not to 'try it at home'. The reason teachers in school sometimes found themselves in hot water. 'Even at your level, Peter, courses get cancelled, don't they!' A reference to one of his own programmes, *The Literature of Colour,* censored by the University on grounds of political bias. So why had he paid such little attention to what was going on around him; heard rather than merely listened to the stories he was told?

'And why,' I demanded, 'did no one come forward to object to such stories at the time?'

Chapter Ten

Flight of Fancy

Helen was not alone in distrusting such stories. Steeped in tradition as our village was, it was hardly tactful for Jimmy to have imbued these stories with notions of democracy and land reform. Worse still, with the war fresh in our mind, tracing our ancestors back to a race of 'Germanic' people. It was not that he set out to cause trouble, but there were certain kinds of adult that seemed perpetually to faze him – those in positions of authority usually, the very ones whose support he most needed and who, in turn, could not seem to leave him be. Chief amongst these was our rector.

'Hardly surprising with all that aping of the ecclesiastic calendar going on at Third Class Cottage.' Helen puffed out her cheeks dismissively.

'He put on quite a performance, though. Gave Jimmy a good run for his money in that respect.'

Colourful vestments, continual crossings of himself, bobbings up and down at unexpected moments, the Rev. Theodore Draper's services never lacked verve. A high-point was the distinctive mode of his responses. High-pitched, strangulated, wavering between octaves – we took bets among ourselves as to how long he could eke them out. More particularly the benediction, concluding with 'the peace of God'; to the uninitiated he appeared to be calling on his Maker for 'a piece of cod'. This was abbreviated by some St

Hugh's swot taking notes on Tudor costume to 'Codpiece' and it was by this sobriquet – unsuspected either by the recipient or our parents, and never fully understood by the younger members of his congregation – that he came to be known.

'Was there no one in the whole village, Peter, for whom you *didn't* have a nick-name?'

'Hardly. Nonentities and incomers perhaps. It was more of a badge of recognition really, a primitive sort of socialisation if you like, telling people that they'd arrived, were part of the community. Or hinting at what was needed if they wanted to be accepted.'

'To conform, you mean? And nobody objected?'

'Better to know yourself for what you are than to be totally neglected,' I said. Which was pretty well the way things stood at the time.

Helen made no reply, merely fixed me with one of her 'more in sadness than anger' stares.

Jimmy was no more popular down at the school. There'd been a succession of teachers following Miss Quintock's departure, incompetent for the most part, their tenure short-lived. Quite naturally they questioned his continued visitation to the classroom, the open relationship he'd built up with the pupils – contrary to good discipline, they claimed. Even when they finally ousted him from the school itself he continued meddling in their homework, or would turn up unexpectedly on one of the woodland trails prepared for them by the inspectorate. There they'd be, trying to fathom the accompanying notes, whilst Jimmy in the background was suggesting a right turn that would take them to Roundabout Paddock, a left to Dishery Piece, or what a shame it was to miss Tandy Gasser at that time of the year. None of which they, or their masters at County Hall, had heard.

But it was with the appointment of a new headteacher that things really began to go wrong.

Eric Stapleton – E. R. Stapleton Esq., BA, DipEd, to give him his full title – arrived in the village not only from military service but a North Korean prisoner of war camp. The school had by then gained a reputation for indiscipline. Parade ground values were required to restore it to the glory days, so he believed, and Eric brought five years of soldiery experience to the task. Battledress was replaced with academic gown, something never before seen in the school. The pupils were to address him as 'Sir', stand to attention in his presence, rise to their feet when he entered the room. They were to march to and from classes in good order; complete their homework not only on time but signed by the teacher who'd set it. A highly regimented cadet corps was introduced for the older boys, first-aid classes for the girls. Least popular of all, his institution of stars for good work, stripes for poor performance, with a series of carefully graded badges awarded according to success or failure; his favourite witticism – the 'ultimate deterrent' – a size ten gym shoe hung behind his door awaiting those disobeying any of his 'four-minute warnings'. My brother, always of a nervous disposition, reacted particularly badly to all this, sleepless nights, bad dreams, sometimes worse, coinciding with the advent of the new regime. The rest of his companions disliked it just as much.

And:

'Sorry, Helen, it was those qualifications – BA, DipEd – that did for him. BadEgg we called him. And deservedly so.'

BadEgg had a deep suspicion of Jimmy's democratic notions, regarding his Jutish stories as a type of proto-communism. As did several long-standing and respected members of the community. For years they'd put up with, welcomed even, anecdotes celebrating the old order: Squire, parson, town crier, publican and so on. We'd sung about them in church most Sundays – *the rich man at his castle, poor man at his gate* – followed immediately by the assurance *God made them high and lowly and ordered their estate.* The more recent of Jimmy's stories were quite another matter. Subversive, they agreed among themselves; undermining the values we'd fought so long to defend, and they were supported by leading members of the armed forces who'd snapped up local properties in the neighbourhood that had been going for a song. Comparable, these latest offerings, to the co-operative movement they'd resisted for so long but which had established a toehold in the village. As was the new health service they'd fought tooth and nail to oppose.

'All might still have been well,' I told her, 'had Sir Desmond, who'd taken earlier tales of the Squirarchy in good part, not objected so strongly to the Jutish saga – with no reason given.'

This could eventually have proved the catalyst, as might Codpiece's religious objections, or the arrival of our new headteacher. It was, however, a single incident unconnected with any one of them that brought matters to a head.

It began, inauspiciously enough, with the arrival of the Grinder Man. He appeared outside the Jugged Hare without warning one Monday morning, tall and swarthy, unshaven but sporting the most splendid moustache. More than compensating for any lack of beard it sat, black and majestic, above a set of sparkling white teeth. These glinted here and there with a hint of gold, matched only by the single ring that dangled rhythmically from his left ear. His hair, jet black also and shoulder-length, had been gathered back into a pigtail, whilst a yellow scarf was flung nonchalantly about his neck. He wore a vividly striped sweater, padded at the elbows; trousers secured at the waist by a heavily embossed leather belt and boots fastened with scarlet laces. Most extraordinary of all, though, was the bicycle he rode.

At first there seemed to be nothing unusual about it. Just a normal gentleman's cycle with wheels, saddle, pedals, brakes, handlebars, etc. The same as those most of us owned, except for the large box fixed above the front mudguard. Closer inspection revealed two supports pulled down, front and back on each side of the frame, raising it a few inches off the ground, allowing it to remain free-standing when dismounted. Having alighted and completed this operation the stranger undid the catch which secured the box, hinged the lid forward over the handlebars, disclosing a small stone wheel, dark grey in colour, rough but shot through with diamond-like iridescence. This was connected by means of a leather belt to a small spindle, part of the cycle's rear axle and, turning to the small crowd that had gathered, he swept his hat from his head and performed an elaborate bow.

'How beautiful a day,' he proclaimed, in an accent that veered from Italian to French with a *soupçon* of Polish, as he did so unfurling a banner proclaiming that here was none other than *Grigorio: Grinder to the Great*. 'See, the sun she shines. The birds they sing. No clouds in sky. All right with world, yes? And now all is the better. Grigorio is come. Problems of garden, kitchen, farmyard, dinings room at end. Ladies, no more bluntness in cookings; gentlemen, the easier become the sawings and the mowings; scouting boys, guiding girls, the badges more quickly won, swift in the sewing ons. And how, you asking? What Grigorio talking about? Come, see. Look and amazing be!'

He produced a knife, passed it round for all to examine, and scraped the blade several times up and down the wall. Then, taking an apple from his pocket he attempted, unsuccessfully, to peel it. Several members of his audience were invited to try but, they too, failed.

'Blunted knife caput,' he informed us. 'No good, man; no good, beast. Also axes, scissors, scythes, mowers. But now, problems over. Grigorio here. Grigorio has answer. Grigorio: Grinder to the Great. Come see!'

And, sitting astride the bicycle, he began pedalling. As he did so, slowly at first, the stone in front of him began to revolve. The faster he pedalled, the greater its momentum, building to a whirring crescendo till, with a high-pitched abrasive screech, the knife was brought down firmly, metal on stone. Sparks sprayed out; there was the strangest of aromas, as if the air itself had been singed. Covering our ears, we crowded forward to get a better view. Grigorio dismounted, took the apple and effortlessly quartered it, sharing the pieces out among the children. Next he demanded a piece of paper and, holding it edge-on to the blade, neatly sliced it end to end, inviting the more responsible among us – the knife was now a lethal instrument – to do likewise. This we did with spectacular results.

The grinder performed another of his bows. 'Just three days only Grigorio is here,' he told us. 'Come, bring all knives, all axes, scissors, scythes, like I says. Six pennies is small. One shillings is large. Machines ten shillings, needing dismantling, blades to discover. But first threes today for frees. Gratis. Come, quick!'

One or two of the men produced penknives and several of the women scurried away to search for blunted instruments about the house. This kept Grigorio busy sharpening well into the afternoon, at the same time providing us with an unseasonable firework display. Howard, as usual, insinuated himself into the group, pushing his way to the front and excitedly interrogating the man as to his origins, details of his travels and the like. We took sparse notice, speculating rather on the wonders of Grigorio's machine. How fast could the wheel turn? Would the metal be worn down completely before he collapsed, or vice-versa? Which of the blades would emit the longest spark, the most excruciating noise? We had cycles of our own, long since modified with pieces of cardboard fastened to the forks, slapping against the spokes as we pedaled and – depending on the size and shape of the attachments – producing any variation of sound, from the low octane growl of a Lancaster to the high-pitched whine of a spitfire. We'd seen pulleys linked to tractors at harvest time, but had never considered using a bicycle in this way. How else might they be adapted? Ice cream making? Generating electricity for

Radio Luxembourg? Bowling cricket balls or shooting at goal? The possibilities were endless.

Howard was even more entranced. 'He's from the forest. Before that abroad. Made the bicycle himself. It took years. Stone belonged to his father, and his father's father before him. Comes from a special place. Only he knows where. Brings it to people everywhere so everyone can benefit. And it's our forest he's chosen. Our forest don't you see…'

We didn't. Not at the time. All of us had grown accustomed to my brother's flights of fancy, wearily promising he could join us when we visited Grigorio the following day. But only if he held his tongue till then.

This could not come soon enough for Howard. Next day he rushed off ahead of us, was nowhere to be seen when we arrived, whilst Grigorio, following an altercation with the landlord, had not turned up at all. This did not worry us. Howard and his schoolmates often went off on forays of their own. We didn't notice his absence for the rest of the afternoon either, nor was I unduly alarmed when I arrived home and he'd still not appeared.

My parents were edgy, but it was not until he'd skipped his tea that they really started worrying. I was sent off to see if he'd overstayed his welcome with any of his friends, protesting all the way and contemplating the most excoriating of reprimands as I dragged him home by the ear. But, as I went from house to house discovering he was not there, nor seen that day, the possibility at last dawned: this was rather more serious than merely a schoolboy prank. Howard might genuinely have gone missing. By now it was getting dark and I began to feel genuine concern for his safety. I racked my brain as to where he might be and recalled his feverish interest in Grigorio. How the man had come from 'the forest'; his obsession with the stone, its mystic origin and magical sharpening powers. Remembered hearing all this before, in a different context. And suddenly I had it. Knew exactly where Howard would be and was off on my bike to fetch him.

Ten minutes later I was banging at the door of Third Class Cottage and Jimmy was confirming that, yes, he'd caught sight of Howard earlier that afternoon, making his way down one of the woodland tracks. He'd called out but the boy had been too distracted to respond. Nor had Jimmy given it much thought at the time. Now, as the story tumbled out, his expression turned from mild interest to real concern. He said nothing but disappeared inside, returning a few minutes later with a powerful torch, a pocket full of spare batteries, and we set off together into the forest.

At first we made good progress. The moon was full and it was a cloudless night. Even so, it seemed to be growing darker by the moment, the trees casting great shadows across the pathway, narrowing down to a track, brambles catching at our ankles, before petering out completely. Jimmy produced the torch and, flashing the beam to either side of us, stooping every so often to examine some depression, studying branches that impeded our progress or here and there a broken reed, we made our tortuous way towards the centre of the wood.

Night had by now closed in around us and I shivered as from afar came the distant call of an owl; closer to hand the sharp bark of a fox. Small animals scurried in the undergrowth about our feet. But nothing deterred Jimmy who pressed on deeper into the wood, saying little but, handing over a piece of chalk, instructed me to mark out the route we had taken. By now I had lost count of time. The hour that had passed since we'd left his cottage seemed more like days, and miserable ones at that. Nor did I realise how cold it was getting. Until…

Jimmy placed his finger to his lips for me to remain silent, sweeping a final curtain of shrubbery aside to reveal a break in the trees. And a clearing no bigger than Third Class Cottage, the grass bleached ashen in the moonlight, fringed at the parameters with jagged shadows. The flashlight swept along the trail now visible before us, played hither and thither among the foliage, then swung back to rest on the solitary figure hunched there among the shadows.

It was Howard right enough, wild eyed, feverish, and muttering incoherently to himself. 'See! It's true. Exactly as he told it. Didn't I tell you, Peter. Didn't I say they were far more than stories?' He pointed towards the centre of the glade.

Jimmy swung the beam across the open space before us, empty but for the silvered grass and shadowy trees. 'Whatever are you doing here, Howard?'

'I had to come. See for myself. After all you told us. But he broke his promise. Didn't come today. As he said he would. On his travels tomorrow, so this is my only chance. Didn't suspect I was on his trail, though. Led me right here.'

'You're not making any sense, Howard. Followed someone, did you say? Whatever possessed you to do such a thing? And at this time of night.' There was real concern in Jimmy's voice.

'It was daytime when we set off. This afternoon. I never expected it to take so long. Didn't notice how dark it was getting. But I had to keep track of him. He had the stone, Jimmy. Don't you see? Knew the secret. The one you told us about. Made knives cut paper. Sharper than anything I'd seen. Just as you said. Came from these woods, too, where they had their home. Was one of them himself. I could tell by his accent. He laughed at me, like Peter and the rest. Said he would be glad to be rid of my pestering. But I tracked him, to the middle of the forest. Then he disappeared. And I couldn't find my way back. Walked and walked. For hours! But I found it. By accident. Not like you, Jimmy. You knew just where to come. All along, you've known exactly where it is.'

'But I know nothing about this part of the woods. And just who was this man?'

'Grigorio, of course. And don't you start pretending, as well.

It's out there! Right in front of you, just the way you described it. Not a thing has changed.' And Howard continued pointing towards the emptiness at the centre of the clearing.

I groaned. 'Not Stoyan! Not the Jutes! You've got them on the brain. Are you never going to give them a rest?' For weeks he'd bombarded us with such stories, besides which I foresaw real trouble for both of us once we got home. Jimmy brushed my objections aside. He draped his coat over Howard's shoulders and squatted down beside him. 'Suppose you tell us exactly what you can see,' he suggested.

Which is precisely what Howard did. There before us was the smithy, the mead hall, mill, ale house and individual huts. Villagers came and went between them, going about their daily business, or tended their gardens. Our attention was drawn to the men, some of them working their plots of land, others fishing in the stream; to the women baking or hanging out clothes to dry. Night had been transformed into day, so that there was hawking in the fields, hunting in the forest. Archery practice was in progress on the village green; at home the girls were sharpening up their culinary skills. We strained our ears to catch the rush of the millrace, the creak of its wheel; arrows thudding into targets; the clang of hammer onto anvil. Couldn't we smell the smoke from the charcoal-burners' fires, the scent of new-mown hay? Individuals, too, were clearly identifiable: Redwald fetching wood to stoke his furnace; Alric dismounting from his horse; Saba circling in the sunlight, the shaman, withdrawn and malevolent, casting the runes.

My brother, I realised, was not shamming. The scenario was as real to him as the leaf of each tree, every blade of grass was to me. Jimmy for the most part remained silent, assenting with nods of the head and positive grunts to the claims that were being made; attempting occasionally to bring matters to an end; telling Howard it was time to go home; putting an arm around the boy's shoulders in an effort to move him off in that direction. Always to be repulsed. 'Wait,' Howard would protest. 'We can't go yet. Not till Stoyan comes.' Or: 'See, his mother awaiting his return. Along with Swidhelm and Tonbert.' And, finally, 'Morgana, Jimmy. She's coming. I know she is. What message do you think she'll bring? What message?'

Such humouring might have continued for hours to come, but it was now well past midnight and getting colder by the minute. Howard refused to be moved other than by force, nor could he be left alone. It was obvious that help was needed, and needed quickly. All along I'd questioned the necessity of those chalk marks, grumbled continuously at time wasted in making them, but I was glad enough of them now as I made my way back, the route plunged into darkness, the trees in constant motion, and with no one there to protect me. Later they estimated I'd made it in half an hour or less, yet I could account for not a minute of it. All I do remember is that, at the moment I heard the distant call of Howard's name, glimpsed the lanterns swinging dimly in the darkness ahead of me, the first drops of rain began to fall.

The rest remains blurred in my memory: leading the searchers back through the woodland; Jimmy fashioning a rudimentary stretcher from branches and lifting the semi-conscious and weakly protesting Howard onto it. The Lone Granger placing a sodden cape over him; the trek back along a now well-beaten pathway; Doctor McNeil examining both of us before a roaring log fire, shaking his head, harsh words, not, as I had expected, for my brother, but Jimmy; then bed, sleep and more sleep.

Chapter Eleven

Closing Ranks

My brother came out of the whole episode very well. Continued feverishness and high temperature kept him in bed for several days, and so immune from blame. Thereafter he was considered too young to have known any better. He'd a strong imagination, so Eric Stapleton testified – too rich to distinguish between make-believe and reality. Not so myself. As his elder I should have taken more care; prevented him from listening to such stories or, at the very least, ensured he did not take them seriously. Which I resented, especially when he became something of a hero among his friends, who crowded round once he recovered, eager to hear every detail of the adventure; wishing they could have been there too.

Howard revelled in the attention, oblivious of the real danger he'd been in or the part we'd played in saving him, elaborating instead on the supposed perils of this hazardous mission into uncharted territory, supplemented with first-hand accounts of Redwald's strength, Stoyan's cunning, Alric's swordsmanship. Any attempt to challenge the veracity of such fantasies resulted in high fever and tantrums. I had my own opinions as to the cause as well as the cure for such behaviour, but medical opinion thought otherwise. Rest and tranquility were the best medicine, the doctor assured us. My brother was therefore to be humoured. So, as they fussed about him, it was resentment I nursed. In time – matched precisely, it seemed to me, to the shelf-life of his stories – he made a complete recovery and things in our household returned to normal. Meanwhile it was Jimmy who shouldered most of the blame.

Previously, and despite growing opposition from several quarters, his sessions up by the war memorial or around the fire in Third Class Cottage had seemed no more than harmless entertainment. After all, Enid Quintock had tolerated them, so they couldn't be all that bad. Now, as rumours of Howard's predicament spread, trust in Jimmy began to waver. Several of our parents placed an embargo on all future contact and, when he remained unrepentant, others withdrew their support completely, playing right into the hands of those who'd opposed him all along. They might not have acted in unison, nor was there anything calculated about the campaign they waged. It was instinctive, intuitive almost, operating through implication via innuendo; the way things were done in Bereden and – for all I know – still are.

The Rev. Theobald Draper – 'Codpiece' as we knew him – again took the lead, speaking out openly in a sermon one Sunday some weeks after the event. Jimmy was not mentioned by name, only 'members of the community operating from their own selfish motives' – those who 'act contrary to the guiding principles manifest in the Scripture'. The sins of which he stood accused were unspecified, but with direct quotations from St Matthew's Gospel – the bit detailing the fate set aside for those who lead children astray – few can have doubted just who he had in mind. Which was the line taken up at Sunday School. There was, it seemed, to be a collective closing of ranks.

This became obvious when, next morning, lessons at Howard's school were called to a halt and the pupils marshalled into the hall. Here the headmaster, in academic dress, accompanied by the fully surpliced rector and senior members of staff, awaited them on stage. Howard had difficulty in conveying precisely what followed. Not so the teachers, several of whom were friendly with our parents; or Albert Florin, the caretaker, who – for the price of a pint at the Jugged Hare – gave impromptu renditions of BadEgg's rhetoric for weeks to come.

'Many of you,' he'd begun, 'will remember the terrible years of the war. For others, your lives will just have begun as it ended. But, if any of you need reminding, or have not been told, just ask your mothers and fathers to take you on a bus ride to Portsmouth or Southampton. Not to visit the cinema or spend your coupons in the shops, but to see for yourselves the houses that have been destroyed, the streets that still lie in ruin, the weeds growing among them.

And it's the same for boys and girls all over the country: in Liverpool or Birmingham, Bristol or Coventry. The war is now over, won by our brave soldiers, sailors and airmen, but not only them. Each of you played his or her part also. By going about your daily lives as normally as the enemy allowed you; by giving up some of the things you like most so he might be defeated; by collecting pans, kettles, train sets to make tanks and aeroplanes; by helping your parents dig for victory.

The "war effort" we called it. And, now that peace is here, you may think that that victory has finally been won. In many ways it has, yet in other ways it continues. We still have our ration books, not quite as much coal as we'd like to keep us warm, and we still need to ask ourselves, "Is my journey really necessary?" And, of course, it's a longer, different kind of journey we've all of us been on these last few years – you, your mothers and fathers, brothers and sisters, friends and relations. Everyone in this room, in Bereden, in fact. All of us together. But I wonder how many of you have asked yourself another question: why did we set out upon it? Why did we accept all the shortages? What was it that we were fighting for? The answer is simple. It was for an ideal. A way of life.'

There was little new in all this. I'd heard it a hundred times before; could supply the parts that Howard and the others omitted, the concluding passage especially. Something along the lines of: 'Freedom of speech. The right to think as you like; within the bounds of decency to write as you wish; without defamation, to say what you please.' So, at long last someone in authority was coming out on Jimmy's side. Well, good for him!

I should have known better. 'A way of life,' BadEgg continued, 'that's been handed down from generation to generation. That is all the more precious for having been fought for. And won, as it has continuously been won down the ages. But, having once more triumphed in the battle for liberty, we must guard the peace with equal vigilance. Not this time against foes from overseas, but those who would challenge it from within. Those who seek to undermine or weaken the very things that have made us strong, by which victory itself has been achieved. Those living among us who set out to challenge the values all of us hold dear; who fight not with bombs or guns, that injure our bodies, but with thoughts that corrupt and poison our minds. Growing like weeds among the remnants of our triumph.'

Howard and his friends were devastated when they realised what had been said – or had it explained to them. As were several of their parents who only a few weeks earlier had complained at the amount of time their offspring spent listening to Jimmy's tales. It was one thing for the rector to make such allegations. He was always sounding off about one sin or another, which was his job after all. But the headmaster; a newcomer to the village, speaking in long words, making accusations they couldn't fully understand? Others defended BadEgg on the grounds that he'd been an army man, captured – possibly tortured – by the enemy, who should know what he was talking about. But explanations such as these failed to satisfy his pupils and a rash of bad behaviour spread like measles through the village. Normally well-behaved children became sullen and disobedient; they had now to be dragged even more unwillingly to church. Truancy –

virtually non-existent in Miss Quintock's day – increased; pupils shunned out-of-school activities; graffiti aimed chiefly against Eric Stapleton and the Rev. Draper began to appear around the village.

And Jimmy? Within the month he'd disappeared, as quietly and unobtrusively as he'd arrived.

* * *

I'd have been content to leave it at that. Would have done but for Helen's new-found interest; as eager now as once she'd been dismissive, insisting there must be more to tell. But all that had happened some thirty years ago; it was now 1985, and there was little further I could remember – chose not to rather – nor anything of substance to add to what she already knew. The Jutes might not have emerged particularly well from her reading of Bede's *History of the English People* or *The Anglo Saxon Chronicle,* but they'd come down to me through childhood as shadowy, omnipresent figures, universally accepted as the founding fathers of the village. I could point her in the direction of one of their warriors, armed for battle with a full range of grave goods that had been excavated nearby; or the remnants of their pottery, darkish red in colour with small circular indentations, unearthed just north of the village, pieced together in Winchester Museum to form the most graceful of vases. I could show her evidence of Ytedenbe, a lost Jutish settlement in the Forest of Bere, or – interesting in the light of Jimmy's stories – the reputation these people had for the sharpening of tools or weapons. And:

Spare of tongue but sharp of wit,
Steadfast in kinship, slow to quit.

I could remind her of the physiological and psychological traces of these people that Jimmy swore still ran through our veins. Not that I took him all that seriously.

Till…

… down at the library, Helen happened upon *England South* by Sydney R. James: the reminiscences of an amateur artist, issued by Studio Publications in 1948 – roughly the time that Jimmy and I had met. Glancing through the book she discovered *Jutes* listed in the index and there they were, on pages 127-133.

Out sketching in the Meon Valley, around Old Winchester Hill, Sydney had met up with *one of the breed of local natives* and, on enquiring as to directions, experienced the local's *monosyllabic… economic style of speech.* Later, he tells his Hampshire cousin about this:

> *'Why,' she cried enthusiastically, 'you have been talking to a Jute!'*
>
> *'This curious stock in the Meon Valley,' she informs him, 'is supposed to have descended from the Jutes. A whole lot of Jutish burial mounds were discovered at Droxford village, which you must have come through… Everybody thinks them rather curious, both in looks and manner, quite different from us true-blue Hampshires.'*
>
> *'So,' Mr James tells his readers, 'it seemed that perhaps I had chanced on a descendent of the marauders who plundered these parts quite early in A.D., who with customary campaigning technique made up to the local girls, produced the goods for succession, and thereby secured a continuance of peculiarities imported from the fatherland, including the mono-staccato in speech.'*

A genuine near-contemporary sighting of a real-live Jute, the first and only one I've come across from that day to this.

'But it was thirty – more like forty – years ago.' Helen was dismissive. 'With no local radio, television in its infancy in those days, travel not back to pre-war standards. Things must have changed enormously since then.'

'True,' I said, 'but go back a generation or two, send a postcard for 1½d in London and you'd have it delivered to Bereden next day. Go back a further hundred years, use our signal tower in the woods and the message would arrive in less than five minutes. So what's a mere thirty years set against a couple of centuries?'

All the same, I wondered just what trace of the Jutes still remained? Just how genuine a presence had they really been? Had they continued to be spoken of at all? The village had increased enormously in size in the forty years since the war ended, the 'forest' shrunk into a shadow of its former self. A large housing estate covered Cowpat Meadow; Joe Wickbourne's forge was now a greengrocer shop. The tanneries had become an exclusive girls' school and traffic rushed headlong on tarmacked roads past the remnants of Harry's toll booth. All of which I learnt from Giles Amberstone – 'Gerundive' – when I booked a room at Amberstone Hall – or BERCEN: Bereden Conference Centre and Residential Retreat as it now was. Helen, the librarian with her knowledge of records; my own experience in the area of research; fieldwork something both of us enjoyed; each having a vested interest in the outcome. The ideal team, apart from the bickering – maybe because of it – to answer such questions. Above all, to discover – first-hand – all we could about Jimmy, his motivation and just what had become of him.

Part Two

Dark Side of The Moon

Chapter Twelve

Tricks of the Light

'Second right, over the bridge, look for a pillar box a bit further on... Slow down. Now what did he say?'

'Past the farmyard. Third, no fourth left. Yes, it's Willow Lane. But none of the houses numbered...'

'Nothing quite so vulgar. This is Surrey, remember!'

'Jacastar. Swan Song. Avalon. But look, there's 57. So, by a process of deduction...'

'... 52 must be three back on the opposite side.'

Twisting in his seat, Peter reversed the car. Back past the well-trimmed hedge, to a gate that stood half-open.

'52 it is.' He eased himself from the driving seat. 'Unless someone's switched letter-boxes.'

'Or we've got the wrong lane entirely.'

Our mission had got off to a disappointing start. A full month gone by since the *Roadshow*; several weeks since we'd begun the preliminary research, but still no response from Chunky, Andrew, Tim and the rest of the gang. Howard, now a successful banker in New Zealand, had little to contribute. Nor had my own efforts via the library network proved any more successful. The breakthrough came via 'Floral Lady'. We'd approached the television company and drawn another blank. Hardly surprising, when the only information we could supply was Peter's two-word epithet and a ham-fisted description of her pictures. Nor was it their policy to divulge personal information. They'd contact the lady should she be traced, but up to her whether or not she responded. As for Frank Murgatroyd, he was off filming in Jamaica, followed by a book tour in America.

Lateral thinking was obviously required, which was Peter's department. He began with the facts as we knew them. The programme had been broadcast from Guildford. Recorded during the summer months if Floral Lady's dress was anything to go by; had contained several references to a royal visitation, which pinpointed the date even more precisely: June. Presumably the target of our research lived in the vicinity, or was visiting it at that time; a lady of uncertain age but, with neither name nor address, either married or single, giving us precious little to go on. So why not place a 'missing persons' advertisement in the papers? Not the nationals; it hardly merited the expense and would attract just the kind of fortune hunters the television company was attempting to avoid. As would any suggestion of a reward. One of the locals then. If displayed prominently enough the lady or her friends might see it; if plaintively worded, she might even respond. The *Writers and Artists Year Book* was consulted for local newspapers serving the area, a telephone call made, and we struck lucky first time. Annabelle, duty receptionist, was not only aware of the event, she'd been there herself.

'Along with my boyfriend, Ted. Lovely two-page spread they made of it, pictures and all. Back-copies? No problem. Yes, a cheque will do nicely.'

The feature was better than we'd dared hope. More photos than text, mostly in colour and all of them helpfully captioned. The cathedral *a spectacular backdrop to this popular series,* shots of the public streaming in, *attics ransacked, heirlooms retrieved from storage,* Frank himself, *the Murgo moment* caught in vivid close-up. Best of all, a half-page portrait of those selected to appear in the programme, with Floral Lady tucked away to one side, clutching *Fiddlers Three* protectively to her bosom. *Miss Mildred Jamieson* according to the caption. A further call to Annabelle was all that was required. Our luck held out. She'd worked in the correspondence department at the time, was certain the lady concerned had ordered a copy of the photo, but:

'More than my job's worth to give you the address.'

Not even to Dr Rayner? The lady his long-lost aunt? At death's door?

'Well, in that case...'

We had the address but attempts at telephonic communication proved unsuccessful. Directory Enquiries came up with no one of that name in the Guildford area, so perhaps she was ex-directory. Which explains how a few weeks later, *en route* south to Bereden and with the help of local residents, we'd pushed open the gate, crunched our way up the gravel driveway, and were knocking, unannounced, at number 52, Willow Lane, Tilswick.

Floral Lady appeared much the same as she had done on television. Shorter perhaps and no longer dressed for the occasion. Somewhat older – well into her forties/early fifties I'd say – wearing a green smock-type dress, with slate-grey hair drawn back into a bun and spliced with a tortoise shell comb. She seemed happy enough to see us, peering cheerfully through glasses hung about her neck on a beaded chain. All of which changed the moment she learnt of our mission. The pictures were not that important; might well be fakes. She'd taken them to the *Roadshow* on impulse; the producer had no permission to divulge her whereabouts. Sensing that the door was about to be slammed in our faces, I pitched in as well. My husband was a university lecturer, celebrated in the field, awarded a doctorate for his studies; he'd known the artist as a child. All to no avail. Peter was about to place his foot in the doorway, I'd taken his arm to drag him away, when there were footsteps advancing from the interior; the sound of a stick beaten briskly on wooden floor.

'Don't stand there all day, Mildred. Can't you see they mean us no harm. For Heaven's sake, let them in!' The voice from the interior was querulous yet sharp.

'Mildred' visibly swayed, torn between the strangers who'd arrived unannounced on her doorstep and the elderly lady who appeared behind her, leaning heavily on a stick.

'Well, what are you waiting for?' She'd turned her attention to us. 'Come in now, before I change my mind, and make sure you wipe your feet. Better still, take your shoes off. Can't have half of Surrey over my carpets!'

Mildred stood reluctantly aside as we were ushered into the front room and settled down to introduce ourselves. Our hosts were unrelated, so we discovered; Floral Lady – I still thought of her that way – the companion ('more of a friend, really') to Mrs Geraldine Leapman, catering for her every need in return for board, lodging and a small stipend. They were not listed in the telephone directory and had no independent postal address, explaining why she'd been so difficult to trace. Meanwhile, I was taking stock of our surroundings: flock rose-burst wallpaper, faded carpet of oriental design, heavy curtains that dropped ceiling to floor. A corded bell-pull, and two large winged armchairs had been drawn up to face the velvet-covered settee on which we lounged. Large oak beams ran wall to wall above our heads. Embers smouldered in an open grate. What light there was came from a number of lamps set into the walls. And between them hung the pictures: a florid version of Tennyson's *Lotos-Eaters*; quite obviously a 'Saintley', directly facing us; beside it a painting in the same style with two illuminated scripts to our right. These were interspersed with a number of embroideries, whilst there, above the mantelpiece, largely in shadow but instantly recognisable, was *Fiddlers Three*.

'Go on, have a closer look.' Geraldine realised that our attention had wandered. 'I know you're dying to.' Peter needed no encouragement. He was on his feet in an instant, striding about the room from one picture to the next.

The old lady followed his progress with interest. 'A great improvement on that ghastly television man. Margo, Mingo, whatever. Made quite an impression on some of us, though.' The companion, who'd retired to a corner, flinched, her eyes darting between the three of us. 'Yes, it was Mildred here you saw playing the starring role. With *my* pictures. Sharing them with the likes of him, and God knows who else once my back was turned.'

'But I thought you'd be pleased. I've told you that a million times. A nice surprise waiting when you got out of hospital.'

'Nice surprise? Anyone, but anyone, might have come knocking on our door! And what's this they're telling me? About their interest in the programme? Explains those letters from the television company, doesn't it? The ones you mislaid. Those telephone calls as well. From the hospital, concerning my recovery so you said. The perfect cover up.'

'None of this would have happened if you'd been open with me. Told me the truth.' Mildred dabbed at her eyes with a miniscule handkerchief.

Geraldine softened. 'Well, I suppose you're right there. I've only myself to blame.' She turned to Peter. 'Go on, have a good look. There can't be many of us around who appreciate them. A university man especially. Might have known you'd grow up that way. One of the "experts" Jimmy hated so much. He'd have disowned you in a second.'

'You knew Jimmy?' Peter swung round to face her. 'Myself as well? Is that what you're suggesting?'

'Forgotten me have you? Well, I don't think I'd have recognised you, either.' The old lady shook her head. 'Not after all these years. Absent-minded I may be; sometimes unable to recall what I did or didn't do an hour ago. But years, they're different. Ten, fifteen, twenty go by and the memories stay put, clear as a bell. Jimmy's bell, in fact. *Saint* wasn't it? Used to sign his pictures that way. And don't look so put out, Peter. It's me that should be shocked. Forgetting me like that when we were so close. Quite led him astray I did.' She'd turned to me, her tone playful, coquettish almost. 'If he'd been just a tad older, a little more experienced, you might well have had yourself a rival, my dear. So, do get him to sit down, won't you?' She moved along the settee and thumped on one of the large cushions beside her. 'And, don't you slope off, Mildred. The poor man looks quite put out. A cup of our special brew, if you please, to restore his memory.'

From the speed with which Mildred regained her composure I guessed upsets of this kind were not unusual in the Leapman household. Putting away her handkerchief, she produced a small mahogany box from one of the cupboards. The kind I'd come across in antique shops, or on show in National Trust properties, but never seen put to any practical use. Compartments on either side contained Chinese and Indian tea; a glass bowl fitted snugly in between them. Mildred removed the silver spoon slotted into the lid and mixed the leaves in roughly equal portions.

In the meantime Geraldine chatted on. 'Quite a ritual, isn't it? Rather more refined than Jimmy's tea-bomb version, but just as effective don't you think? The wonder is you didn't die of food poisoning, the lot of you. Still, there was rationing then, which gave him some excuse, I suppose. What was it, two and a half ounces a week? And stop looking so surprised, Peter. The wind will change and your face will stay fixed, as that schoolteacher would have said. Quigley, Quantock, whatever her name was. And don't go thinking I'm following in her footsteps, poor soul. Like I say, the older one gets, the sharper one's long-term memories.' She tapped her head. 'All the same, it's not very flattering for a lady not to be recognised. You tell him, dear.'

Her last comment was addressed to me. Peter had taken his place, as instructed, cup balanced precariously on knee, beside her. Wondering, he told me later, if this was a dream. Whether it was he, Geraldine, or both of them who'd lost their mind. Now, the mention of Miss Quintock brought him forward in the seat, suddenly all attention.

'Coming back to you now, is it?' Geraldine's tone was conciliatory. 'Just like the old days, in fact. So eager to help you were then, remember? When there was no one else I could rely on. All fifteen years of you. So willing to please.'

'Wait a minute! Just give me time to think.' Peter slurped down the rest of his tea and Mildred sprang forward to rescue cup and saucer as he slumped back, eyes closed, vigorously massaging his forehead. 'The reporter. On the track of Jimmy's paintings. Tricked me into believing in her. Got me into all sorts of trouble. Jimmy too. Trusted every word you said when all along...'

'... I meant you harm?' The old lady shook her head. 'Believe me, Peter, if anyone had a secret, something to hide, it was Jimmy not me. I never meant to hurt him. Why else do you think I've kept his pictures all these years? And I'm sorry, really I am, if I got you into trouble, but think back, honestly now. Did any harm come from it? Isn't the truth of it that you were getting just the tiny bit tired of all those stories? You weren't all that complimentary about them, you know. Not the way I remember it. Quite the little grown-up in fact; condescending about his popularity with the 'little ones' – yes, that's really what you called them! High-minded about the need to protect him, but no holding back. Not once I turned on the charm.' She reached out, depressed a switch, plunging her part of the room into semi-darkness. 'One of my "tricks of the light". Remember?'

Peter made no reply. No need. He remembered alright. And I could tell that, just as certainly, took no pleasure in doing so...

* * *

She'd appeared one evening. A lonely figure, muffled against the March wind, there at the bus stop. Meeting someone from town, I'd assumed from my vantage-point on the top deck, except that I knew everyone in the village – their friends, and their relatives; in those days Bereden was that sort of place – but she was a stranger. I gave it no further thought, until:

'It's Peter, isn't it?'

She'd stepped aside to let the few late shoppers pass; was smiling down at me and, as she spoke, the street lamp overhead flared suddenly into life. Later it became a joke between us. One of her tricks of the light we called it. That part I did remember – and being instantly on my guard. We were a close-knit community in those days and wary of strangers. Came with the territory, I suppose, or a legacy of war-time stories carried over into the peace: foreign agents and German spies, poisoned apples left for children to eat along with booby-trapped toys. The fact that she knew my name made me doubly suspicious, so it must have been her confidence that won me round.

Together with the flattery. She treated me as an equal, unlike my parents or the teachers at my new school where all the questions, so it seemed, were designed to catch you out. Quite the 'little grown up' as Geraldine said, distancing me from childhood and everything associated with it. She was right about my attitude to Jimmy as well. Only a few years had passed since I'd been enthralled with his stories yet already they'd been relegated, along with nursery rhymes and fairy tales, to the realms of infancy. I'd humoured Howard by listening to his re-telling of the Jutish saga in a patronising sort of way whilst dismissing it, as did my teachers, and as all good GCE students should.

All of which I'd chosen to forget – until Geraldine appeared and brought it back to my attention.

I'd not have recognised her otherwise; never have taken the angular bird-like figure eyeing me from across the room, silver haired, chair-bound almost, for the attractive, well-proportioned creature who'd waylaid me all those years ago. Thirty by a quick estimation: the same, approximately, as the difference in our ages. That gimmick with the table lamp was typical, though, as was the smile accompanying it, the slight shrug of the shoulders, the way she held her body. Shrunk into herself now, dependent upon her stick, but the personality remained intact. Except that in those days she was calling herself Veronica – Veronica Flack.

Just passing through the village, she said. As if anyone 'passed through' Bereden. Interested in local history she was: the church, Amberstone Hall, Toll Booth Lane, the Tanneries. She even had a map of sorts. Had tried all the usual sources, but the vicar had been away, they'd been uncommunicative at the Jugged Hare and she didn't feel up to disturbing Sir Desmond. No one, in fact, had been willing to talk to her; well, that figured. Then someone had mentioned my name. Too busy to spare the time themselves, but young Master Rayner was her best bet. 'Young Master' – a brilliant stroke that, elevating me several rungs up the social ladder whilst playing to my vanity. It had a splendid ring to it as well, Dickensian almost; I imagined the unknown villager – I never did get round to asking her who it was – doffing his cap as he spoke. It was only later, months after she'd gone, that I reflected on the improbability of such a scenario, the skill with which she'd baited her hook. But she'd not won me over yet. Not quite. For all the naivety there was still an inborn distrust of strangers lingering down there beneath the surface.

She'd picked up on this almost immediately and changed tack; rummaged through her handbag, shook loose a cigarette from the packet and – the very last thing I expected – offered me one! I'd never yet smoked, let alone been invited to; was flattered beyond measure, yet had no idea how to respond. I'd seen it done a thousand times on screen: the casual selection from the pack, the tapping of the cigarette on the back of one's hand, a single flick of the lighter, better still, the shared intimacy of a single match. As for me, I stood dumb, wide-eyed, no doubt jaw-sagging, for what seemed an eternity. Veronica appeared neither to notice nor to care. Cradling her fingers against the breeze, she lit up, green eyes narrowing above high cheekbones as she inhaled, settled down on one of the benches beneath the glass canopy, indicating that I should join her. By now she'd removed her beret, releasing an auburn-red cascade that danced about her shoulders, down onto the tightly belted, pleasantly bulging raincoat, as she spoke. This she did in a straightforward, uninhibited manner whilst I, unaccustomed to such treatment, merely sat, half-listening and admired. It was love at first sight.

My knowledge of the village was her first concern, she said, whilst my fervid imaginings conjured up what the others might be. They'd told her I was the person to ask, and good advice, no mistake about it; wasn't that a St Hugh's badge on my blazer? So kind, as well, prepared to talk like this to a perfect stranger. Prepared to talk? I would have granted her anything. The hook well and truly baited, she now proceeded to reel me in.

The information she required appeared straightforward enough, nor was there anything suspicious about her being here. Bereden was an attractive village; church, turnpike, hall and mill were of historic interest and quite obviously there were stories to be told. And it was the telling as much as the content in which she seemed interested, which again should have put me on my guard when, for all their distrust of outsiders, there were others older and more knowledgeable who might have been persuaded to oblige. Naturally, I did little to solicit such help, leaving her delightfully in my charge. A difficulty was my being at school all day with her needing to be at home in the evenings and at weekends. If, however, I caught a later bus one afternoon, we might find a mutually agreeable time in town. Warning signs again. Such enthusiasm for a further meeting well away from the village, yet this continued eagerness to hear tell of it. All of which I neglected, convinced as to the magnetism of my personality; the brilliance of my narrative skills.

So, a further meeting – assignation I liked to consider it – was arranged, about a fortnight later, in the park, the excuse I provided for my parents being a long-delayed reunion with Andrew. Matters did not go quite as I had expected, though. Her interest in local history remained undiminished, and she seemed as enthralled as ever with the folk tales I'd heard since childhood. The mistake I made was in associating Jimmy with such stories, whereupon the focus of her attention switched immediately to him. No matter what I said, no matter how I embellished the events, elaborated on the characterisation, the initiative had passed out of my hands. Nor did my efforts at disparagement – the inaccuracy of the man's material, his facility for making enemies, the obscurity of his verse – have any effect. All it did was to enhance his appeal – Jimmy the romantic, a dark, enigmatic figure, origins unknown, future uncertain, had captured her imagination. Dejected at this hijacking of our conversation, I suggested she meet the man himself, realising it would bring the interrogation to a close, but wanting, above all to please her. Nor did her dismissal of the idea seem strange. It was the obvious solution; except that by now I was convinced there was a bond between us and that she was using him as a means of furthering it.

That was it, of course. It had all come round to Jimmy in the end. So surprised to hear about him, yet fascinated once his name had been mentioned – when she'd led me to it, rather. Then, suddenly, all attention switching to him. Eager to learn everything she could; pulling the very soul from me. Finally, vanishing without a word as suddenly as she had come. Jimmy had been her target all along. The reason was soon to become obvious, the consequences still loitering in the background of my subconscious some thirty years later. And Veronica Flack's explanation – if she had one – long overdue.

Chapter Thirteen

Carnations and Roses

'Come now, Peter, surely you're not still holding it against me? A little mild flirtation? Not all one-sided either. So, what was the harm in it?'

Back in 1985 now, with all three of them staring at me, and Veronica – Geraldine Leapman rather – still acting the innocent. What harm? She had the gall to ask me that. Just what kind of fool did she take me for? Helen laid a restraining hand on my arm.

But there was more to come: 'You're blowing this out of all proportion, Peter, really you are. All I wanted was your help. No one else seemed willing to give it and there was no guidebook, so why all the song and dance?'

I didn't believe a word of it. Why the make-believe if she'd been nothing more than a tourist? Such an elaborate façade, as well, for someone interested merely in beauty spots or local history.

'You've a far sharper memory than mine, that's for certain.' She seemed amused rather than offended. 'Except for a point of detail that seems to have eluded you. Your diffidence back in those days; the unwillingness to unbend. Only to be expected in a teenager, I suppose. And a Beredonian at that. No fraternisation with outsiders, anyone not born within a musket-shot of the village, in fact. Prided ourselves in being different, as well, didn't we? So adult and sophisticated. I can see you now, sitting there, prim and proper, in your grammar school blazer.' She brought herself upright in the chair, stick clasped before her, smiling beatifically; a parody as infuriating as it was accurate. Just the tiniest bit of encouragement on my part, that's all that it took.'

She was right. I had been susceptible, prone to flattery, but she wasn't escaping that easily. Not after the damage she'd caused. One minute pumping me for all the information she could obtain, off to the four winds the next. Veronica/Geraldine had known exactly what she was after.

But now a change of tack: 'You're serious aren't you, Peter? Storing it up all this time. You must have been genuinely struck on me. Well, I'm sorry, but it was just a ruse to get you talking, something I'd quite forgotten till you arrived at our doorstep. What can I say? Sorry for my pretence? For all the upset I seem to have caused, leading you on in that way? I suppose I just didn't think.'

She'd thought alright. The whole plot, through from beginning to end. There'd been no chance meeting. Her insistence that I alone, who'd been so close to Jimmy, should be the one to help her was nothing but a ruse. Then, having discovered all that I knew, off into the unknown. She must have thought she'd got away with it as well. Would have done – but for Mildred's five minutes of fame. It had taken half a lifetime but the play-acting was at an end. As was her sham interest in the village. We were through with the make-believe and excuses.

I don't remember just how much of this I said, but: 'That's quite enough, Peter! We're visitors here, and can't you see they're only trying to help.' It might have been worse, but for Helen's intervention.

Mildred, silent throughout my accusations, stepped forward and opened the door. 'I think you'd better leave, now!'

'She's right, we should go home. And I think Mrs Leapman

is due an apology. It's all past history, as she says, so where's the harm in it?'

'Owe her an apology? When you've only heard one side of the story?' Helen's suggestion goaded me still further. 'What's the harm? Go on, Veronica, tell us what happened after you hightailed it into the blue yonder. If you dreamt up the worst of his nightmares, multiplied it a hundred times over, you couldn't have done worse.'

'Honestly, Peter, I've no idea what you're talking about.' Geraldine seemed genuinely perplexed. 'Jimmy, as you call him, was my sole interest. No point in denying it after all these years. Whatever happened later was no concern of mine.'

'Coincidence, then, the ones that came after you? Press, reporters, photographers hotfoot down from London. Strange, how no one on God's earth's heard of Jimmy till she appears on the scene. Then exit Veronica and hey presto her friends arrive mob-handed!'

'Peter!' Again, Helen's remonstrance.

I shook her off. 'Tell us what more there was to it then. You must have known from all I told you how much Jimmy detested publicity of any kind, let alone flash-lights and cameras. He just couldn't work that one out. His pictures – the press might have got hold of them, the *Shakespheres* possibly. But they knew about the stories, so it must have been one of us children that had blabbed.'

'And that's what all this fuss is about?' Mildred snorted her disdain. 'Hardly the crime of the century.'

'The only people in the village he really trusted.' Once started I was in no mind to listen. 'Stupid of him, wasn't it? With half of Bereden cursing him for bringing such a visitation down upon our heads, the rest accusing one another of the responsibility, and only I knowing who was to blame. Realising what I'd done yet not daring to own up. Terrified that Jimmy would learn how much I'd betrayed him, that the others might get to know who'd let them down. I don't think I've ever felt quite as lonely in my life. Part of me never has.'

'So that's it! You thought that I was a reporter! Or some stringer from the tabloids. I don't know whether to be upset or flattered.' Geraldine was taking my accusations in good part. 'But you've got it wrong, Peter.' She shook her head. 'So far off the mark that I hardly know where to begin.'

'His own guilty conscience working overtime.' Mildred had no such doubts.

'That's quite enough.' A single glance from Geraldine silenced her. 'Seems to me there's a far simpler explanation. One based on fact rather than whimsy.' She sounded far more confident now. 'Jimmy wasn't completely unknown; you've said that yourself. Those *Shakespheres* were just coming onto the market and he'd made a hero of himself, saving your brother that way. Yes, Peter, another piece of information you were quite eager to let slip. So, isn't it just possible – no, likely – that an editor out there somewhere, or an eager journalist, picked up the story? Not me, I promise. Just look around you if you doubt my word. Those are Jimmy's pictures on the walls, aren't they? Brilliant, some of them, but hardly commercial. As Mildred discovered, not worth a fortune. So, why else do you think I've kept them? You should be grateful rather. They're all we have left of him.'

'All we have left of him.' It was Helen who'd spoken, whispered rather. Sitting beside her, I hardly caught the words.

* * *

...All we have left of him.' There was something in Geraldine's tone that caught my attention. As she spoke her face had softened, taking on a gentleness wholly out of keeping with the harshness of Peter's attack. Regret. The kind of thing captured a hundred times over by the old masters. Or Shakespearean actors at their best. Yet there was more to it than this. Grief certainly, but tenderness also. An indefinable yearning, impossible to counterfeit. The precise duplicate of the one I'd witnessed first-hand some time back…

…the anniversary of Daddy's death, that was it. The third it must have been. Since when I'd stayed clear; away from the turmoil and recriminations, the never-ending check-list of his inadequacies, Mother's interminable rage. Aimed chiefly at the hours we'd spent together. The way I'd listened to his fantasies, encouraging them even; developing the wayward side of his character, so she claimed. When I'd been every bit as devastated as she had been. And just as unforgiving.

Nevertheless, finding myself in the area, a few minutes' drive from home, it was Daddy I decided to visit. There'd be problems tracing the grave. Overgrown and neglected last time I'd seen it. Down from the lichen-covered cross, I remembered, a single granite slab among the toys and plastic dolls, the jam-jars stuffed with artificial flowers; his name, dates of birth and death inlaid in black. All we had left. With Mother begrudging him this much even. Given her way, like as not he'd have been unceremoniously dumped into an unmarked grave. I'd come prepared: kneeler, trowel, clippers purchased from an ironmonger en route, roses from the car-park stall. No need. The grass, I observed from a distance, was mown. The pathway had been raked. His headstone scrubbed free of moss. And there was a figure crouched down beside it, placing flowers in a glass container, coaxing the blooms lovingly into position. Young, female, tastefully dressed, hair tucked under the brim of a hat conforming to the latest of fashions. Unaware of my approach till she glanced up. There was a fleeting moment of recognition. And she was gone.

Alison, of course. Who'd been uninvited to the funeral, ostracised by the family, lampooned by the press. Neither as young as Mother maintained, nor as 'tarty' as she implied. Keeping her lonely vigil at the grave she'd tended these last few years. I made no attempt to follow; simply placed my roses alongside the bouquet she'd brought.

Carnations. Expensive, out of season, and – how could I have forgotten? – his favourites. And there was a note, four words only: *As you like it.* Of all the expressions she might have chosen, why that one? The picture, of course. I remembered telling Peter how much Mother hated it; how Daddy had smuggled it up to the study. A coincidence? I'd thrust all other thoughts aside, determined not to dwell on them…

But the image I've carried down the years. Her expression especially. The moment before she looked up and caught my eye; the moment before the moment rather. Hard to describe. Regret. Emptiness. Loss. Every last nuance played out in fine detail. Recaptured now by Geraldine, at Willow Drive, five years down the line.

'You must have been very fond of him,' I said.

'Jimmy?' It was there in her tone also. 'You might say that, my dear. Considering I married him.'

Chapter Fourteen

Birds of Pray

We spent a sleepless night in The Spurs and Stirrup, a drab hotel of Mildred's choosing. Geraldine had been tired. She'd put up a spirited defence, but the cross-examination had taken a lot out of her so we must wait till morning. Then and then only would we get the rest of her tale. Peter was still in shock, as much from the old lady's revelations as his own reactions. They'd surprised me, too. His embarrassment I could understand. All of us, at some time or other, have had crushes of this kind. And true, it had been thoughtless, blurting it out in that way. But his turning on her, the viciousness of his response – inexcusable, considering her age and condition. Till, thinking it over, I realised it was his betrayal of Jimmy that was really troubling him, a guilt he must have been nursing down the years. Something the two of us shared; the betrayal of, or by, someone who'd been close. How long, I sometimes wonder, would it have taken for such disclosures to emerge had we missed that television programme; if our search had ended at this point?

But it didn't. Next day the old lady was in a forgiving mood. As was Mildred. Still smarting, though, from the dressing down she'd been given. Hurt that Geraldine had not confided in her. Just how much, we wondered, did she know about Jimmy? When precisely had they met? Geraldine in pursuit of an artistic husband; Jimmy – I quipped – nursing a passion for assertive women. Veronica Flack, Enid Quintock and Alice Amberstone – a formidable triumvirate.

Yet never once did either of us picture him in an ecclesiastical setting. Back in the mid-1920s that would have been. No more than eleven or twelve as Geraldine took up the story; marching in crocodile along with the orphanage children, to church each Sunday.

Derek he'd been then. With Geraldine – Veronica rather – some three years younger, watching as they sat in rows, girls at the front, boys at the back, just as they'd done for as long as she could remember. Jimmy an orphan? The first Peter had heard of it. Veronica had been curious as well. Later, after they were married, she'd tried to trace the records, but the paperwork had been destroyed during the war.

'And a miserable time he had of it. You can check that out for yourselves.' She jabbed with her stick at a small picture high up on the opposite wall. '"Twenty or more sisters and not a mother between them," that's all I could get out of him. Nor did I realise just how bitter he was, not till I found that painting.'

Mildred moved her armchair to one side and the three of us gathered round the picture. *Birds of Pray* was much in the *Home Thoughts* style, the title, subject matter and artwork merging to form a visual pun. Here the 'B' of *Birds* took the form of the enormously busted, big-bellied abbess, a switch grasped in one hand whilst with the other she points to a text above her head: *God is Love.* The second letter – 'i' – had become an opened bottle labelled *brimstone*; the third – 'r'– the figure of a small child cowering before her; 'd' through to the 'y' in *Pray* a line of nuns, heads respectably wimpled, wearing ebony black – the habit of the order – their bodies contorted into prayerful subjugation. Or so it appeared. On closer inspection what had been vestments became pairs of enormous wings. The folds in their garments were individual feathers. Silver chains hobbled each of their delicate white feet to the branch on which they were sitting.

'My God, how he hated us!'

An unguarded exclamation, but Geraldine picked up on it immediately. 'A Catholic? How tactless of me. And convent-educated as well?' Surely I'd not crossed myself. 'I'm so sorry, my dear, that's the last of his pictures I'd have shown you had I known.' She beckoned us over, indicating that I should resume my seat beside her. 'He was just as offensive to the Anglicans, you know. Would have let fly at the Methodists, too, given half a chance. Atheists even.' The arthritic fingers that rested on my wrist were ice-cold yet comforting. 'Nothing like your own teachers, I'm sure. It was a love/hate relationship between them really, Derek and those nuns. Grateful after his fashion for what they'd done for him, taking him in after he'd been abandoned, feeding and educating him, but resenting it all the same. All his life long, the threats and the beatings, the hellfire and the strap. Surprise was that, one way or another, either because or in spite of it – and don't ask me which – he emerged such a brilliant teacher. Good enough to be put in charge of the orphanage Sunday School, then asked to help out down at the church. Only too glad of the opportunity as well, no matter how much he was to look back at it as exploitation. The "birds of pray" exacting their pound of flesh.'

'Wonder is he didn't add *The Merchant of Venice* to the *Shakesphere* series.' Peter seemed to have recovered his humour but, I could tell, remained suspicious.

It had been later at the Sunday School that Derek had taken her eye. After all those years of paying no heed to the orphans – the "Awful-ens" as she'd called them – fidgeting away at the back of the church. Not that she had time for boys in any shape or form till, called upon to help him out, she'd become entranced with his story-telling prowess. Those found in the *Old Testament* especially. Talking donkeys, plagues of locusts, boils or serpents, staffs miraculously transformed into snakes or blossoming into leaf, ghostly writings on the wall – the more outlandish the plot, the better he seemed pleased.

'Not so the rest of teachers.' Geraldine smiled impishly. '"Inculcating the wrong sort of values entirely"' – an impersonation presumably –' took the matter straight to the rector. Poor man. With Derek in the fold he might well lose one or other of his voluntary helpers; without him – and the parents only too eager to be shot of their offspring on a Sunday afternoon – he'd have none of the congregation left.'

'Couldn't get enough of him myself.' Her sense of fun was infectious. Carry on this way, I thought, and she'd have Peter won over completely. 'Began taking an adult interest in my appearance, all fourteen years of me. Went out of my way to please him in every way – and I mean "every way" – possible. Not that Derek noticed.' Geraldine sighed. 'All fire and energy inside the classroom, yet withdrawn and passive once the books were closed, the church door locked behind us.'

'A great hit with the "birds of pray", though. "Think what you might achieve" they told him' – another of her impromptu impressions – '"away from unwelcome distractions" – meaning yours truly. "Build on your natural talent", they said. "Give it greater focus, more direction. You should be grateful for the chance we're giving you."'

This, he discovered, was Pendarrell House, a college far away in North Wales, which fitted their purpose precisely.

'Poor lad.' There was genuine sadness in her voice. 'His sole notion of childhood was what the orphanage had to offer. Till the Sunday School gave him a glimpse of something different. His pupils returning "home" once their lessons were over. To "families", something he'd only read about in books, or seen on the movies shown of a Saturday night at the convent. Children of his age or younger speaking of their "mothers", their sisters even, with genuine warmth. Pendarrell offered him means of escape into the world beyond the convent.'

One that Derek had seized with both hands, leaving Veronica nursing a broken heart.

Chapter Fifteen

Different Drummer

Geraldine's long-term memory turned out to be as sharp as she'd claimed; the events of those days as clear now, in 1985, as when she'd first heard them over half a century ago. It had taken her some time to discover just what had happened to Derek at Pendarrell House; wheedling it out of him, piece by piece over the years; uncertain even now that she knew all there was to know, nor fully understanding everything she'd been told. But for us it was an opportunity too good to be missed. The University vacation had several weeks to run, Helen dreamt up some excuse explaining her extended leave; a 'phone call was all that it took to put our trip to Bereden temporarily on hold. Far more important, the opening up of a part of his life Jimmy always kept hidden; a chance – together with our subsequent discoveries, a touch of extrapolation from what we already knew – to discover the dark side of his moon.

* * *

Beginning with Pendarrell House as it had been in the mid-twenties. Named after the twelfth-century owner of the land, so Geraldine told us; selected now for its isolation, with no expense spared on the conversion. What remained of the farm buildings had been demolished, to be replaced with an office block and refectory; the milking-parlour becoming dormitories, silos refurbished with state-of-the-art equipment as the community's central meeting hall; a cowshed sanctified as their chapel.

A strict regime, Derek had been warned, but they seemed docile enough. About a dozen of them altogether, the 'brothers', mostly in their thirties, some considerably older, each of them adopting the name of a British river. The better to accommodate the individual needs of the noviciate, he later discovered, a reminder also as to the dangers of excess. Brother Derwent, for example: as thrusting and forward-looking in his thinking as that particular stretch of water, but having always to curb the wilder, more reckless aspects of his nature. Brother Arun: quiet, reflective, gently carrying the scholars with him, yet with a tendency to procrastination. And Brother Ouse: bringing together a multitude of minor detail into a single flowing argument, just as his namesake gathered tributaries, but somewhat bombastic when doing so. Unity of purpose was stressed by their mode of dress. Grey roll-neck sweaters, *PH* in green silk lettering above the chest, dark slacks, tightly-buckled belt and white canvas shoes laced according to house style – specifically designed, so the rumour went, for soundless access into any part of the building. Above them, the elusive yet omnipresent figure of their benefactor.

Little was known about Soroyan other than what could be seen or heard. Wheelchair-bound, with a shock of snowy hair, he lived in a luxury apartment somewhere on site, but had the run of the place. American, according to those who had heard him speak; fabulously rich and an art-lover, if the rumours were true; deferred to in all things, that much was obvious. Occasionally he'd be seen trundling to-and-fro between buildings, yet seldom witnessed in his comings and goings. He'd appear without warning or invitation at their discussions, always interested in what was said yet never taking part; one minute he'd be there, attentive at the back of the room, and the next he'd disappeared. Or there he was in the pew specially prepared for him at the back of the chapel, head bowed in prayer, but when they next looked he'd be gone. The one constant was his Monday meetings – ten o'clock sharp, with senior members of the staff, but Heaven help any one of them if they were late. No doubt about that.

The discipline might have been rigorous; mild, though, in comparison with what Derek had come to expect; the programme – lectures, prayer, group seminars, solitary afternoons set aside for 'individual inventories' or 'encellments' – tedious yet tolerable. Worse was the 'public confession' when each novice was expected to reveal how they'd found their way to God, or *vice versa.* And nothing had quite prepared him for Pendarrell's handling of Biblical studies. The same tales he'd told a hundred times at Sunday School but recounted with infinitely less verve, each part of every verse being analysed in minute detail. They stood for different aspects of God's graciousness, so the brothers assured him, and only when decoded could the message be fully understood.

He'd accepted this at first, understanding little of it, but was content to give them the benefit of the doubt. There came a time, though, when Brother Arun – not many years his senior – chose the story of Daniel in the Lion's Den, then handled it with less competence than the most unimaginative of the teachers from his previous school. No stress on the personality of each of the characters, no background detail; no feeling for the storyline, gripping incident following incident leading up to the grand finale. No dramatic pauses, no aping of King Darius' villainy, feigned distress at Daniel's plight; his companions showing no dismay at being eaten, nor the lions smacking their lips in anticipation. Brother Arun's sole concern, it seemed, was to label each with some obtuse allegorical meaning or other, so that the inevitable inquisition might begin.

Derek's protest was greeted with an indulgence more infuriating than had they shouted him down, beaten him even. The truth, the brethren insisted, turning to one another for confirmation, had been revealed to them. It was there in the Scriptures for those that had eyes to see. So perhaps he should retire to his cell for a few days' contemplation and, whilst he was no longer among them, they would pray for his enlightenment.

He was well familiar with the room by now. It measured no more than a few footsteps across in either direction, stripped of all furniture save for a single table and chair, pine and scrubbed clean to match; its floor uncarpeted, the walls uniformly bare. On the table lay a leather-bound Bible, beside it an oil lamp, the only other illumination coming from a small window set way out of reach. With little else to occupy the mind and keen to verify the accuracy of his position, he turned at once to the Bible. Only to find that it had been doctored. The story was there right enough, precisely as he had remembered it. So, too, were a series of numbers or symbols placed alongside most of the verses, directing his attention to notes at the foot of the page where the Pendarrell version of the Scriptures was expanded upon.

Little help then, nor anywhere else within the cell. The brothers had seen to that, insulating him from every trace of normal existence, or what, for them, passed as normal. All save the sounds of everyday life reaching him from the world outside. This was the room that had been his for daily prayer, as well as the fairly regular periods of encellment, and it had not taken him long to distinguish each one of the brothers by their footsteps alone: the solemnity of Brother Wye's measured tread, Brother Eden striding energetically about someone else's business, Brother Trent in unhurried contemplation, young Avon's somewhat mincing gait. And so the experiment that was to engage him over the months had begun.

He'd realised quite early that there were other sounds out there that the brothers had failed to eliminate. The birdsong that awoke him each morning, for instance. He'd never paid much heed to it before but now he came to recognise variations within the pitch and combination of notes, wondering whether individual wrens, thrushes, blackbirds, etc. recognised one another this way, or if there was a single song common to all their species. Not that he'd be able to tell them one from the other in the first place. Just as previously he'd always considered the sun as no more than a source of heat and light, depicted in picture books as a standard yellow orb in a blue sky. Now, with little else to occupy his mind, he came to appreciate the subtle changes as its beams slanting in from the window inched their way, brick by brick, across the cell. Differences in the quality almost of the light; each of its tinctures – cerise, silver, crimson, orange, gold, copper and a multiple of variations in between – during the course of a single day. Changes in the wind and rain as well: the smattering of hail on that same window, the buffeting it received from autumnal gales; times when daylight was almost obliterated by snow, others from falling leaves – each took on added significance during these periods of encellment, enforced or otherwise.

As did the relationship between all such factors: how creatures, heard yet never seen, modified their conversations, adjusted their tone at the first sign of danger, in advance of climatic change even; warning one to the other, or anyone who chose to hear. Which became the nub of his experimentation. The cells had been constructed to facilitate personal 'inventories', so why not put them to the test? Not the Pendarrell model of introspective soul-searching; something far more direct and practical, involving what could be heard only, experienced without his actual presence. How much more might be learnt in this way? Just what would be lost? The investigation had been in progress for several months now, at prayer time and during punitive encellments, but there was yet more to discover. Moving the table across the room and lifting the chair onto it, he clambered up, placing the Bible on the narrow sill to act as an arm rest, and adopted his usual stance: peering out through the window.

The stretch of grass between the building and the perimeter wall had been familiar to him from the outset, as was the pathway that crossed it to a doorway, kept locked at all times. He found himself looking out onto a hundred yards or so of open countryside; bleak, mossy and untended, a dozen or more sheep grazing contentedly upon it. This sloped gradually upwards, past a fringe of wild brambles, before giving way to a stretch of coppice, then open woodland that reached out as far as the eye could see to where distant hills fringed the horizon. A thin column of smoke rose from among the trees – neither wind nor breeze then – overhead birds wheeling cloud-like about the sky before plummeting suddenly downwards.

As he watched there was a disturbance in the foreground, sheep scattering in all directions as a large horse was led across the pasture dragging the trunk of a recently felled tree behind it. Could he hear, or did he imagine, the clink of the chains, the cries of the woodsmen? Later, another group of men emerged from the woodland, chatting – it appeared – among themselves. After which the sheep made their leisurely way to what he presumed was their night-time shelter. By now the sun was setting and the faintest of mists carpeted the meadow. The sound of church bells reached him, melodious from a far distance. Closer to hand the clanking of the chapel bell reminded him of evensong within the chapel. He climbed down from what had become his daily perch, watching the world go by unnoticed and unhindered, all part of a regular routine, unknowing one of the other, yet each of them interdependent. Far more satisfying than the brotherhood's wearisome certainty.

This had been going on for several weeks when the binoculars appeared – powerful ones, if size and weight were anything to go by. Now the smallest of leaves on the furthest of trees swam instantly into view, the minimum of practice combined with his customary patience soon enabled him to identify individual markings on each of the sheep and match these up with their owners; to recognise patterns of behaviour among birds and animals previously heard but not seen. The source of his new window on the world remained a mystery, though. It was not as if they'd been left there by accident. They were meant to be discovered, and discovered by him. Nor was he in any doubt that he was using them in the manner for which they'd been intended. Divine intervention, as the brothers would doubtless claim. He thought not, although this might be a hoax to persuade him such was the case. He carried out a roll-call of their individual characteristics, eliminating each of them in turn. Nor could they have come from anyone beyond the walls. If he had been unable to make his escape, then certainly no one could break in. And, after all his subterfuge, who could know of his secret obsession?

Then, a week or so later the book appeared: *Walden*, by Henry David Thoreau, with a series of bookmarks slipped between the pages, telling, so he discovered, of another man's obsession with the world of nature surrounding him. An American, this Thoreau, who'd delighted in a voluntary solitude that was his for the taking. His decamping to the woodlands of Concord, Massachusetts, was interesting enough, so too descriptions of the wildlife and vegetation. The philosophy, though, was hard to take. Garrulous, home spun, countless allusions to writers who seemed to have little to offer beyond what Henry David himself had to say. But the passages marked for his attention were another matter entirely:

> *One may almost doubt if the wisest man has learned anything of absolute value by living. Practically, the old have no very important advice to give to the young; their own experience has been so partial, and their lives have*

been such miserable failures, for private reasons, as they must believe, and it may be that they have some faith left which belies that experience, and they are only less young than they were. I have lived some thirty years on this planet, and I have yet to hear the first syllable of valuable or even earnest advice from my seniors. They have told me nothing, and probably cannot tell me anything to the purpose. Here is life, an experiment to a great extent untried by me, but it does not avail me that they have tried it. If I have any experience which I think valuable, I am sure to reflect that this my mentors said nothing about.

and:

If one advances confidently in the direction of his dreams, and endeavours to live the life which he has imagined, he will meet with a success unexpected in common hours. He will put some things behind, will pass an invisible boundary; new universal, and more liberal, laws will begin to establish themselves around and within him; or the old laws be expanded, and interpreted in his favour in a more liberal sense, and he will live with the license of a higher order of beings. In proportion as he simplifies his life, the laws of the universe will appear less complex, and solitude will not be solitude, poverty not poverty, nor weakness. If you have built castles in the air, your work need not be lost; that is where they should be. Now put the foundations under them.

Finally:

If a man does not keep pace with his companions, perhaps it is because he hears a different drummer. Let him step to the music he hears, however measured or far away.

Ideas half-formed in his own mind, expressed in a way he'd never considered possible. But who at Pendarrell House would think this way? Anathema to all of them, surely. The same person who'd provided the binoculars, obviously, who knew of his secret. But what was the purpose of these gifts?

I have yet to hear the first syllable of valuable or even earnest advice from my seniors; *different drummers*; *stepping to the music*: he resolved to put it to the test. Summoned back into the community a few days after the Daniel incident, he was questioned once more about his interpretation of the story. During his absence the brothers had prayed that the truth might be revealed to him and were eager to hear confirmation of the fact. Indeed, he informed them, assuming the benign expression appropriate for such occasions, no further arguments would be necessary. He, too, had prayed, in precisely the way they'd taught him, and such intercessions had been answered, just as they'd promised. Never again would he doubt the benefits of encellment. The brothers turned to one another, praising themselves on the efficacy of their treatment. Only to be silenced as their pupil proceeded to a reaffirmation of the views he'd previously held. But pride, he continued, was among the greatest of sins. Had not those more worthy interceded also on his behalf? Credit should be theirs also. What a mighty volume of prayerfulness they must have raised – he and the brothers together – enabling him to arrive finally at the truth.

A hushed silence fell over the hall but, from the back, came a burst of deep-throated laughter. All eyes swivelled to catch Soroyan, head thrown back in a paroxysm of mirth, trundling his way from the building.

Chapter Sixteen

Embracing the Emptiness

He was still laughing half an hour later, as he had been all the way from the hall.

'Strikes me, son, you ain't never been housetrained!' The abruptness of the introduction, directness of the idiom, took Derek completely by surprise. He'd seen Soroyan often enough around the college, heard the rumours, but never confronted him face-to-face. Nor any American, come to that.

'Like I sez, seems to me as no one's gotta round ter telling yew when to keep yer God-damned mouth shut.'

It helped to concentrate as much on the way the man spoke as to what he actually said; the tone of his voice, the slow rhythm occasionally broken by clipped emphasis on certain words or phrases; the wheelchair responding to the slightest of his touches.

'When, damn it, all as required is learnin' from tha Good Lord's own example.' The relaxed southern drawl was accompanied with a benign smile. 'Bin a pestering Him these five years a more now, them brothers. But that don't bother Him. Not one mite. Might learn a little from tha Good Lord's patience, don't yer think?'

Soroyan and Thoreau, both Americans. No doubt as to where the book had come from, nor its appropriateness, and the binoculars had proved a life-line, an inspiration. But how could a complete stranger have known that?

'Weren't nothing in-spirational about it.' The man's laughter filled the room. 'Gave tha game away yerself. Same as tha abbot I heard about. Had his wicked way wi tha nuns. Left tha toilet seat left up fer all ta see. Yours, the chair lifted up on tha table. "Committing suicide" thinks part of me. "Never" says tha other, "His mind a-searching for different ways to escape, no more!" Right on tha button, too. Could be, son, you an' me's tha only sane ones as left in this here asylum.'

Soroyan executed a neat three-point turn and, signalling Derek to follow, wheeled his way vigorously down the corridor, out into the courtyard, past the meeting hall towards the opposite end of the college. He expected they'd be apprehended at any moment, but the brothers they encountered passed by without a word, even wishing the two of them a respectful 'Goodnight'. Finally they reached what must once have been the stables. These adjoined the main building but were completely separate from it and regarded as out of bounds to all but the most senior members of the establishment. Soroyan handed him the key to a side door, which opened silently on well-oiled hinges, leading them along several broad passages into what he came to know as 'The Sanctum'.

This, he learnt, was the American's sole preserve, a low-ceilinged room, softly carpeted and furnished at one end with an enormous knee-hole desk raised still further above the floor by bricks placed one at each corner. Above the desk hung a painting he'd come across frequently, at the convent, or in books that he'd read: *The Light of the World*, life-sized, in an elaborate gold frame; by the Victorian artist Holman Hunt, if he remembered correctly. Facing it at the other end of the room was a well-polished mahogany table surrounded by a number of ornate, richly tapestried chairs. Three of the walls had been lined, floor to ceiling, with books, their shelves interspersed with other paintings that seemed vaguely familiar – Italian, so he'd been told – the 'old masters'. The fourth side of the room consisted mainly of a recess dominated by a large silver crucifix. All this taken in within a few minutes, before Soroyan, wheeling adroitly about, instructed him to return to his room. Not a word was to be said to the brothers, but he was to report back to 'The Sanctum' in the morning.

Here a young man was clearing away the breakfast things. Not a word was said as he went about his domestic chores – moving the table back into the alcove, rearranging papers on the desk and replenishing the jug of water that stood there – communicating with Soroyan in a form of sign language. Finally, having received what could only have been his instructions for the day, the valet was dismissed, after which there was a crunch of gravel as he cycled off on his errands.

'Ronnie says tell ya "Hi!"' Soroyan swung round to face him. 'Wishes could do so his-self, 'cept he got no tongue. Might take a leaf from his book there, son, as far as them out thars concerned. We's prisoners, tha both of us. Knew it tha moment I saw that chair on tha table; caught you a-staring outta window day after day. So now's yer chance ta help along the both of us. Be-come ma Fra Lippo.'

Derek had no idea what this meant and was too timid to ask but, over the next few weeks, settled into a daily routine: transcribing passages from reference books kept on the shelves or looking out others in preparation for Soroyan's research, collecting parcels newly arrived from publishers; reading through the papers, fetched by Ronnie each morning, and extracting anything he considered to be of local interest. Best of all, permission was granted for him to make trips out into the countryside viewed previously only through binoculars, exploring each and every aspect, carrying a sketchpad and pencil at all times, and returning several hours later with a minute report on everything he'd seen. Evidence of the world into which the American could not, or would not, venture.

It was not till some time later, asked to check up on an obscure line from Robert Browning, he came upon the poem 'Fra Lippo Lippi.' There was not much of it Derek understood, but the plot had been tersely summarised in a series of footnotes. Lippo Lippi, a supreme artist of the Medici period, breathing life into everything he painted, had been obliged to spend his days in a monastery producing characterless saints and angels to order. His inspiration, though, had come not from contemplation of the Almighty but everyday life spotted beyond the monastic walls. Unable to resist the temptation, he'd clambered through a window, out into the streets, following a carnival into the heart of Florence, where he'd been apprehended by the night watchman, returned to the monastery and 'encelled' once more. 'Fra Lippo': the nick-name was as obvious as it was appropriate.

And it was on a Sunday, during one of his expeditions that Derek traced the bells first heard during his earlier Lippo-like incarceration. He'd arrived at St Asalph's, a small stone-built church with an unusually large belfry, just as they'd been ringing, summoning the last of the congregation in for Matins. The service had been in Welsh, but the Rev. Eli Jenkins – tall, craggy as the surrounding hills, seemingly not much younger himself – had a rhythmic command of English and, once acquainted, Derek made regular visits, taking rubbings from the tombs and churchyard memorials, receiving his first stumbling lessons in bell-ringing, but chiefly to hear Eli's lilting rendition of the *Mabinogion*. Tales of Prince Pwyll and Branwen, her suitors, Math and Gwydion, their deeds passed down from generation to generation by word-of-mouth. Fantasies maybe, the old man told him, heathen even, pre-dating the written word. Intended for the telling, yet holding truths beyond the power of speech.

Pity the nation that had no such legends, yet beware of those who make them their master.

The American agreed. Just as the *Old Testament* stories through which he, Derek, had made his reputation.

'It's th' et-ernal choppin' up an' di-secting of tha Scriptures as got our friends out thar all fired up.' Soroyan nodded in the direction of the brethren's quarters. 'No mor' an' hackin' down them trees – the ones ya bin a-sketchin' – ter count tha rings. Get ta know their age that way. Tha condition, too: dis-eased or healthy. But then what's there left ta look at? One God-damned empty space, that's all. So, onto tha next tree. An' the next. Till, before ya knows it, ain't no more trees left. No forest. Jest one damn desert. Findin' it cost me ma legs. Got Him cut down completely.' He'd swung round, silhouetted now against the gold-framed image of Christ, lantern in hand, addressing the painting almost. 'Even then they could have em-braced th' empti-ness; listened fer His voice beyond tha silence. But no. What they go an' do? Gathers up tha timber an' fashens themselves a new church.'

Which stood in direct contradiction to everything he'd been told about the man. 'But it's you that supported them all this time,' he protested. 'Without your help the brotherhood couldn't exist; there'd be no Pendarrell House.'

But Soroyan refused to be drawn any further and it fell to the valet to explain, using the sign-language he and Soroyan had developed and which Derek had been eager to learn. This had grown in complexity through practice, as did their friendship.

'Not told you about the "guest ant"?' Ronnie signed.

He hadn't. '"Shiny guest ant", *Formicoxenus nitidulus*.' Ronnie struggled with the terminology, scribbling it down on the back of an envelope. 'Makes its home among other colonies; lives there undetected, but if discovered exudes a bitter off-putting secretion. Just his way, the name-calling; he's done it as long as I can remember. How else do you think the brothers got their names? The "Fra Lippo" tag? Take it as a compliment,' he added. 'It's not till he really knows someone that he comes up with something suitable.'

An American millionaire seeking refuge from fortune hunters; Pendarrell House the perfect hideaway. But financing a whole community whose ideas he himself questioned sounded more like craziness as far as Derek was concerned. 'And now these hints that somehow it was this that crippled him!'

'As it was!' An instant response, instantly regretted. 'But that's not for me to say.'

Nothing could persuade Ronnie to take the matter further, neither then, nor in the days that followed. Avoiding his company whenever possible and sullen when they met, it seemed to Derek that his curiosity had brought their friendship to an end. Till some two weeks later when he volunteered to accompany Derek to the post office.

'Can't think how he allowed matters to develop this far and still stay silent,' he signed, once the gates were passed. 'Putting you in harm's way with never a word of warning. Lost sleep thinking about it.'

A practical joke? Not Ronnie's style. Nor had the man been drinking. Soroyan's evasiveness tipping him over the edge?

'The brothers finally got to you?' he ribbed.

'They've nothing to do with it. Innocent bystanders; kept in the dark, just as you've been.' Ronnie seemed to have taken him seriously. 'Not me. I came into it with my eyes open. Known all along; willing to take the consequences. But you, devoted to the man, involved as either of us but with no notion as to what's really going on. No, just hear me out.' Ronnie pulled him to one side, and they settled on a low platform alongside the milk-churns. 'And promise me one thing. You'll be wanting to leave us after you've heard what I tell you, but he must never know why. Give whatever reason you want. Loss of faith; impatience with his manner; distrust of the brothers; a falling-out between us – anything. But never that you know his secret. Nor how you discovered it.'

He reached into his pocket and handed over a book: *Old Testament Mythology: Synthesis, Assimilation and Accretion.* Nondescript, its cover faded from black to grey, with dense pages of close-knit text, time-charts, the occasional line drawing or diagram. Self-published in Delaware, USA, 1924, by one Raymond K. Lansdale III. But it was the author's sepia photograph accompanying the introduction that caught Derek's attention. Middle-aged, bespectacled, standing before a map of the Holy Land, his dark hair neatly parted: a younger, smarter version, of the man he knew as Soroyan.

Chapter Sevemteen

The Night Watch

An anti-climax, unexpected, but hardly world-shattering; Soroyan was not the only author to write under a pseudonym. Nor did there seem anything unusual about the content; nothing more, and certainly nothing less than what they'd been studying these last six months.

'Nothing unusual?' Ronnie's concern couldn't have been more evident had he spoken the words. 'Not here, perhaps, given your background. Guided by an expert, permitted to make your own way to the truth. Think back just a few months, though. To the way the brothers treated you, just for disagreeing with what they said. Multiply that a hundred, no a thousand times, and you get some idea of the reaction to the book. Printed privately – no publisher would touch it – not in the southern States. You'll have heard of the Scopes trial?' Derek shook his head.

'Monkeyville?'

Now he had it. 'The American schoolteacher charged with propagating Darwin's view of creation?'

'That's the one. Well, this was a few months earlier, a curtain-raiser you might call it. Giving a non-literal slant not only to *Genesis* but the *Old Testament* as a whole. Got him dismissed from the University where he taught; denounced by the faculty, together with churches right across the south. Accompanied by ceremonial burnings of the book, along with effigies of

Lansdale. Same fate as awaited the printers, their premises fire-bombed. Divine intervention, according to God's Intent that is, the most diehard of all the fundamentalist sects, with "Praise the Lord" Malone - yes, that's what they christened him, Praise the Lord - leading his followers in prayers of thanksgiving. There's a photograph of him in one of the papers brandishing a shotgun from the pulpit: "Always keep one of these by me for the elimination of vermin", he's quoted as saying. Whilst behind him, just in case there were those who misunderstood the message, Lansdale's picture, with a target superimposed over the heart.'

'Hence the pseudonym?'

'That's the part I'm coming to now.' Ronnie was not to be rushed. 'Three days later a hooded man was seen entering the Lansdale household. Shots were fired and he was left for dead. As he would have been, had it not been for two hours on the operating table, which saved his life, but not the legs; they caught the full blast, hence the wheelchair. Meanwhile a shotgun was unearthed from Praise the Lord 's back garden, a perfect match for the one used in the assault. An open-and-shut case, you'd have thought - when they dared to bring it. Hundreds of spectators had poured into town, queuing for hours to get admission to the courtroom; the proceedings continuously interrupted, and state troopers called in to restrain those waiting outside. But nothing compared to the pandemonium that erupted when the "Guilty" verdict was announced: insults hurled at the defending lawyers, windows smashed, the courtroom having to be cleared, the terrified jury led out under police protection.'

A break in the narrative as a tractor with hay-stacked trailer rumbled past, Ronnie greeting the driver with a cheery wave before continuing. 'The judge himself was clearly nervous, but there was nothing for it: the death sentence had to be passed. Nor did Malone go quietly, threatening Lansdale from the electric chair itself, vowing God's Intent would be avenged. No matter how long they had to wait, wherever the man hid, he'd never be at peace. No more would those protecting him, "even if we have to claw our way down to Hell to reach them" – his own words, just a few minutes before he died. By which time Raymond K. Lansdale had become Soroyan and disappeared, apparently, from the face of the earth. But not before he'd promised a sequel, doing for the *New Testament* what *Mythology* had done for the Old.'

'Bringing him to Wales: the "the ant in the ants' nest"?'

'With a fortune to spend on renovating Pendarrell House.' The tractor had pulled into a field down the lane, birds wheeling above it as the unloading commenced. 'He'd inherited the family estate, which was enormous, together with a lifetime's collection of Renaissance art. Which is how I came to meet him. Americans love English butlers, particularly if "art-wise and savvy". Especially so if they can't answer back.'

'Explaining why I've been on the look-out for strangers; the paper-chase each morning?'

'The Thoreau book and the binoculars, put there for a purpose. Same as everything he does. Don't think you found out about the 'Fra Lippo' by chance, do you? With Browning being his favourite poet, knowing the man's work backwards. And *Adoration in the Forest*, up there on the wall in the study from the moment you started pestering him over the nickname.'

Ronnie paused, some response obviously expected. 'Fra Lippo's masterpiece?' He shook his head sadly. 'No point, then, in mentioning the picture he chose specially for you. The one he had me put up in your bedroom.'

'Rembrandt's *Night Watch*.' Derek had lived with the picture, night and day, for several months now. '*Amsterdam, 1642. City worthies setting off on evening patrol*.' He rattled off the caption.

'Headed up by the local aristocracy, on the look-out for vagrants and ne'er-do-wells. Seventeenth rather than fifteenth century; not Florence, Amsterdam this time, but same sort of group that arrested Fra Lippo. And here the both of us are today, on the alert in the same kind of fashion.'

Had this been Soroyan's sole interest in him, then, as an unknowing accomplice, to act as an early warning beacon should danger appear on the horizon? Not trusted to share in the secret. A big one, of course; the man's life depended upon it.

Ronnie seemed to have read his thoughts: 'Wondered so myself, why he never shared this with you. Different for me, knowing the dangers, experiencing them first-hand; how nothing will stop them. Made him promise time and again he'd come clean; tell you everything. Never seemed fair, putting you at risk yet not daring to tell you the truth.'

'In case I absconded?'

'Got to see it his way, I suppose.' Ronnie had picked up on the indignation in Derek's voice. 'Robbed of his livelihood, made out to be a figure of hate across half the States; blown almost into kingdom-come, then chased from his homeland by those eager to finish the job. His life's work at an end when suddenly the organisation he's created to mask his activities throws up someone with real talent. No, hear me out.' Derek had half risen in protest. 'No mere novice, a kindred spirit rather. Providing him with a possible means of escape; vicariously through eyes that see things the way he does, ears that pick up what others have missed.'

'So, if he thought that much of me, why not come straight out with it? Questions rather than answers. Hints, suggestions, pointers. Anything but a straightforward explanation.'

'Had to be sure of you, I guess. Get to know you better before he came clean, but the closer you got the more difficult it became. Used the clues – nicknames, the paintings, that poem, those quotes from Thoreau – to salve his conscience. Kidding himself you'd catch on, save him the embarrassment of telling it straight. Self-inflicted wounds, if you ask me. And a victory of sorts for God's Intent.'

'"Self-inflicted wounds", "victory of sorts"? You're beginning to sound like the man himself.'

Ronnie seemed not to have heard him. 'Forced forever to hide under a cloak of deception. Never knowing when or how they might strike, or who to trust. Driven to communicate through clues in case he let something slip and they got wind of his hiding-place. Until it became second-nature; a way of life. A victory for God's Intent, like I say, achieved without raising a finger. Not that he'd see it that way. Just as, hopefully, those following in Praise the Lord's footsteps are never going to learn of their success.'

* * *

There never was a conscious decision as to his future. Derek did not tell the American what had passed between them nor, as far as he could tell, had Ronnie warned Soroyan that his secret was out. Life at Pendarrell continued very much as before, although now he took extra care in perusing the local press, was especially on the look-out for strangers crossing his path. Till gradually the novelty of the situation wore off; *Old Testament Mythology* became a distant memory.

Until the arrival of Veronica's letters: ten of them altogether, addressed to Derek, written at regular intervals, dating back to his first week at Pendarrell. They'd been intercepted by Brother Arun who, responsible for checking all incoming mail and fearing worldly distractions, had failed to pass them on.

She'd made her feelings clear. Nor did she disguise her disappointment at Derek's failure to reply, begging a response of some kind, promising – to the goggle-eyed Brother Arun's acute embarrassment – to do anything he wished. Finally, the threat. Life without him was not worth living; if he cared that little, she would bring it to an end. At which point Soroyan had been consulted. He'd written personally to the girl, apologising for the situation and explaining that distraction of any kind was forbidden during the probationary period. Her letters would be kept and given to the recipient once he was permitted to read them. Fury on Veronica's part had given way to resignation but now, with the fictitious 'probationary period' at an end, she'd written demanding an answer of some kind, and this time directly from the object of her affection.

The outcome was disastrous. A few lines of the most vapid prose were all Derek could muster, nor did further attempts prove any more successful. Till Soroyan sat the boy down at the desk and, gyrating about the room, dictated precisely what should be written. How he – Derek – had settled down at the college; his gratitude for all that had been done for him; his delight at receiving her letters; that she'd been persuaded not to carry out her threat. How he thought about her often, looked forward to the time when they could meet again. No more than a stop-gap, the tutor assured him; by the time Derek left Pendarrell she'd have forgotten about him.

But Veronica's reply came by return of post, as frank and amorous as the original. Bringing old memories unexpectedly to mind: the sound of her voice, the excuses she'd made to be near him, her delight at the smallest of favours. Derek found himself strangely moved, made several clandestine attempts to reply, was forced eventually to creep disconcertedly back for his tutor's advice. There'd been an initial show of reluctance, following which the American rose eloquently to the occasion. And so the pattern was set, with Derek eagerly awaiting her replies, reading and rereading them till he had each one off by heart, guessing and reguessing what form his responses might take. Always he was mistaken, whilst Soroyan – as ever – came up with the exact sentiments he wished so badly to convey, together with nuances he would never have guessed were his.

Less than a year, Veronica had written, and they'd be together.

More like a century it seemed, but the months became weeks, weeks dissolved into days until, three years after his first arrival, the time of departure came. The whole college assembled in the chapel to hear the few sentences that Brother Trent had cobbled together. Prayers were said for the well-being of his soul. There was a valedictory blessing, and the few possessions he'd brought with him were returned to his room. Ronnie's hands fluttered emotionally as they said goodbye, and now it only remained for Soroyan to make his farewells. Derek waited in the study where they'd spent so much time together, rehearsing and rerehearsing the thanks he'd planned. Inadequate now the moment had arrived. Nor did his mentor appear to have any final words of wisdom. Instead, curt good wishes and a package placed in his hands. Thin and oblong, one side hard and flat – glass he realised – ridged along the edges with sharp corners. No need to guess at the contents: *The Night Watch.*

But, before he'd opened it, proffered his thanks, the American had wheeled himself from the room.

Chapter Eighteen

The Stained Glass Conscience

'It was a very different Derek that returned home from Pendarrell'

Our second day at Willow Lane, Peter's accusations seemingly forgotten, with Geraldine well into her stride. A window stood open, curtains billowed out in the breeze and I remember hearing the rest of her reminiscences to the accompaniment of bird song from the garden.

'Every bit as shy and reserved, liking to keep himself to himself, but eager for my company now.' A complete change of tone, as well. Geraldine – Veronica a she'd been then – no longer the bystander, reporting dispassionately on what she'd picked up over the years. Reliving her time with Derek – or should that be Jimmy? – told first-hand in a direct, very personal manner. 'Meeting me each night after work, taking me for walks in the countryside, bringing presents, forever knocking on the door or finding ways of pleasing me. Mum disapproved from the start. I'd been apprenticed to a dressmaker for several months by then and she'd got it into her head I could do better. Threats, emotional blackmail, Dad turning in his grave; God knows what would have happened if she'd known the content of those letters. Copied out from magazines most of them, or films I'd seen. But much more explicit. And, if that wasn't bad enough, Derek was in trouble with the church. They'd given him back his old job at the Sunday School, but he'd returned with his head full of the weirdest ideas. Comparing Abraham's devotion to God with heathen practices, teaching the flood was not from the Scriptures but barbaric writings, reading pagan sacrifices into the way we worship God. "Confusing the sacred with the profane", according to the rector.'

'Quite normal in *university* circles.' Mildred's disapproval was quite obviously aimed at Peter.

Geraldine glared across at her. 'Be that as it may, it earned Derek the sack. After which there was little chance of further employment. My own work suffered as well; treasuring every moment we had together, concentrating on little else. All of which he took in his stride, quite unperturbed by what was going on around him. He'd become pedestrian in his wooing as well. I'd remind him of the letters, read them back to him, suggest he put his thoughts down on paper if that's what turned him on. Till eventually he confessed how they'd come to be written. In the end there was only one thing for it. I reminded him of just what I had to offer, hinted as to how far I'd go to please him. But no. Derek was as deaf to subtlety as I was to Mum and the rest, all of them counselling caution. Caution? Try telling that to a eighteen-year-old with only one thought on her mind. Or a fifteen-year-old grammar school boy in a St Hugh's blazer at the bus stop, eh, Peter?'

He tensed, seemed about to enter the fray. 'Don't you dare,' I mouthed. Here, at last, was part of the background he'd always withheld and I was not to be deprived of it. I nodded across at the old lady to continue.

Which she did almost without pause. 'Reading those old letters brought the suicide ruse to mind. The ploy had worked once, brought Derek to his senses, so how much more effective when operated at close quarters? Dramatic, as well: two empty pill bottles at the bedside, some scribbled last words and my loved one's picture clutched in my hand. A cliché, I know, but tell me a suicide that isn't. And I signalled my intentions: that last desperate 'phone call to the doctor. Timing as well, with Mum due home within the hour. And it worked, better than I'd expected. Derek and I were engaged within a fortnight; married once I'd turned twenty-one. Made my bed, so then I had to lie in it. There's another cliché for you. Mum quoted it back at me often enough. Together with that other one: about marrying in haste, repenting at leisure. Except it wasn't really in haste and I never did repent. No matter what she or the others had to say. And I'd clichés of my own. Going into the marriage with my eyes open, for instance, believing that love conquers all. What's it they always trot out at wedding ceremonies, Mildred, about Christian longsuffering and forbearance?'

'"Love bears all things, believes all things, hopes all things, endures all things?"'

'That's it. Fine. Except the part they leave out. How love takes different forms, means different things to different people. That what you most admire in a man can become the thing that drives you apart. Constancy, for example. The thing all of us look for in a husband. Derek had it in spades. Continual, undemonstrative devotion, forever willing to please. Disguising his distaste at my reading habits, the films I liked best, the radio programmes I enjoyed. Taking care to explain his own interests, the ones I failed to understand. Our walks seasoned with historic detail or botanical curiosities. His refusal to respond in kind if ever I lost my patience. Even found myself picking quarrels, over the smallest of things, just to get some response.'

'Are you sure you want to share this with us, Geraldine?' My turn to break into her narrative. 'We didn't come here to pry.'

'You wouldn't be hearing about it if that's what I thought, dear. Truth is, I've been nursing it to myself all these years; rehearsing what it might sound like if ever I got round to telling it.' She beamed across at me. 'So, don't go stopping me now, just when I'm about to find out!'

'Nor you, Peter. I know you idolised the man. Which is something we have in common. Difference is, it wasn't you that married him.

Not so romantic, all that determination, the self-reliance when you live with it twenty-four hours a day. Suppose I thought it would be different once we were together, when I had him all to myself. But no. He made no distinctions. As determined to retain his independence inside the home as he had been out of it. Willing to share in the household chores, as long as he was not asked to do so. Turning his hand to any number of tasks, yet grudging any suggestion I made. Not that he'd argue. Just the pursed lips, a shaking of the head, or the sudden recollection of odd jobs requiring instant attention elsewhere. That, and the silences. Used to great effect if ever I crossed him. World champion in that department was Derek. Come to think of it, he did have some crazy notion about it. Silences, I mean. Each one of them different and far more than merely the absence of sound. The split second pause in an argument, the air charged with malice; the moment a trigger is squeezed; a dying breath; those precious seconds that precede a kiss. Shot through with emotion; tangible almost…'

'That crazy notion? He tried it out on us kids once. Thought they might be caught on tape, or whatever recording device the BBC used. An anthology maybe.' Peter interrupted, his embarrassment forgotten.

'One of his "magpie moments" more like.' Mildred tossed the comment, grenade-like, into the discussion before turning her attention once more to what her companion was saying.

'Wasted his time on matters such as that, with things going from bad to worse on the employment front,' Geraldine continued. 'Folk knew how matters stood between us, were sympathetic. Several jobs were his for the taking, but he couldn't hold them down. He'd stand it for a time. Till someone got obstreperous, or he'd make a mistake and have to be corrected. Often enough just thought his own way was best. Then, rather than listen, he'd up and off. Time after time it happened until the goodwill ran out and I was left making excuses for him: he'd been brought up in an orphanage; educated by strangers; fended for himself all these years. Hiding the fact it made no more sense to me than it did to them. Not realising that you don't have to like someone to be in love with them. The attraction of opposites, I suppose. Hating them almost, yet adoring them at the same time. Anyway, Derek's patience was wearing thin as well as mine. Instead of the silences or excuses to be somewhere else within the house, he took to solitary walks in the countryside. Which was where he really wanted to be, had we been able to afford it.'

By now the room had darkened. Not that any of us noticed, nor how cold it was getting. We blinked as she switched on a lamp behind her and I found myself shivering. The chill air, or was the story affecting me more than I'd imagined? The 'attraction of opposites', just as it'd been with myself and Peter; 'picking quarrels just to get some response' the way our relationship could have gone, but for the 'living in' sin. Veronica might have realised her mistake if only she and Derek had followed our example. Not that such options would have been open to them in the 1930s, any more than they'd been to Enid Quintock and her 'Reg' some twenty years earlier. Veronica at least had grasped the inconsistencies in Jimmy's character. Unlike Peter, who'd idolised the man – unconditionally – then betrayed him. Or thought that he had. I reached for his hand as our host switched on the electric fire, assuring us yet again she felt no embarrassment. Mildred closed the window, and she resumed her narrative...

War was very much in the air by then and, with it, the matter of conscription. Veronica had prepared herself for the worst, dreading the thought of separation, never suspecting that Derek would refuse the draft. As he did, giving neither reason, nor permitting discussion. Others did not hold back. Accusations began the moment he took himself down to the labour exchange, where separate booths had been set up, conscientious objectors lined up on one side of the room, four or five of them only, far outnumbered by conscripts on the other. There'd been angry mutterings. Some of the would-be soldiers turned their backs, waved their papers, called out the names of brothers who'd answered the call; fathers who'd died in the trenches. One man detached himself from the group, strode across the room and began haranguing them on their patriotic duty – the defence of King and Country. 'Conchies!' He spat out the name.

It was not the first time Veronica had heard the term, nor was it to be the last: conscientious objectors denounced from the pulpit; council employees – office workers, teachers, Sunday School helpers and the like – dismissed from their post; biblical texts legitimising the 'righteous war' pushed through their letterbox. As were items of an even more repugnant nature. There'd been the neighbours who passed them by in the street, shopkeepers who refused to serve them. Worst of all the commiseration of her friends, on hand as they always were when her husband proved difficult. 'As if there was a bereavement in the family,' she told us. 'The tribunal to which Derek was summoned came almost as a relief.'

The room had been stripped of all furniture save only for a trestle table covered with a green baise cloth. Behind this sat the four members of the panel. At the centre an imposing figure: the chairman, a judge. He was flanked on his left by the town clerk: dark suit, balding and bespectacled, determined that correct records were kept and procedures ran on time. On the right sat the 'union representative': intent, angular, about Derek's age; dusty both in appearance and opinion. The fourth member of the group was noticeably younger. Withdrawn slightly to the clerk's left and introduced as 'Sir John' but Derek was unable to remember the rest of the man's title.

Geraldine recounted as much of the proceedings as she could remember, and I'm sure she dressed it up, giving Derek all the best lines. '*Jimmy*,' insisted Peter, 'and he'd never have spoken in such a pompous manner.'

Be this as it may, from what we could gather the hearing seems to have proceeded somewhat as follows:

TU Rep: The note from your current employer seems fine enough, but he's only known you for, let's see now, four months. Tell us about your previous work.
Derek: Varied really. I tried my hand at a number of skills.
TU Rep: But master at none. A drifter, in fact. Does loyalty mean nothing to you?
Derek: Certainly. To myself; to my family.
Judge: And your country?
Derek: As I've said, a man's prime loyalty is to his own.
Judge: Nothing beyond this? It says here you were once a Sunday School teacher.
Derek: Where I taught the children to love their enemies; do good to those who hated them.
TU Rep: It also says you were sacked.
Derek: As was the person who said those words. Got Him thrown out of the building, too.
Clerk: That's not what it says in my Bible.
Derek: Mine has Him teaching out in the open, by the roadside, in the hills, from a boat. Why else would He have done that?
Judge: Forget the theology for a moment. Don't you recognise the rule of law? The necessity for each one of us, as citizens, to follow it. Regardless of our feelings?
Derek: I was created human before it was decided I was a citizen. Born free before anyone claimed my obedience. A man's conscience is not democratic. It belongs to him and him alone.
Clerk: (clapping his hands) You've got the gift of the gab, I'll give you that. I never in my whole life heard cowardice so eloquently described!
TU Rep: Convenient as well!! Supposing you explain just how you know what your 'conscience' is telling you? What proof is there you have one at all?
Derek: How can I prove such a thing? Conscience is like a pane of glass: the clearer it is, the more difficult it is to see.
Judge: See through more like! (General guffawing.)

TU Rep: A stained glass conscience!
Sir John: Church attendance might do, the Sunday School possibly. How about membership of one of the humanitarian organisations?
Clerk: Vegetarianism, for example. You eat meat, don't you? So it can't be the thought of killing that deters you.
Derek: Pork and beef perhaps, but not sentient creatures. Remarkable how you know every detail of a man's life when it comes to taxation yet otherwise can't tell them from cattle!
TU Rep: Sentient creatures! Swallowed the dictionary have you? What...'
Judge: ...I see you have never actually broken the law. Nor, it seems, failed in your civic duty. Can't you see, it's that same law that requires you to enlist?
Derek: It's the establishment's war, not mine. Let those who wish to take part in the slaughter do so; it's none of my business. Nor the state's to tell me what is.
Sir John: So, you'd stand by and let others do the fighting? Do nothing to prevent it? Have I got that right?
Derek: Correct. It's their business, not mine.
Sir John: And, as they've answered their conscience just as much as you have yours, support the decision they've arrived at?
Derek: Why should I hinder someone in pursuit of their conscience?
Sir John: Assist them, even? If some way could be found which did not involve you in the action?
Derek: Certainly, provided I took no part in the killing.
Sir John: Just so. Then the answer seems obvious.

For all Derek's impertinence, maybe because his was the last case of the morning and they were getting hungry, most probably because Sir John's solution, though irregular, carried weight, the tribunal was lenient. War on the home front was taking its toll. London had been subjected to almost continuous bombing by night and day; Bristol, Coventry, Birmingham suffered in similar fashion.

Ambulance drivers, stretcher bearers, firemen were all required to assist the professionals in their work. It was to the latter that Derek was seconded.

For what should have been the duration. To Veronica's relief, following basic training he'd been posted not to the capital, but the industrial cities of the North West.

'Occasionally he wrote; mundane stuff, heavily censored, of course.' She smiled wistfully. 'So different from the letters he sent from Pendarrell. He'd arrive back unexpectedly as well. Tired and dishevelled, but distant as ever, still with little to say. I was thankful he returned at all; the part of the Midlands where we lived saw so little of the conflict. The occasional air-raid siren, that's all. The sound of distant gunfire perhaps, and, sometimes, at night, an orange tint in the sky.'

One raid in particular lived with her always: Liverpool, 12th March, 1941.

'I'd heard the siren, taken cover in the shelter, peered up at aircraft streaming in. Saw them disappear to the north and waited for the all-clear. Thought nothing of it till I read the newspapers next morning, listened to the details broadcast on the radio.'

Some 400 aircraft there'd been. Heinkels for the most part, four at least brought down by Hurricanes and Defiants, one of the pilots rescued from the Mersey. Shipping, factories, cranes and warehouses their targets, the surrounding area, Wallasey, peppered with parachute mines, incendiary bombs and high explosives. Over 630 people killed. And one of them had been Derek.

They'd not let her see the body. Or what was left of it, together with remnants of his helmet, buttons and buckle from the uniform melded and misshapen. His possessions had been boxed together and returned to her: wallet, key ring, the book he'd been reading, the watch she'd given him, its hands set permanently at 11.52 – together with the obligatory note of condolence. She'd attended the funeral alongside her mother, half a dozen or so of her friends, the last of his employers and a representative of one or other of the Conscientious Objectors' Groups.

'So sympathetic they were. The lot of them.' For the first time there was a catch in Geraldine's voice. 'Advised that I put it behind me; make a new life for myself. And so I did. But, no matter what they said, there was this one image I couldn't get out of my mind. I've never quite rid myself of it. Nor wanted to. Those aircraft, dark shapes up there in the moonlight. Only part of the raid, I know, and maybe not the bombers. But they could have been. One in particular among them. Course set, bomb-sights checked. All in readiness, whilst I stood by and watched. Silly, I know, all of them told me so at the time. But it could have been the one. Really it could...'

Chapter Nineteen

Love in a Mist

Geraldine's story was far from finished, calling for an additional night at The Spurs and Stirrup, spent in the room with the cracked washbasin and creaking floorboards, myself attempting to square the Jimmy that I'd known with the Willow Lane revelations, and Helen – bless her – trying valiantly to suppress that 'I told you so' expression. Could Jimmy and Derek be one and the same person? The evidence seemed incontrovertible, yet I remained unconvinced. The orphanage, a taste for the more fanciful of Biblical narrative: yes. Rejection of conscription and teaching in a Sunday School: possibly. But penning love letters? And married? Hardly the Jimmy I remembered. A case of mistaken identity, then? How else could the same person be a victim of the 1941 Liverpool bombings, then telling his stories, painting his pictures, several years later in Bereden?

'So follow it through rationally, as if it were a piece of academic research. "Begin at the beginning. Start with the facts that are known to us. Then, and only then, decide on the questions we must ask."' Something I'd driven into my students' heads a hundred times over, and Helen, leaning back against the side-table, thumbs tucked into the lapels of her jacket, gave a very good impression of my doing it.

Well then, if Geraldine – or Veronica as she then called herself – was to be believed, Derek would have slipped out of her life at the moment – give or take a few years – Jimmy had entered mine. She'd got the background right as well. Neither Bereden nor Northampton – where they'd lived at the time – had been targeted during the Blitz, but each lay on routes favoured by enemy bombers; hers to the industrial north, mine to the south coast dockyards. She remembering the decoy Liverpool over to the west, luring the bombers away from more valuable targets; I the make-believe artillery emplacements set up around the village, no resemblance to the real thing but an enticing target at 15,000 feet. And we shared the experience of waking to the sound of sirens in the night, being hurried to the safety of a shelter, the pulsing drone of aircraft far above, later the spluttering of V2s, the woof of distant gunfire; most memorable, the glow of cities burning in the distance. Thereafter our memories differed somewhat: hers of Coventry in ruins; my own of Bargate, Southampton, bombed-out end-to-end, as was the King's Road, Portsmouth.

Which got us very little further; the 'research' angle even less successful when applied to matters of the heart. 'In the early days,' I conceded, 'he might – just might – have fallen for her wiles. He seems to have lost interest once he returned home, so I suppose he could have faked his own death? Marriage would have seemed like imprisonment for him.'

'Just as it would for Veronica,' Helen had no doubts. 'The demure little housewife, doing what she was told without a murmur, whilst he took himself off, or out into the countryside whenever things got too hot to handle. An "open prison" by comparison. Come on, Peter, even you grew out of him. She spotted it the moment you met.'

'That was completely different. I was hardly into my teens. Showing off, I admit it; trying to prove how grown-up I was.'

Which must have been the reason I reacted so badly when reintroduced to Veronica – or Geraldine as she was now. Embarrassment; the reminder of all that adolescent lust; of a betrayal I thought I'd left behind me. Ushering this woman into Jimmy's life – reushering if what she said was true. A reporter, I'd been sure, following up on Jimmy's *Shakesphere* success, or his tracking down and rescue of Howard – together with the unwelcome hoard that followed in her wake. But why had Veronica, who'd made all the running, disappeared so suddenly once she'd discovered the deception and run him to ground? As, with my help and her artifice, we agreed she must have done.

'A mistake; it must have been,' I concluded. "Veronica in pursuit of the husband she'd given up for dead catches up with him; finds it's the wrong man, beats a hasty retreat.'

Nothing, though, would be achieved by further confrontation. This was no longer the auburn-haired siren who'd beguiled me all those years ago but an old lady well into her seventies, and we were guests in her house. Far better to play it her way and see what emerged, as we did from the moment we arrived at 52 Willow Lane next morning.

'Did my best to be a good wife,' she now told us.' Waited in vain for him to notice the care I'd taken over the darning of his socks or the sewing on of his buttons. But no. Far too engaged with his inner self or spats with one employer after another.'

Yet it was precisely these talents – the sewing, running up of dresses, emergency repairs; her flair at 'make do and mend' – that was to bring her face to face with Derek fifteen or so years after she'd seen him buried. The route as indirect as it had been fortuitous.

Her mother's death had followed on shortly from her husband's. There'd been a small legacy, but for the most part she'd scraped a living through needlework and the embroidery that was beginning to find its way into nearby craft shops. And so things might have gone on indefinitely, but for a set of table decorations – *Field of the Cloth of Gold* – that came to the attention of the county magazine. A feature article was commissioned, followed by a complete series, *Behind Every Man*, suggesting how the hard-pressed housewife might send her smartly dressed spouse off to work each morning. From there her interests had broadened out, into the regional and historic aspects of fabric design. Features by 'Geraldine Leapman' – a combination of her mother's Christian and her own maiden name – now appeared in glossy magazines and, almost without knowing it, she found herself consultant to one of the newer television companies. She was now able to establish her own business, specialising in folk art, coming by chance upon the work of an obscure artist from the rural depths of Hampshire whose paintings seemed ideal for embroidery and taking herself off to meet him.

It was, of course, Derek.

'Recognised him the moment I set eyes on him.' Geraldine paused, selected a cigarette from a silver box on the table beside her and, both of us having declined to join her, lit up. 'Not got into the habit then?' Her eyes narrowed as she inhaled. 'Not after all these years? Almost killed you last time, remember? Trying so hard to be grown up, he was.' This to Helen. 'Still, it's not done me any harm, no matter what the doctor, or Mildred here, says. Derek most of all. And, God help me, I do believe I had one of these in my hand the moment I saw him there.' The fingers that held the cigarette trembled slightly. It glowed momentarily as she gazed through the twisting smoke into her past. 'Like I say, knew it right away, him propped up there against the war memorial, surrounded by children. Older, of course, eyes sunken, but not in an unattractive kind of way. Hair beginning to recede and he'd grown a beard. Taken to wearing a medallion as well, which he'd never have done the whole of the time I knew him. Relaxed and smiling; that's the thing I remember most of all, always will. Derek smiling, just as he used to in the early days. Not that he'd seen me. Before I'd time to say or do anything he was up and away, with the children swarming after him. And I knew. Instantly. What he'd done and why he'd done it.'

She leant forward and stubbed out the cigarette. 'The doubts came later. Had I really seen what I'd seen? Or was it my imagination? Like in the days after the funeral, when I'd catch sight of him everywhere I looked. Well, no problem this time. Merely a question of slipping back to the village, watching everything he did; asking questions from the locals, delicately, in case after all I'd been mistaken, but getting no replies. Finally latching onto the one person who seemed willing to talk. Using all my charms on him. And most susceptible he turned out to be, didn't you, Peter? A rotten trick to play on a kid, I realise that now.'

'And when you were sure, what then?' Helen came in quickly, unsure as to what my own response might be.

'Once I'd got over the first shock I began to see things more clearly. This was Derek right enough. Just as reserved, as determined in his outlook, impatient with those who failed to see things his way, detesting authority in any shape or form. Just as you told it, Peter. Discovered that for myself all those afternoons I stood and watched. As skilled at story-telling as he'd always been, but far more relaxed, comfortable in his new lifestyle. Talented in other ways, too. I remember you telling me about his "doodlings". Never imagined one day I'd travel half-way across the country to search them out. Quite obviously he'd regained his old self; discovered something I could never supply, and found something more precious: contentment, self-fulfilment, so, how could I destroy it? He'd deserted me, it's true, and who's to say he wasn't right to do so? Minor feelings – indignation, anger, resentment, humiliation – didn't come into it. The test of my love was the distance I would now put between us.'

Helen's words, both of us realised, almost precisely, that time she left me. 'You never went back?' I heard her ask.

No response; exchanged glances with Mildred, rather; another cigarette lit, smoke exhaled. So, did her resolve break? Had she returned to find her Derek?'

'Let that wait. It's about time we heard your side of the story, Peter.' The abrupt change-of-topic clinched the matter; so she *had* gone back. Just as Helen had returned to me.

'What exactly did happen after I'd left?' she was asking. 'Reporters, photographers you said. You're right, he'd have hated it. Nothing to do with me, though, I promise. So, what precisely *were* they after?'

Which was the strange thing about the affair. No one ever did discover just what all the excitement was about. It had been the talk of the village for weeks. They'd just appeared from nowhere, poring over maps, looking at compasses, not one of them saying why they were there or what they wanted. The rectory was their first port of call, but Codpiece was out, so it was off to take photographs of the bell-tower and Third Class Cottage. Jimmy was apoplectic, of course; took himself into the woods, with the lot of them trailing after him. At which point Sir Desmond arrived on the scene. Not that they listened to him either. A novel experience that, the best part of it for some of us. Anyway, he stalks back to the Hall, makes a telephone call – a London number according Andrew's mother, who worked there at the time. Next thing we know the Lone Granger's summoned from his lunch by God knows who, astride Wild Silver, and two black cars with enormous headlights and swept-back mudguards pull into the village. Six or seven men leap out, meet up with the PC Granger, consult Sir Desmond; the reporters are bundled into the cars, their cameras and notebooks confiscated and the Squire waves them off.

'Which was the last any of us heard about it,' I told her.

Geraldine was shaking her head. 'And you thought that somehow I was responsible? Do I look like a reporter?'

That had been the popular opinion. Obvious really: glamorous outsider appears from nowhere; is fascinated by the village and its past; noses around for a day or two asking silly questions;

disappears as suddenly as she'd arrived; then, for whatever reason, sends in the heavy mob. Jimmy's rescue of Howard after the escapade in the forest was the most common explanation – the kind of human interest story we devoured so avidly in the tabloid press. Except this was happening on our doorstep; involved one of our own. Bereden closed ranks, protecting my brother from the results of his stupidity; unaware of how far Veronica, as she then was, had duped her way into my confidence, wheedled enough information from me to fill a dozen or so articles, then summoned up the cavalry and all that followed: Jimmy' in disgrace, his sudden departure, Third Class Cottage trashed, the forest placed out of bounds. For all of which I felt personally culpable.

'Never really forgiven yourself, have you?' Geraldine seemed to have read my thoughts. 'Nor me, either. Took an age to put it all behind me and, if you take my advice, that's what you'll do. Move on, I mean.'

'Just as he did.' Mildred would have none of it. 'First as Derek, then Jimmy. Made quite a habit of it in fact, and for all we know, there's a third version lurking out there somewhere. A fourth or fifth even, doomed like the Wandering Jew or the Flying Dutchman to roam the world forever. If you ask me, Frank Murgatroyd came nearest the truth. Said the man didn't really know who he was, and I reckon he got it about right!'

'Unpopular by all accounts. Third Class Cottage trashed. Attacked by villagers with flaming torches?' Geraldine stepped in quickly to preserve the peace.

'Hardly. And, in any case, that was after he'd gone.' Her version, unpalatable though it was, had begun to make sense; interlocking with the facts as I knew them, like the jigsaw puzzles we'd pieced together under Miss Quintock's watchful eye. There were gaps, just as there always had been, some of the pieces lost forever, those that remained belonging to another set, but an overall picture was emerging and Jimmy was not coming too well out of it.

'His home,' she repeated. 'Destroyed, and after he left?'

'That's right. Vandals must have got in. They had a wonderful time, turning everything upside down, smashing the furniture – what there was of it – even up-ended floorboards. No doubt looking for what loot they could find, but a complete waste of time. Anyone could have told them Jimmy earned very little and that was spent almost immediately. The books had been removed, apart from which there was very little of value to be had.'

The wildest notion crossed my mind: Geraldine returning to wreak vengeance on Jimmy's home, or sending Mildred to do so.

'And they were never caught?' Further glances between the two of them.

'No. PC Granger made some enquiries, but they never amounted to much. And he had more serious crimes on his hands.'

'What about the Squire? Didn't you say he once worked for Intelligence? Helped Jimmy find a new identity?'

'Well, yes, but that was during the war and another branch entirely. He might have been able to pull a few strings for Jimmy when he first he arrived – ration book, identity card, etc. – but this was several years later. Nor was he minded to help Jimmy last time they met.'

'And the press, when they arrived, made straight for the bell tower?' It was to Mildred rather than myself that the question had been directed.

'And then to the forest,' her companion replied.

'Squire on the spot in an instant,' the litany continued.

'One phone call from him sends them packing…'

'… the local police not unduly perturbed; not a word of it appearing in the press…'

'… Jimmy suddenly out of favour. Disappears…'

'… and his cottage is trashed.'

'Well, there you have it.' Geraldine sat back contentedly.

'Just as we suspected.' Mildred nodded her agreement.

'You knew all this already?' It might be their usual mode of discourse, but my patience was giving way. 'Having gone back to Bereden again to find Jimmy, or Derek as you call him. Discovered all this for yourselves and not said a word about it?'

'Oh no, dear. It was guesswork on our part. Conjecture only once you told us about the press visit. But yes, we did go back again.'

'But not looking for Jimmy,' added Mildred. 'He'd made good his escape by then.'

'And do you intend to tell us about this second visit, or just keep us guessing?' By now even Helen was becoming tetchy.

'Sorry, my dear.' Geraldine patted her knee reassuringly. 'We've only just appreciated the significance of what Peter's told us. Meeting you both the way we did yesterday, the realisation that I'd known him all those years ago put everything else out of my mind. It was Mildred saw it first; grasped how the different strands fell into place, understands now how guilty Peter must have felt over the years.' She paused, glanced at her companion, saw that contrition was the last thing on Mildred's mind, and hurried on. 'But I'm the one to blame. Unintentionally; I'd never have teased you that way had I known. And I'm afraid you're not going to be any more pleased with me when you've heard the rest of it. Derek might not have come up to the expectations I had of him, Peter, but then neither was Jimmy quite the person you took him to be.'

Chapter Twenty

Small Talk Among the Roses

Neither Peter nor I knew what further surprises Geraldine had in mind. Whatever they were, she was determined to keep us waiting till after lunch. And no discussing the matter over the ham and egg salad; not till she'd had her afternoon nap. In the meantime, Mildred could show us round the garden.

She seemed to share my opinion of Jimmy, did Mildred, but kept it very much to herself. Aggrieved, maybe, at being excluded from Geraldine's matrimonial secrets, to say nothing of the drubbing she'd received following the *Roadshow* debacle. Peter was withdrawn, wondering – so he told me later – how badly Jimmy might emerge from any further reminiscences. All attempts at small-talk were, in any case, cut short by the ringing of a hand-bell. Mildred scuttled off to see what was required of her, returning a few minutes later to say she was needed in the house. Her companion would not be ready to see us for at least forty minutes. Which must have been as much of a relief to her as it was to us.

They'd made good use of their time. When we re-entered the house the furniture had been pushed back against the wall, chairs brought to the centre of the room and arranged around a table upon which a number of documents had been laid out. The *Field of the Cloth of Gold* article caught my eye. Alongside it photographs of Geraldine in her youth, certificates, congratulatory letters, newspapers, preliminary sketches of handiwork she never got round to completing, a scrapbook bulging with press-cuttings. All tracing her career from her earliest days in journalism and forming a back-cloth to the story which she now continued.

Her break with Derek had been complete. Having discovered his deception she needed to be as far from him as possible. Immediately, before her resolve weakened. 'Escaping from myself as much as from him,' she mused. 'If only that had been possible. But, in spite of everything, I loved him still. Addicted to the man. As surely as an alcoholic to the bottle; a junky to heroin.' And the only known cure, she reminded us, was total abstinence.

This had proved difficult. A well-advertised series she'd planned on the work of this Hampshire genius was cancelled; lucrative offers to write about him turned down. All part of the withdrawal cure, but it was not long before the inevitable happened.

'Quite sudden it was,' Geraldine recalled. 'Without warning, at the end of a lecture I'd been giving. A member of the audience stayed behind, the way they often do, you know how it is, Peter. I'd not uttered a word about Derek or his paintings from beginning to end, but suddenly this woman starts asking me questions about him. How she'd taken my advice, used his technique as a starting point for her embroidery. And suddenly, before I could stop her, she'd produced a picture from a bag she'd been carrying.'

A 'Saintley', there'd been no doubt about it. Original design, complementary range of colours, perspective delicately handled; the perfect example of the style she'd championed so strenuously. How complicated would the conversion to embroidery be, the lady had asked. How long would it take? What of the cost? The advice she gave was to prove a turning point for both of them.

The embroiderer carried off top prize in a regional competition, went on to achieve national fame and, having no further use for the picture, donated it to Geraldine. And there it was, a rococo blending of text and image; Jimmy's version of Tennyson's *Lotos-Eaters* brought down from the wall where we'd first seen it, handed over to Peter.

The gift had redetermined the course of Veronica's life. If she could not have the man who deserted her, she'd make do with his pictures. *Lotos-Eaters* was the first in her collection. The next – *A Stitch in Time* – was knocked down to £15 among miscellaneous items at an auction. *Birds of Pray* – still hanging on the wall opposite – she'd acquired through business contacts. From that point she'd begun her collection in earnest, searching high and low for the works of this obscure Hampshire backwoodsman. Word of her obsession percolated among the artistic community. A biography, they supposed – that or a retrospective exhibition. Not much of the oeuvre survived; what did was retrieved from outhouses or cowsheds, hauled down from dusty attics to be sold at exorbitant prices – or faked.

'Thinking they'd taken her in.' Mildred relieved Peter of the painting. 'But she was much too sharp for that. Pity she couldn't recognise the man himself as a phoney.'

The early sixties that had been. Before long, she'd acquired fifteen genuine Saintleys, become an authority in the field. 'Hardly a field.' Geraldine pushed *Lotos Eaters* to one side. 'More of a lawn. A small and largely untended one at that.'

Which must have been the reason one of the dailies had asked her to contribute an outline of his work for their forthcoming supplement on British art. 'Not a matter of expertise.' She shook her head dismissively. 'Just the fact that no one else was capable of doing it.'

The realisation of what was coming crystallised slowly. Neither of us knew the precise point it became a certainty, but there it was in the scrapbook: the article on Saintley's art from *The Encyclopaedic History of British Art* we'd read a few days earlier, fixed at the four corners with stamp-hinges. Concluding with the initials GL: Geraldine Leapman. Neither of us said a word. Partly surprise, partly thinking through the implications. But mostly because we were anxious to hear the rest of her story.

It was in building up the collection that word of *Mappa Mundi* first reached her. The last of the 'Saintleys', it was said. His final protest; content and style unknown but believed to be the most irreverent of them all. Nothing more than hearsay really, but consistent enough for it to become her Holy Grail, and Bereden its most likely hiding place. Return she must, but how? Peter and her husband – the man he called Jimmy – might still be around, to say nothing of the countless people she'd contacted on her first visit, and there must be no hint of her marriage – for Derek's sake as much as her own. Not even her newly-appointed secretary, later companion, Mildred, might be told. Her resolve wavered. Till finally, some fifteen years after the chance encounter with teenage Peter and her erstwhile husband, much firmer evidence arrived.

'Makes perfect sense now we've heard both sides of the story.' Mildred could contain herself no longer. 'Little wonder Derek, Jimmy, Saintley or whatever he chose to call himself, left in such a hurry. Same reason nothing about him appeared in the press. The perfect cover-up, till someone let the cat out of the bag all those years later. I wonder...'

'Why don't you just let them read it for themselves?' Geraldine hauled herself up. 'Half hour's pruning will do me a power of good.' She pushed the final piece of evidence across the table and hobbled off on her stick.

It was a whole page feature in what had been *The South Hampshire Observer,* dated 11th March, 1971, that Mildred passed across to us:

Now it can be told: Bereden's 'Secret Army'

'What did you do in the War, Daddy?' – ask this question around Bereden and the answer could surprise you. If the truth is told, that is. Some will tell you of military service, in the army, navy or air force. Show you their medals or demob papers. Others recall duty as special constables or air-raid wardens. Or how they were excused service on medical grounds. A few, though, will give you no answer. You may dismiss their war effort as negligible; believe them to have been malingerers even.

Be careful before you make such accusations, though. And read the recently published story of the part played by 'Churchill's underground army', recruited to harry the enemy at a time when invasion seemed imminent. Think before you pass judgement. You could very well be speaking to an unsung hero of World War II.

One of the best kept secrets of that life-and-death struggle, when this Island – and with it Europe – stood on the verge of defeat, was the existence of the Auxiliary Units. Never heard of them? Nor were you meant to. These men and women, recruited for their bravery, knowledge of the countryside – and the ability to keep their mouths shut – were trained in the arts of guerrilla warfare: to kill without question; wound without compunction; destroy road or rail networks rather than see them fall into enemy hands. As they would have done. Before disappearing into the hinterland. Had the invasion come.

Only in the last few years has their cover been blown. By an American, David Lampe, in a book Last Ditch. This some thirty years after the last of them had been stood down. And, all over the south of England, the question is being asked: 'Did we play our part in such operations?' 'Was there an "underground army" hidden in our neck of the woods?'*

Take Bereden, for example. Is it possible that whilst most of us went about our daily activities, a unit such as this was plotting the disruption and downfall of an invading force? Meeting in secret, at some out-of-the-way farm shed, disused cottage, church belfry even? Under the leadership of a respected figure; someone accustomed to command, with experience in the armed forces. With previous knowledge of espionage, maybe? And, given the nature of the terrain, might it not have been possible for an operation base to be established, far from prying eyes, out there in the woodlands? Carefully hidden, with a secret entry – at the base of an oak-tree, say? In which weapons could be stored; from which they could launch attacks should the homeland be occupied? Observation posts also. The battlements of a castle, a high tree, or some obsolete signal tower. Anywhere that overlooked the surrounding countryside.

All speculation, of course. In other parts of the south, maybe, but here in peaceful Bereden? Surely not! Elsewhere, David Lampe now tells us, such men and women – postmen, gamekeepers, poachers even – each of them knowing the countryside like the back of their hand, were trained in the arts of guerrilla warfare. At the 'sharp end' were those expected to inflict direct damage on the enemy, through sabotage or disposing of them as surely and silently as possible. The tools of their trade were plastic explosives, incendiary bombs, pistols and sten guns fitted with silencers and commando knives honed to perfection. Many of them took to creating their own weaponry, 'swords from ploughshares' one might almost say.

Targets for such sorties were selected by a second group, the 'special duty section', who'd probably lived in the area all their lives, coming to know the people who lived there and those among them they could trust. Having 'run with the hare' each day, they 'hunt with the hounds' by night. Others – woodsmen, gamekeepers or tramps – eking out an existence in third-class accommodation yet steeped in country lore, could well have used their skills at tracking of wild animals to hunt down the enemy, knowing precisely where explosives might be set to cause the maximum of damage.

Communication between each of these groups or to the War Office in London was essential. A number of dead letter drops would be set up around the locality, younger men acting as runners between them and a radio transmitter operated by trained signals staff or a competent local 'ham', the aerial hidden high up in the trees or concealed within the chimney of some large building. Disinformation was just as important. Putting the enemy off the scent and encouraging him to concentrate his efforts where they would prove least effective.

The local citizenry needed to be put off the scent also. It could have proved disastrous had some local busy-bodies found one of the letter drops, stumbled on one of the observation posts, or children out playing discovered the base itself. Secrecy and camouflage were part of the answer, that and stories spun to keep the young and the faint-hearted at a distance.

Yet all this going on beneath their noses. Churchill's 'underground army' waiting in readiness. Across the whole of the south, their world map constricted to that of these islands. Waiting for the invasion that never came. And not a word spoken of it. Till now. What part, one wonders, did Bereden play? Perhaps we shall never know. Unless someone steps forward – as David Lampe has done – to paint a broader picture, chart more detailed a map..

**See, David Lampe, Last Ditch, Cassell, 1968, ISBN: 0304925195*

I finished the article several minutes before Peter; watched as his curiosity gave way to amazement, then incredulity. 'Who wrote this stuff?' He pushed it angrily aside.

'Someone with a good deal of inside information, I'd say.' Geraldine had returned and taken her place beside me on the couch.

'But it's all nonsense! Don't you think that if there'd been some secret outfit masquerading about the village I'd have known about it? Unless it was the gang Andrew and I set up! Or the home guard maybe?'

'Hardly likely. No disrespect, but this wasn't your fireside run-of-the-mill operation. These boys meant business. Fully trained in the techniques of underground warfare, having the weaponry to go with it; they'd have made life very unpleasant for the Germans had there really been an invasion.'

'More like the script for some Errol Flynn movie, if you ask me.' Peter had taken back the article, was stabbing at the offending passages as if to obliterate them. 'Shadowy figures flitting round the countryside with sten guns and semtex? Their faces blackened? Tracking one another through the forest? Sending secret messages? Just the kind of thing we acted out as kids. About as credible as well. Circumstantial evidence. Not a fact from beginning to end. If he's so sure of himself why doesn't he name names, tell us who these people were?'

'Why bother when it's all there in front of you?' Geraldine was not to be intimidated. 'Their leader a respected figure who'd served in the army, experienced in espionage. His headquarters crenulated, so probably a titled gentleman. I wonder who that could have been? Communicating with London via "observation posts", signal towers out there in the forest perhaps, four minutes from Portsmouth to the capital I think you told us. Aided and abetted by someone living in "third class accommodation", "steeped in country law"...

... 'whose job was "disinformation", keeping the "young or faint-hearted at a distance" with stories of cockatrices and grampuses, spectres roaming underground passages.' Mildred was determined not to be excluded from Peter's discomfiture. 'Circumstantial evidence? When the truth was out there for the asking?'

'So you *did* go back!' It must have been triumphalism in her voice; Peter was onto it in a trice.

Geraldine sighed expansively. 'Yes, we went back to the village. As I was about to tell you. And, if you don't mind, I'd like to do it in my own way.' To my relief, Peter eased himself back into his chair, arms folded, prepared – I could tell – to believe none of it.

'All of you obsessed with the organisational details, where it happened, who ran what, from whom they took their orders. Missing the most important part of the whole piece. Or giving up before you reached it. Here, see for yourself. The final paragraph: "Their world map constricted to that of these islands".' She'd dumped the scrapbook in Peter's lap. 'World map – *Mappa Mundi.* And there again, right at the bottom, almost the last words in the piece: someone coming forward to paint "a broader picture, chart more detailed a map". All those years building up the collection. On the track of that one picture. No notion as to what it was, where it might be. Then the first and only lead to come my way. You bet we went back to the village.'

Clutching at straws, I'd have said, and I could tell Peter agreed. But back to Bereden she'd gone using a false name and booking into a hotel some five miles away. Whilst Mildred, aware only of her professional interest in Derek – 'Jimmy' muttered Peter – was dispatched into the village to seek out anyone who might have known him and ferret any information she could from them.

He was long gone by then, but the rest of the village was seething. All of them had read the article, but no one would admit to having anything to do with it, pointing the finger, rather, at the figure of the 'woodsman' who'd featured so prominently in the text. A member of the unit 'steeped in country lore', knowing the area like 'the back of his hand', and that reference to "third class accommodation" – their scepticism about the secret army evaporating as they warmed to the theme. He it was who must have written the article, supplied the information at least; the man had a track-record after all. They, too, remembered the sudden incursion of all those reporters back in the fifties, but already part of local folk history. How Sir Desmond – the 'respected figure', 'accustomed to command', 'experienced in the armed forces', with 'previous knowledge of espionage' – obviously leader of the group, had been so concerned. Understandable now the way he'd by-passed PC Granger, summoned up the flying squad in their black cars with swept-back mudguards, expelling them from the village – just as Peter had told it. An explanation also for why Jimmy had fallen so unexpectedly out of favour, his hurried exit. His cottage had been identified as well. Used as storage by then but, prompted by Mildred, vague memories of a break-in emerged. Shortly after Jimmy's departure the place had been trashed, but – again – no mention of this in the press. Nothing either of *Mappa Mundi,* or any other painting come to that.

Geraldine had gone to Bereden hoping to find the solution to one problem, but she'd uncovered something far more disturbing. Previously I'd suspected Jimmy of crude indoctrination, perpetrated for his own selfish ends, but darker undertones were emerging. The auxiliary units, of which he'd been a member, had remained the closest of secrets till 1968, when the story was leaked. They'd been operational in the early forties, at a time of war. If what the article was hinting at was correct, then he had not only betrayed the trust of those around him; Jimmy was a traitor to his country, too.

Peter refused to take the suggestion seriously. Mildred rounded on him. 'Make what you like of it,' she growled. 'It certainly ties up all the loose ends.'

Chapter Twenty-One

His Last Duchess

'So many loose ends: Jimmy's falling out with the Squire, his unpopularity in the village.' Mildred counted out the incidents on her fingers. 'The sudden departure, following that visitation from the press.' Peter might have been some child learning his catechism. 'Reporters scrambling over themselves to reach all the places mentioned in the article, photographers to take their pictures. Yet one brief telephone call from Sir Desmond sends them packing, and not a word heard about it for the next fifteen years. Not till that American spilt the beans on the auxiliary units. "Churchill's underground army", isn't that what he called them? With the *South Hants Observer* filling in the local details, in their *Now It Can Be Told* article. No doubt among the villagers as to who leaked the information either. Someone who'd been a member of the group himself; living in "third-class accommodation", "steeped in county lore". A tracker, able to "hunt down the enemy" – just as he did that time Howard needed to be rescued.'

She might have gone further. Campanologists meeting regularly, yet not a bell rung till the war was over. Chosen for their knowledge of the countryside, rather; one of them who'd "run with the hare, hunted with the hounds".

'And it wasn't only him that disappeared, was it?' Geraldine took up the story. 'What about that last picture of his: *Mappa Mundi*? The reason we were there in the first place.'

'Whatever's that got to do with it?' Up to this point Peter had remained silent, mesmerised so it seemed, by Mildred's accusations.

'Everything, if you ask me. All of us know how he liked to play games in his paintings. Using *Birds of Pray* to get back at the nuns, popping the bishop into *Fiddlers Three*, even parodying himself in *Home Thoughts*.' Mildred recommenced her finger-ticking litany. 'Caught the habit from that American tutor, most like. *Adoration in the Forest* was it? *The Night Watch?* So isn't it possible that he might have used the Squire's wartime activities in the same sort of way? Painted out on canvas what had been hinted at in the *Now It Can Be Told* article? That this was the final straw; first all that trouble over the Jutish stories, then giving away wartime secrets? No wonder the Squire decided that enough was enough. Sent him packing. After which the picture had to be destroyed.'

Accounting for the trashing of Third Class Cottage. The hallmarks of the search procedures we were then beginning to read about in the papers. MI5 turning the place over in their search for the picture, then wrecking the cottage to make it appear there'd been a run-of-the-mill burglary? All fitting together to form an alternative scenario.

Incontrovertible, as far as Mildred was concerned: 'Not that you'd have known much about it, occupied as you were with your grown-up friends.'

'Just because I saw less of him after I changed schools doesn't mean we weren't close.' Peter had not hit it off with her, that much was obvious. First the notion of cockatrices, grampuses and the like, dreamt up merely to keep his gang clear of the woods. Now the suggestion that he'd deserted his hero at his hour of need. 'He'd begun treating me as an adult by then, showed me all of his later works. If there'd been a *Mappa Mundi* I'd have known about it. As for his last painting: nothing but a daub.'

Mildred pounced: 'Meaning that you actually saw the picture?'

'And you've not thought to mention it till now?' Geraldine's stick clattered to the floor.

'It was nothing, I promise you.' Peter shrugged his dismissal. 'Something he'd given up on, had difficulty with, or hadn't the heart to finish. Probably left behind when the cottage was trashed.'

* * *

There was no great mystery, regardless of what Helen or the other two wanted to make of it. There'd been no mention of *Mappa Mundi* till the day before, by which time revelations of my teenage indiscretions had driven all other matters clear from my mind. One brief glimpse of the picture – if you could call it a picture – was all I'd had, following hard on the heels of the Grigorio incident. Little wonder it had slipped my memory. Till Mildred's mention of Jimmy's skills as a tracker brought it flooding back.

The blame had fallen squarely on his shoulders. Howard's escapade in the woods, the way Jimmy handled the situation, both of them ignored. Thanks largely to Codpiece's sermon, BadEgg's diatribes. All our parents remembered was the outlandish nature of the tales he told and the affect they'd had on Howard – sensitive lad as he was. My brother milked the situation for all it was worth, but those who sneaked a visit to Third Class Cottage in the days that followed found the door locked, the curtains drawn, garden unattended. There was no reply, no matter how hard or how long they knocked or rattled the handle; no response to their tapping at the window. Yet smoke could be seen rising from the chimney, refuse was put out regularly and, if they stood still and listened, someone could be heard moving about inside. Jimmy was in there right enough, sulking like a five-year-old and determined to take no further part in village life. And, as the weeks passed, it seemed that this was no idle threat. His door remained shut to all comers; the patch of worn grass beside the war memorial remained unoccupied. Milk and groceries were delivered, payment in tattered envelopes pushed through the letterbox. We had fleeting glimpses of him disappearing into the woods; besides which, nothing.

All my doing, I was certain of it. Veronica, ace reporter, determined to discover all she could about him, closing in on a scoop, her sudden disappearance coinciding with the arrival, mob-handed, of the press – there had to be a connection. Worse still, Jimmy must have realised that one of 'his own' had betrayed him, hence the self-imposed incarceration. The more I thought about it, the more convinced I became – and the more I knew what was required of me.

My parents were told I was going camping. Nothing unusual about this; I'd spent several weekends under canvas, they themselves having given me a tent on my recent birthday. The weather was fine and they didn't worry as long as they knew where I was and when I would return. This, however, was to be the only occasion on which I deceived them. My destination was not Scapegoat Heathland, as I'd said, but Third Class Cottage. No doubt they would get to know this sooner or later, but there was always the excuse that I'd sprained my ankle or the weather had turned bad. Besides which, the lie was a white one, and well worth the telling.

On arrival I banged on Jimmy's door, shouted through the letterbox that I knew he was there and had no intention of leaving until he let me in. There was a shuffling inside, but no response. I had his attention at least. So, if I wasn't to be admitted, he'd better come out to me. I was camping in the front garden, brewing up; tea made the old way, ready in half an hour, and willing to share it – provided he brought his own condensed milk and newspaper. There were provisions enough and I intended to stay for as long as it took. Still no reply. I think I caught a glimpse of him at the window as I pitched the tent, set up the primus stove, boiled the saucepan and performed the tea-bomb ritual in time-honoured fashion. The results, which I'd recalled as ambrosial, were revolting. Nevertheless, I marched up the pathway and banged on the door once more. Again, no response. Not at first, but then I heard movement, a key was turned in the lock, a bolt shot back, and Jimmy's head appeared.

'Come in and bring the water with you. I've got all the rest of the ingredients ready.'

I fetched another cup from the tent and followed him into the cottage, not knowing what I would find, but expecting to be greeted with harsh words and accusations. His attitude, though, differed little from normal, but it was obvious that things were far from well. I don't think he'd slept for several nights, nor changed his clothes in days. His beard, usually short and well trimmed, was ragged, as was his hair. Streaks of stubble ran down either side of his face, there was bruised colouration to the skin; his eyes, permanently deep-set, appeared now to have been gouged still further into their sockets.

'Quite like old times. Here's to absent friends.' The cup quivered in his hand. 'Friendly absents more like. Well, I'm glad you especially could make it, knowing the whole story the way that you do.'

He knew of my disloyalty, then. The excuses I'd been rehearsing all these weeks came out in a garbled rush: 'I meant no harm, Jimmy, honestly. It was all a trick. Her ruse to get a good story for the newspaper. They warned me about it but I wouldn't listen. All that's happened – the reporters, photographers, prying into your business, tramping all over your garden – it's my fault, I know that now.'

His reaction was the opposite of the one I'd expected. 'Conned by the power of the press, were you?' Tipping back in the chair, laughing, the whole of his demeanour transformed. 'It's their job, lad, what they're trained to do. Given half a chance and they're over you like fleas. Blood-suckers the lot of them. Shame you found out the hard way, it happens to the best of us.' Seeing my surprise, he leaned forward and patted my shoulder. 'A lesson well learnt if you ask me. And just you remember it.'

So Jimmy knew I'd spoken to the press, but only *after* they arrived in the village. A reprieve; the smallest, most acceptable, of betrayals. 'Howard should have come to thank you,' I said, eager to move the conversation forward. 'After all you did for him. As should the rest of them.'

'He's young, knows no better. And I suppose I'm just as much to blame.' Jimmy swirled the dregs of the tea around the cup, found it had gone cold and pushed it aside. 'As to the others, wouldn't have expected any more of them, really.' He got up, adjusted the gaslight and took my cup through to the kitchen, refusing my offer of help with the washing up. The furniture, I now realised, had been drawn back, making space for an easel which had been set up at the other end of the room; beneath it a sheet, daubed with paint that had splashed down from the canvas above. A *Shakesphere* from the look of it, or what had started that way, sketched out on the rectangular canvas. There was the space reserved for the text at the centre, the bare outline of figures clustering round it on all sides. An old man, some courtiers maybe, a dog – rabbit perhaps – a jester, or was it Punch, or Harlequin? Clouds, young people joking, plotting, gambling. *King Lear*? *Othello*? *Twelfth Night*? It might have been any one of them, but for the two ragged brushstrokes, virulent green, that ran corner to corner across the canvas, obliterating most of what lay beneath.

'*My Last Duchess*,' Jimmy called through from the kitchen. 'Outstayed our welcome, the both us.' I heard him moving hurriedly about, shifting furniture so it seemed, whilst the radio, muffled yet audible, announced the weather forecast. 'Time I was moving on, anyway.'

It was the obvious ploy: to make himself scarce for a week or two. 'Just let us know where to find you,' I said, searching for the elusive Duchess amid the welter of green paint, 'and we'll let you know when it's safe to return.'

''Fraid it's going to be rather longer than that.' He'd rejoined me, wiping his hands on an ink-splashed tea towel.

'You don't mean you're leaving us?'

'Seems like it.'

"What, forever?'

Jimmy stood contemplating the picture for a moment. In the background the weather forecast had given way to a news bulletin. He threw the towel aside. 'Come and see.'

As I followed him the reason for so much frenetic activity became apparent. He'd been emptying the drawers and bookcases, piling most of the contents in heaps on the floor, placing a few items of clothing into a battered suitcase, stacking what crockery he had onto the draining board, the chairs up onto the table. Without a word to any of us, or the hint of an explanation, he'd been preparing to leave – and leave in a hurry.

'No need to worry. I've a talisman as looks after me.' He held the medallion he wore around his neck up to the light. '*Constant Companion*.' It pirouetted in the gas-flame. 'Where I go she goes. We've seen a good few adventures together, the two of us. And no doubt there's more to come.'

Which was all I got out of him. Within the week, both he and the picture were gone. I never set eyes on either of them again. Never having fully confessed the part I'd played, or thought that I'd played, in his departure.

* * *

'...Outstayed his welcome.' Mildred picked up on Peter's words immediately. 'Seems fairly obvious to me. It was the auxiliary units rather than the *Shakesphere* prints or his rescue of Howard that attracted the press; Jimmy himself who tipped them off. Destroyed the picture he was working on – the *Duchess* was it? In a fit of pique.'

'Browning actually,' I told them. '*His Last Duchess.* An apologia from the Duke of Ferrara on his ex-wife's fall from grace. Wanting to keep her all to himself.'

'And another example of his following in his master's footsteps.' Mildred was onto it almost before I'd finished. 'First, the penchant for messages hidden in pictures, now aping that American's love of Browning. Or is that just another in the long line of coincidences as far as that man – Derek, Jimmy, Saintley, or whatever he chose to call himself – is concerned? How many more of them must there be before you start taking him and what he was up to seriously?'

Peter was cornered and outnumbered. 'If we didn't take him seriously why do you think we're here?'

Which was where we left it. There was little more to be said. Apart from Peter's: 'Soroyan, I swear I've heard that name somewhere. Just can't place it. Infuriating.'

And Geraldine, taking me on one side before we departed: 'You will follow this through, my dear, won't you? Everyone Mildred spoke to was convinced *Mappa Mundi* existed. I know she's got it into her head it's been destroyed, but somehow I can't believe it. Peter's made his mind up, I know, but there might be something he missed; some detail that meant nothing to him at the time? Or, how can I put it...'

'He's gone out of his way to forget?'

'For the kindest of reasons. It's good that he respects your beliefs. Count yourself lucky if it's all he's hidden from you. Something you must have realised over the last few days.' She took both my hands in hers. 'Believe me, Helen, I'm not asking you to be disloyal, but there must have been more to it than that. The whole truth may never be known, it's been thirty years after all, but if any trace still exists or there's anyone else who actually saw it – and remembers – then you're heading in the right direction.'

Even then, not yet married to the man, I knew Peter better than she did. He'd dismissed her story, to begin with at least; taken it as deluded, the ramblings of an old lady, with Mildred's hostility doing nothing to convince him otherwise. Now, though, he'd begun to reconsider. As Geraldine had said, the chances of corroborating her suspicions were slim, but at least they provided a framework for the next stage in our investigations. And, should any such evidence remain, it was at Bereden it was most likely to be found.

Part Three

Mappa Mundi

Chapter Twenty-Two

A Stranger in my Own Land

'*Trapped in a pincer movement between Portsmouth and Southampton, progressively criss-crossed by commuter traffic and diesel highways, its chalkface the bedrock of some future Solent City.*' Helen was reading from a guidebook she'd purloined from the library.

'Trapped' explained exactly how I felt. I'd roamed this countryside every day of my childhood; cycled to villages that could not be reached on foot; thought I was intimate with every inch of it. But now I was lost. Scapegoat Heathland swallowed up by bungaloid detritus, Harry buried together with his tollgate beneath a five-way roundabout. Gone, the easy-going signposts of my youth –single uprights, their wooden arms pointing finger-shaped: Bishops Waltham four miles, Swanmore five; Wickham merely two miles to the west, but no hint that it was uphill all the way, with a further five miles' hard cycling back to Bereden. Vanished, the lot of them, once the fear of invasion took hold, to be replaced by peacetime's metal monstrosities. Occasionally there was a pub sign I recognised; a church tower that seemed familiar; the brick wall along which the Americans – 'Got any gum, chum?' – had camped prior to D-Day. The landmarks had been uprooted, the boundaries forgotten, just as Jimmy had predicted. I found myself a stranger in my own land.

Bereden remained bordered by woodlands to the north, even less a 'forest' than I remembered, fenced off from the roadside with official-looking notices declaring it remained part of the Amberstone Estate, and that *trespassers would be prosecuted.* The Square remained much as it had always been, smaller than I remembered, more contained, buildings and shops far more of an entity. A few of the houses, Georgian mostly, remained intact, but Carter's Fish-Fry Delight had become a travel agency, the newsagent's was now an up-market wine bar, and a bus shelter now stood where the greengrocer had set out his goods. Later we wandered past St Matthias, stopping to place a posy of cornflowers – always her favourite – on Enid Quintock's grave, and searched among the ivy for the spot where Tobias still guarded the east transept. Over the bridge, past Cowpat Meadow, we paid respect to the house where I'd been born, a further ten-minute walk taking us past the Amberstone Estate *No Entry* notices, to trace, beyond the high wire fencing, what remained of Third Class Cottage.

'Another country,' Helen consoled me. 'They do things differently there.'

'Clever,' I said.

'L. P. Hartley,' she replied. '*The Go-Between*.'

We had no such problems in locating Amberstone Hall, a matter only of following signs pointing us in the direction of Bereden Conference Centre and Residential Retreat (BERCEN). Mounting debts and school fees had obliged Giles – 'Gerundive' as we'd once called him – to sell the property, together with most of the estate, reserving a small but comfortable apartment for the family use. Now a member of the board of management, he'd arranged for us to have one of the dozen or so rooms reserved for visiting tutors. The director, hovering in the foyer, was expecting us. Giles had been called away on business and sent his apologies for not being there in person. His wife was visiting their daughter –currently completing her education in Switzerland – but hoped we'd join him for dinner at the Amberstone Arms that evening.

The Jugged Hare as it had been in my day. Giles was full of apologies. The change of nomenclature had been the brewery's brainwave, wanting to 'add a little class' to the establishment, nor was there much he could have done to stop them, the Squirarchy having more or less died out with his father. He seemed to have lost none of his personal influence though, being treated with the greatest deference by the waiters as we entered, and pausing to shake hands with several of the guests as we made our way to the private dining room.

The loss of the estate had proved less calamitous than it might have been. Some years back he'd established a consultancy advising those faced with a predicament similar to his own; Giles, with his soft-spoken manner and the pale blue Amberstone eyes, having no difficulty in winning their confidence. He'd always been tall, currently around the six-foot mark by my estimation, with square shoulders and cleft chin – even more pronounced now than when we'd teased him about it as children – lending him a rugged charm. He'd made quite a name for himself on the rugby field as well, hence the scar now visible beneath the receding hairline and the loss of an ear lobe. But this, again, was a matter of history; currently he coached a team made up of youngsters from the surrounding villages.

It was not until coffee had been served and we'd settled into easy chairs at the bay window overlooking the square that childhood days were mentioned. We were unsure how much Giles knew about his father's wartime activity, nor was I certain there was much to be told. We'd selected our drinks from decanters set out on a silver tray and Giles was bringing us up-to-date on how the old gang had fared.

'Andrew became a teacher, head of a school in the Midlands

last I heard. Must have retired by now. Charlie Dowse – nose always in a comic – went into journalism, wrote for the tabloids. No messing with Chunky, into the army the moment he left school, demobbed as a sergeant, but our paths never crossed. And Tim's no longer with us you may have heard. Died a few years back, behind the counter of his tobacconist shop.'

'And Jimmy?' I asked, seizing the moment. 'He never returned? No clue as to what happened to him?'

'Not even in the runes.' Giles laughed. 'Remember his teaching us the script? How to sign our names, with your lot using it to send secret messages? His pictures are worth quite a bit these days, so I'm told, thanks largely to that television programme.'

The perfect cue. I was into the narrative almost before I knew it: Floral Lady and her pictures, Frank's assessment of *Fiddlers Three* – Giles, if he remembered, had had a hand in its creation. ('But only as a bystander. Nor there to see it through to the end. God, how I envied you that!'). Helen's memories of her father's print; her distrust of the artist – we'd agreed to be quite open about this; the 'coincidence' which had led to our undertaking this joint mission. ('"Quest", "mission", "venture"… you're beginning to talk like Jimmy himself.') Onto the Quintock papers, *Songs of Innocence and Experience*, then forward to our meeting with Geraldine. An aficionado dedicated to Jimmy's art and the nearest he'd come to a biographer, if GL's encyclopaedic entry counted as such – was all that we said. Next the Grigorio incident – Giles had been away at school ('Remember the old man cursing that damn-fool brother of yours') – that and the Codpiece sermon, which the Squire, apparently, had done his best to prevent ('far too sanctimonious for my father's taste').

'Yet he took the church's side when it came to those stories about the Jutes, along with all the others, just when Jimmy needed him most.'

Giles shook his head. 'Never quite understood just how that

happened. 'Nor, for that matter, how the two of them came to be so close.'

'Nothing to do with campanology, then?' I eased gently into the real purpose of our visit. 'Those wartime meetings in the church tower when no bells were to be rung, discussing signal towers or arms dumps?'

'Observation posts and dead letter drops, runners and plastic explosives? Don't look so surprised, Peter, you're not the only one to read the *South Hants Observer.* No point denying it, either. Not after all these years.'

The very last response I'd expected. After the hours I'd spent rehearsing what to say, arguing over it with Helen, steeling myself for all eventualities: denial, ignorance, prevarication, ejection from the house even.

'Turns out there were units run in similar lines operating all along the coast.' Giles gazed out of the window for a moment, gathering his thoughts. 'Vital at the time but forgotten about once peace had arrived. Rather like those unexploded bombs that keep turning up. Normally it's fine; they're defused or there's a controlled explosion, till someone steps on them or starts monkeying around with their innards, and people get hurt. That article's a case in point. Jimmy and my father clearly identifiable, reminding folk of the great press invasion back in the fifties. Making a bee-line for all the places associated with the unit, followed by the falling-out between the two of them and Jimmy's sudden departure. What more proof of his perfidy was needed? Which was when the old man came clean – he had no option once *The Observer* got hold of the story – and told me what had really been going on under our noses out there in the woods. As far as he felt able, that is.'

'With Jimmy leaving of his own free will? Not one of those unexploded bombs that needed defusing before it did any further damage? Your father suspecting him of God knows what and sending him packing?'

'Not a bit of it. Others might have had their suspicions but the old man gave him the benefit of the doubt. An unguarded comment, he reckoned. Sounding off about those *Shakesphere* prints most like. Bringing the press swarming like bees round a honey-pot.'

Jimmy guilty of loose talk? Collaborating with the media? Unbelievable, unless he really *was* guilty as charged. Or had Geraldine played an even more active part in his downfall than I'd imagined? Arriving in the village on the track of Saintleys but finding the husband who'd deserted her; knowing how much he detested publicity and unleashing the press upon him. Unaware that he'd been recruited into a secret army, how serious the repercussions would be. Not at the time, but later maybe, in advance of her second visit. Well known as a writer by then, so she might well have picked up the story on the grapevine - would have had no problem in planting it. Might well have written the article herself. An even more protracted form of revenge. This time calculated. And taken cold.

But could there be a yet more devious twist to the plot?

'Jimmy wasn't the only one to go missing,' I said. 'His last picture disappeared almost as soon as it was painted. Some say he destroyed it.' More false information from Geraldine, of course, along with her allegations that it contained further incriminating evidence, branding Jimmy even more of a traitor. With her being the only one with any real information concerning that painting - if it ever existed.

But it had.

'*Mappa Mundi* you mean?' Giles, again one step ahead of us. 'The picture that upset the rector so much? Would have had it publically burnt, given half a chance. Might well have got his way, too, if the old man hadn't acted quickly; devised a less conspicuous way of disposal.'

There came a discreet tap at the door: the proprietor, advising us the restaurant was closing in half an hour's time and asking if there was anything else we required.

'Not like the old days, I'm afraid. It's no longer the Jugged Hare, Alf Thomas is no longer the landlord.' Giles returned to his seat, poured us liberal portions of brandy, selected a cigar from the tray, noted my expression and returned it. 'And the Lone Granger's successor somewhat more zealous about closing time.' He nodded at the police car discreetly parked opposite.

'So there really was a *Mappa Mundi*,' I said, wrenching him back on track. 'And your father "disposed of it"?'

'Proves our point, though, doesn't it?' Helen pushed her drink to one side. 'There just *has* to be something in that picture that had to remain hidden.'

'Just as there *has to* be something the pair of you are keeping to yourselves,' Giles leant back in his chair, arms folded. 'Such as how precisely you've discovered so much about a painting known only to the rector and my father, both of them dead, with myself making a threesome?' The silence lengthened between us.

No option, then, but to reveal what we'd gleaned of Jimmy's – or should that be Derek's – pre-Bereden existence, his marriage and supposed death. An edited version, omitting my youthful dalliance with Geraldine, a recent acquaintance, we claimed, who harboured suspicions that *Mappa Mundi* had been Jimmy's way of revealing the Amberstones' wartime secrets.

'You don't really think there's any truth in her story?' I asked, attempting to sound confident. 'Did your father give you no idea as to the nature of the picture?'

'Nor why it worried him so much that he got rid of it?' Helen's belief in Geraldine remained unshaken.

'Got rid of it?' Giles was smugness personified. 'The "last of the Saintleys". He thought far too much of it for that. "Disposed of" was what I said. Took his inspiration from that break-in at Third Class Cottage, otherwise it might really have been a goner.

Put it around that *Mappa Mundi* had been moved there whilst the gallery was cleaned, that it got stolen along with the other nick-nacks. Not much of a cover story, I know, and don't ask me what good the picture would have been to tearaways like that. Still, it seemed to work, right through to this day, apparently.'

'Which means…'

'… that the picture still exists.' I finished Helen's sentence.

No denial from Giles; the silence that followed would have had pride of place in Jimmy's audio collection. As it lengthened I swear I actually heard the implications rippling outwards, like pebbles slipped quietly into some woodland pool.

'And no need for me to answer any more of your questions.' He swirled the last of the brandy in his glass before downing it. 'Unfair, maybe, stringing you along the way I have, but it's a game two can play and I needed to find out just how many of the family secrets you knew – or how badly you'd got them twisted – before I opened up completely. Would have saved us no end of time if you'd come clean from the start, told me about your embroiderer friend's suspicions. Never mind, now we've got all that out of the way I'll introduce you to *Mappa Mundi* and you can decide for yourselves whether she was right or wrong.'

There was a shout of 'Time, gentlemen, please' from downstairs, the saloon bar was pushed open, the sound of cars revving up.

'Which is what I suggest you do tomorrow. After breakfast shall we say? And, remembering the way the two of you bicker, we've a long day ahead of us!'

Chapter Twenty-Three

Moment of Intimacy

Nothing distinguished Giles's apartment from the rest of the building but, once inside, BERCEN's drab institutionalism gave way to clean lime-coloured walls. Darkish carpet tiles contrasted with light teak furniture of modern design. A set of neatly framed impressionist prints had been strategically placed about the room. But it was the photographs, arranged on a small table by the door, that caught my eye. Family portraits, so Peter told me. Pride of place having been given to a young man in RAF uniform, cap resting on knee, the emblem of his squadron on the desk beside him. Vernon, Giles's elder brother, son and heir to the Amberstone estate, lost in the air during the African campaign, whose memorial we'd visited the previous day. An artist, I remembered, and those must be his pictures hung about the walls. Watercolours mainly: still lives, pastoral views, rood screens, stained glass windows. An expressionist portrait of what could have only been the old Squire, and, a little to one side, *Some corner of a foreign field that is for ever England* – the first-draft of Jimmy's tribute to the fallen hero.

Peter was tugging on my arm, reminding me of the purpose of our visit: *Mappa Mundi.* And there it stood, leaning up against the back of a chair in the corner, draped in a sheet and looking for all the world like some conjuror's prop. Giles had the sense of theatre to accompany it. No sneak previews, never a hint as to what he was about to reveal. Not till he'd completed the preliminary patter.

'The old man acted with strict military precision,' he quipped. 'Phase one: outflank the clergy. Phase two: pre-emptive strike. Phase three: secure picture. Phase four: cover tracks, outwitting the local press completely. "Burglary at Third Class Cottage", according to the headlines. But all it took was some rummaging among the vaults, a little light cleaning. And, hey presto!' Giles whipped the sheet aside. Revealing…

Something of an anti-climax. The picture was blasphemous, no doubt about it. Unerring in its target, subverting the accepted version of history, calling into question everything the rector must have held dear. A persuasive piece of propaganda certainly, but not nearly as extreme as I'd expected.

The painting was a map of sorts, mounted in a thin gilt frame; the setting pre-conquest times, but most of the features recognisable from what I'd been told. There, at the centre, was the site of the future St Matthias. To one side was the crossing point on the river where the bridge now stood. Near it an age-old pathway led into the forest. There was Frogspawn Shallows where Peter and his chums once swam; tucked away in one corner, Cow Pat Meadow. It was larger than most of Jimmy's other works – those that I knew – and he'd found yet another way of combining graphics and text. Events taking place over a period of weeks were seen occurring simultaneously, on different parts of the canvas.

The villagers, so a small plaque at the bottom of the picture informed us, have gathered by the river, calling on the gods to provide them with a bountiful supply of fish. But, when their nets are pulled ashore, they've caught nothing but shells. An itinerant priest arrives. He confers with the Heavens, then stretches a net from bank to bank. Soon it is writhing with creatures of all shapes and sizes. The holy man is pleased with his quickness of wit; delighted at the outcome he leaps for joy into the river. The fish are gathered up and taken to the church where, to celebrate this miraculous conversion of the heathen, a feast day is proclaimed. The grateful villagers cut corn for the Harvest Festival. They present the best of their catch to the missionary, who is last seen cheered on his way to a well-earned fish-and-chip supper.

But *Mappa Mundi* had quite a different tale to tell. Brief notations appeared alongside each incident. Here and there a sentence had been printed beneath their feet. Thoughts or motivation floated cloud-like above their heads; speech bubbles allowed us to eavesdrop on the conversations they were having. Jimmy had, in fact, adopted techniques used in mediaeval times to provide his own commentary on the events portrayed.

The deity in question was Morgana, associated from time immemorial with that stretch of the river, where the earliest settlers had made their home. These were Jutes, of course, who'd accepted the goddess' rights over the surrounding woodlands. Thanks to her their wells had remained fresh, their crops abundant, the river well stocked. In Jimmy's *sub rosa* version the villagers are delighted, not downcast, at their catch. The surfeit of shells indicates Morgana's permission to proceed with the fishing. And it's strands of myrtle they – not the priest – cut with their sickles, weaving themselves a net, this being her emblem. It is to a site hallowed to her memory that the people take their catch, depositing it at the entrance to the sacred grove. The blunted sickles are taken in, to be placed reverently on the high altar. The priest is presented as a figure of fun throughout. Aren't those birds hovering above him as he casts his gaze skyward? Can we detect a scar on his bald head, or something more fundamental? There he is diving ecstatically into the waters. But could that be a mediaeval boot assisting his trajectory?

The villagers now take themselves off to the mid-centre of the picture, jubilant at the razor-sharpness of their previously blunted sickles. Meanwhile the priest exits top-right, not in triumph but reeking with the remnant of last week's catch ignominiously pinned to his habit. Meanwhile the river flows on into the far distance, revealing a large building in flames mid-canvas. Several of the surrounding houses are also on fire. Loot is piled into boats drawn up along the quayside. Stones are hacked from the more substantial of the properties. A column of ant-like figures carries them to the old pagan shrine where the new church is about to be consecrated. A smaller group scurries into the forest. They're led by a figure identified only by the letter 'S' on his tunic. A kite of sorts hovers above their heads.

'Nothing suspicious there,' Peter was saying. 'No booby-traps, hidden explosives, commando units massing in the woods. Anti-religious propaganda, I'll give you that. But bland, as Helen says, compared with the rest of his stuff.'

'Exactly what I thought first time I saw it.' Giles straightened the picture on its easel. 'What a chance I had. No sooner did it arrive in the house than Father whisked it away. Not that I would have known there was anything suspicious about it, the auxiliary units being a closely guarded secret until that article appeared sixteen years later. Caused a major sensation in the village: suspicions aroused, Jimmy accused of blowing their cover, outsiders wanting to know more.' Mildred one of them, I realised. 'It wasn't till then my father told me as much as he felt able, or could remember – the old boy was going the way of that schoolteacher, Enid...'

'Quintock.' Peter was quick to supply the information. His reaction to Jimmy's involvement in the unit's activities – overreaction rather – had begun to worry me. Here, at least, he was on surer ground.

'That's right. Anyway, I recalled his fondness for that picture, how he'd saved it from Codpiece's clutches, and came up with the bright idea that sight of it might restore some of his memories. He caught me at it though, hunting around for where *Mappa Mundi* was hidden. Went ballistic, threatened – him in his eighties, myself approaching thirty – to give me a good hiding. Which really set me thinking. Codpiece had left the parish by then. The new parson was much more amenable, so why was it my father kept something he admired so much stowed away in that fashion all those years? And why the apoplectics when I went searching for it? Made it my business to discover what, ferreted out the picture – not so difficult once I put my mind to it – secretly, of course. Only this time I had a good look at it.'

Theatrical as ever, he paused, holding the both of us in suspense.

'And?'

'And nothing. Believe me, I searched it top to bottom. If there'd been anything suspicious I'd have found it, especially knowing his pictures the way I do, the kind of clues to look for.'

Another anti-climax. 'And no one had got at the picture?' I asked. 'It hadn't been doctored in any way? Secret ink, a coded message in the text?'

'Hardly Jimmy's style. And no one else has laid a finger on it, known of its existence even. Here, take a look for yourself.' He produced a torch and magnifying glass from one of the drawers.

A cursory two-minute inspection was all Peter gave it. 'I knew all along we'd find nothing.' He turned away from the painting. 'But she was so certain. Had me persuaded almost. Doubting all I knew about him.' I joined him at the easel, slid my arm around his waist. I'd been there before; knew exactly how he felt.

Giles might have left it at that. He'd every intention of doing so; regretted having taken us this far into his confidence. Uncertain, he was later somewhat sheepishly to admit, as to how far I was to be trusted with the Amberstone family secrets. Quite flattering really; never in my life had I been viewed as a *femme fatale.* But it was that moment of intimacy that changed his mind; the revelation as to how much we meant to each other. Together, as he was also to confess, self-satisfaction at having turned the tables on a couple of academics. A throw-back even to the days when he'd been excluded from Peter's gang.

'Didn't give up that easily myself.' Placing a hand on each of our shoulders he shepherded us back to our seats.

'Drew a blank at first. The content's mild compared with some of Jimmy's other stuff. My father paid no attention to Codpiece's ramblings before, so why now, after the man had gone; hitting the roof, even, when I mentioned it? Making me even more determined to get at the truth, as I could after he died and I was able to take my time. Hours I must have spent searching for clues hidden in the paintwork, decoding each and every piece of text. But it wasn't till I'd given up searching it from every angle that it came to me. Obvious once you think about it. There in the title, *Mappa Mundi*.'

Giles glanced from one of us to the other; if he'd hoped for a response he was disappointed. 'No? It was a map!'

Blank looks from the both of us.

'One of Jimmy's weaknesses, remember? Think of all the trouble he got you into, Peter, "helping out" with your geography homework? So why the sudden change of heart, adopting a style he avoided like the plague unless he was drawing our attention to a specific location?'

Still no response. 'Not *what* he painted but *where* the events took place. Which is when I came at it from quite another angle, following through the story out there where it really happened. I remembered him sitting alongside the war memorial. Thought it might hide some sort of message. But it didn't. Drew a blank in the church, and nothing down by the river.' Giles had retained the torch and was using it as a spotlight. 'Nor up at the rapids where all that carnage is taking place. Otherwise he was spot-on regarding the geography of the village. Which brought me to this fellow' – the beam settled on the figure making off into the woods whilst the Mead Hall went up in flames. 'Remind you of anyone?'

It didn't.

'Hero of the *Jutish Chronicle*. His shield marked with an "S"?'

'Stoyan!' Peter's confirmation was hardly necessary; the identity was obvious once drawn to our attention. 'I know your father hated those stories, Giles, but you're not telling us that's the reason he kept the picture hidden all those years?' He'd snatched the torch and was feverously examining that part of the canvas.

'No disrespect,' I added, 'but he was getting on by then and we all know how old people sometimes blow things out of proportion.'

'Like father, like son you mean?'

We protested but it was exactly what I was beginning to think.

'A joke!' Giles held up his hands in an exaggerated fashion. 'Not that I blame you. What with all those weeks trekking back and forth armed only with a sketch I'd made of *Mappa Mundi* and an ordnance survey map, I was beginning to believe it myself. Till I lighted on – what was it they called him, Peter? – "the Jute of Jutes" and decided to follow his lead.'

'Which seems to me the best tack for all of us here on in.' He snapped off the torch and returned it to the drawer. 'From now on we do things Jimmy's way. What was it, "treasure, tale and travel"? Well, you've had the first – *Mappa Mundi* – and I've told you the "tale". Now for the "travel". Don't worry, the reconnaissance's been done. I'll be there to point you in the right direction. And there's no option really.' He held open the door and we trooped downstairs. 'Unless you see with your own eyes what I discovered you're not going to believe the half of it.'

Chapter Twenty-Four

Unpacking the Hamper

Outside the weather was fine, the going easy across fields of rough grass. Sheep chomping nonchalantly among rocky outcrops paused momentarily to gaze up at us as we passed. Giles, no more forthcoming, said little, whilst Peter had given up on his questioning, more interested in childhood reminiscences: the old mill house, a leafy clump that once had served them as a tank, and there was the sentinel pine they used to climb to watch the liners steaming in.

'First of the signposts.' Giles brought us to a halt, pointing out traces of the hoofs, antlers, rampant masculinity of a large stag, carved out centuries ago beneath the surface. Briefly he checked the makeshift map he'd prepared before hurrying us on to find the next 'clue'.

This turned out to be a stream some quarter of a mile off, neither wide nor fast-flowing but impossible to cross. 'Might never have done so,' he mused, 'till I noticed the oak tree over there and decided to investigate.' We followed him downstream to where, beneath its branches, the water broadened out, bubbled over a series of strategically placed rocks. Gingerly we made our way across, to the point on the opposite bank where a number of pathways branched off in different directions.

'Had me foxed at first,' he admitted. 'No means of telling which route to take without my map. Or a compass. Shinning up the pine would have given us a bird's eye view. That of a falcon, even. Up there, sky-high, leading the way forward. Leastways, that's how Jimmy told it. Sounds familiar?'

'Saba!' Peter was on to it. 'Belonging to Alric; the one guiding Stoyan in the *Jutish Chronicles*, on the mission to return his father's sword.'

'Which you mistook for a kite on the painting,' Giles reminded us.

'And the figure tagged with an "S",' I added.'

'The whole thing scaled right down, yards rather than miles,' he continued. 'Took me weeks to get right, but the route's straightforward enough when you know where to look. Direction north, according to the symbols on Tonbert's stone.'

And there was the first of several white markers he'd used to show the way once he'd discovered it. Leading us first through the 'wasteland', reduced to a piece of ragged terrain not a hundred yards across, where Swidhelm had performed his culinary magic; next, the impenetrable forest, through which Redwald had battered his way, now merely a stretch of closely clustered pine trees. Then the 'rocky heathland' via a drover's track, sloping upward through stunted outgrowth, towards a weather-beaten hillock. Beyond this lay a stretch of fairly open countryside and, last of all, the position marked with an 'X' on Giles's map. Ceowulf's final resting place, where he'd been reunited with Eanfled, his sword; taken final leave of his son.

I looked about, searching for a burial mound or barrow; crypt, cave or scattered sarsens. Nothing but arid scrubland, the occasional bush; here and there patches of hawthorn or nettle; solitary trees, bent over, sculptured by wind and weather. Then I remembered it was only a story. So why had we been brought here? Revenge for the way this *femme fatale* had doubted Jimmy's loyalty? An example of what for the Jutes passed as humour?

Giles said nothing. Placing his fingers conspiratorially to his lips, he indicated we were to stay where we were and disappeared behind the last of the trees. The final *denouement*, his parting shot – leaving us to find our own way home? Hardly had the thought occurred than there was a metallic creaking, the kind of sound I associate with a ship weighing anchor, and with a crash the ground not six feet ahead of us opened up.

'Ceowulf's tomb.' Giles reappeared, wiping oily hands on what had been a clean handkerchief. We peered down into an opening about the size of a manhole, neatly squared off, with metal rungs set into a narrow brick-lined shaft.

'Somewhat claustrophobic, I'm afraid. Think you'll be alright?' Obviously the man had no experience of lonely hours spent classifying books in the murky gloom of a county library.

'Don't worry about the rungs, I keep them in good nick.' Unfamiliar, as well, with the rickety ladders we used to reach the higher shelves.

The descent was as easy as he'd promised. Twenty-two rungs, all rather slippery, but Giles had brought a torch and the width of the shaft left no room for accidents. We stood in a narrow red-brick tunnel, the ceiling only a couple of inches above our heads, a heavy metal door a few paces before us. He produced a key which turned easily in the lock, heaved, and the door swung open. Dank chill struck instantly to the bone. Decay mingled incongruously with a hint of fresh paint. Giles's footsteps echoed on concrete flooring as he disappeared into the darkness. A match was struck, an oil lamp flared, and the room – if one could call it that – took shape around us. An extension of the tunnel really, about the size of an average garage, roughly tubular in shape with uneven flooring, a corrugated iron roof and brickwork at either end forming a semi-roundel. A second, then a third lamp was lit and further details swam into view. The side walls had the same fluted appearance as the ceiling, plastered and painted dull beige, with a series of black nodules prised into them along the full length of the room. Several pipes descended through the roofing. What I'd taken as shelving was now recognisable as a crude form of bedding. A table occupied the centre of the room. Several chairs had been drawn up beneath it, whilst the cubicle to one end displaying a *Vacant* sign could only have been some sort of toilet.

'I don't recommend we stay too long.' Giles flashed his torch around, picking out brown stains that had broken through the plaster. He ran his fingers down one of the walls, flicked away the condensation. 'We did our best with it, but it's hardly a health cure.'

'And hardly Ceowulf's tomb either.' Peter had taken one of the oil lamps and was examining the construction. Shadows loomed, enormous, then shrank down to nothingness. 'A shelter left over from the war?'

Giles shook his head. 'Rather more interesting than that. Those are gun-racks you're looking at, and the trap-door over there is where the ammunition was kept. Tinned food and water to last a fortnight or more on the shelving, bedding of a kind for half a dozen or so men, with the greatest of care taken in keeping the entrance secret. And, in case that was discovered, there's an emergency exit hidden in the brickwork opposite. All evidence of what you were hoping to find, in fact.'

'The auxiliary units?'

'Right. The operational base to be precise, just as described in the article. "Elephant shelter" to those who were supposed to live down here. Produced by the War Office in kit-form – corrugated sheeting, blast-proof walls, with drainage, ventilation and sanitary matters all considered – constructed secretly by the sappers according to the local conditions. Once the balloon went up, they'd hightail it down here, waiting for the right moment to emerge and wreak vengeance upon the enemy. Which is what I suggest we do now – get some fresh air in our lungs, I mean. God knows how they would have lasted a fortnight down here. Half an hour is the most I've endured!'

He led the way back into the sunshine, showing us how the trap-door was operated – via a cable that ran underground to a lever and counter-balances hidden amongst the roots of a tree. We sat eating packed lunches provided by the conference centre and contemplated the problem. Concealing the entrance once the trap had closed was something his father had never solved. Neither had Giles, who'd been intent on restoring the base to its former glory and opening it up to the public. Damp, the roots of trees, shifts in the soil had defeated him though. In any case it was too far off the beaten track to be anything like a worthwhile proposition.

The same notion had occurred to his father, who'd had great affection for the 'funk hole', as he called it. He, at least, had got as far as having the rusty iron replaced, overlaid with a non-porous covering, the drainage seen to and fresh ventilation installed.

'God knows where the money came from.' Giles poured out coffee from the flask and handed it round. 'All carried out long before word of the unit's existence got out. Employed only those who'd been members of the unit, or people he thought he could trust.' He swatted at a wasp buzzing noisily about his head. 'Swore them to secrecy, though just how he thought he could keep the lid on it beats me. As it did him eventually. One of them must have spoken too freely in the pub, tipped the wink to the press, bringing them to Jimmy's doorstep, seen off by the old man.'

At last a plausible explanation for their descent on the village. Neither Peter nor Geraldine had been responsible. Someone 'in the know' rather, a member of the auxiliary unit who the Squire thought 'he could trust'. And, from what had been said, there was only one odd-man-out among them.

Peter was onto it already. 'You really do believe the rumours, don't you?' He rounded on Giles. 'That Jimmy not only joined your father's outfit, but was the one who betrayed them?'

'Not so difficult finding your way here, was it? Once I set you going, pointed you in the right direction.' The wasp had returned. One swipe and Giles sent it flying. 'More than a coincidence I'd say, using Stoyan's journey as a route-map. With Jimmy's picture pin-pointing the starting point. *Mappa Mundi*: the perfect title. "Every story tells a picture" – isn't that what he always told us?'

'With this whole business of the auxiliary units blowing his pacifism clean out of the water,' I said, eager to change the subject.

Giles shook his head. 'I think he was genuine enough in that respect. My father reckoned it was a principle that had been burnt out of him at some point in the war; that he'd witnessed things – and Jimmy would never say what they were – that made it indefensible. Even so, he vowed to have nothing to do with the killings, should it come to that. Agreed to do everything else to support the units: scout for them, identify dead letter drops, ensure the operation base kept free of prying eyes. Either way, he'd not have had much time on "active service". No sooner had he arrived than the units were closed down.'

Hardly a compromise the pacifists I'd known would have settled for. But there was another aspect of the events that didn't add up. 'The war had been over ten years by then,' I put it to them carefully, needing to be sure of the facts. 'The units disbanded in the mid 1940s. So why keep them a secret all that time? I can see why operations such as Bletchley Park should be kept under cover. Their code-breaking work might still be useful to the enemy, but not the units'. And those involved were real heroes. So what possible harm could there be in letting it be known?'

'Modesty?' Giles shrugged. 'Wanting to put the war behind them. Not wishing those near to them to know how they'd been deceived, or that they'd been living all those years with trained killers? Whatever the reason, the secret held through to 1970. And it was an American that broke it.'

Little of which interested Peter. 'But no problem in landing the blame on Jimmy,' he fumed. 'What possible motives could he have had? A valuable addition to the unit from what you've said, trustworthy all that time. Why suddenly turn against it?'

'I couldn't believe it myself.' Giles shrugged. 'Not at the time. Thought maybe it was just an act of revenge. Lampooning the church to get back at Codpiece and that schoolteacher after the attacks they made on him. When that article appeared and I began to follow-through on the clues. So accurate, and the rumours about Jimmy being a stool-pigeon. At long last, despite all my father told me – how it was pride in his work that attracted the press – the *real* reason they fell out so badly. Everything fitted perfectly into place.'

'With Peter blaming himself all these years. Convinced he'd sold out on Jimmy.' I'd hoped to boost his morale. Realised, too late, that we'd kept this last part of the story to ourselves. Giles was ignorant of Peter's assignations with Geraldine; his supposed 'betrayal'. There was nothing for it but to come clean. Back-track once again and tell him the truth. Accurate as far as it went: a rogue reporter from one of the tabloids inveigling a naïve Peter into revealing Jimmy's whereabouts then sending in the heavy mob to ferret him out. Concluding with a touching operatic finale: penitent Peter laying siege to *Third Class Cottage,* receives absolution from his childhood hero, who takes his final bow.

'So you camped out, actually gained admittance; that last day before Jimmy did a runner? No, hear me out!' Peter had half-risen in protest, taking offence at that stool-pigeon expression. 'It's exactly what he did, though. Letting you believe it was his rescue of Howard or the celebrated *Shakesphere* prints that brought the press to his door? As good a cover as ever. Precisely the one Father fed me. When all along it was a very different game Jimmy was playing.'

Peter stared at Giles in disbelief. 'You're not telling us that newspaper got it right, that Jimmy really was…'

'Guilty as charged? Led us straight to the funk hole, didn't he? And the rest of the article as near the truth as makes no difference.'

'An exaggeration, it's got to be. Gutter-press journalism at its worst.'

But Giles had believed it. The respected local figure whose family went back generations, had a stake in the land. Who'd remained in Bereden long after others had left to find their fortunes. He, if anyone, would know the truth.

'Well, I did warn you, right from the start, that your faith in the man would be challenged.' He'd got to his feet, was brushing himself down, hand held out to assist Peter.

To be shaken off: 'There must be some other explanation. You can't think that of Jimmy. Headstrong, against authority in all shapes and form. Misguided, even. But betraying the one man he trusted? Together with Danny Earl, Tom Carter and the rest of them? Never!' And before I realised his intentions, Peter had taken me by the arm and we were making off. Having no idea, he later admitted, which direction to head.

'Neither of you interested in *why* he did it?' Giles called after us.

Peter slackened his pace.

'The *wheres* and *whens*? Just *what* it was drove him to it?'

Stopping us dead in our tracks.

'Turns out both of us have been living with guilty consciences all these years.'

Giles caught up with us and paused for breath.

'Self-justification, I suppose you'd call it, the old man showing how far-sighted he'd been. The guy who saved the day for Britain. Broke every rule in the book the moment he put pen to paper.'

'You mean there's first-hand evidence of what really happened?' Peter broke away and squared up, all five and a half feet of him to Giles's six foot.

'And all this time, after all we've been through, you've been sitting on it?' I interposed myself between them.

'Didn't realise just how much it meant to you, not till a moment ago. Nor how much you already knew, changing your story every couple of minutes. Do you think I'd have held back otherwise?' Giles seemed genuinely contrite. 'A miscalculation as well, assuming that if I took you through it, clue by clue, you'd have cottoned onto it by now.' He smiled ruefully. 'And Peter a university man. Two out of ten, I'd say, D minus at the most.'

'Okay, Giles, so we failed. Dismally. What next: fifty lines, detention, or six-of-the-best in true public school tradition?' The first and only time I'd heard Peter refer to differences in their background other than in jest.

'And if you've no intention of telling us where we've gone wrong, there's plenty of mess here that needs our attention.' Time to draw a line before they actually came to blows. I began tidying the remnants of our picnic.

'It's not something I'm proud of, you know.' Giles squatted down beside me, collecting up the cutlery. 'The old man comes badly enough out of this as it is. God knows what would happen if it got out he'd written it up. A rival to Churchill's war diaries to his way of thinking.' He gathered up the rug. 'And, having got this far, you'd better have a second chance; see what you make of the rest of it. As long as you're sure there's nothing else you've left out.' He held one end of it out to me to be folded, 'and what you read remains between the three of us.'

'*Spare of tongue,* my Peter,' I quipped taking the other end of the rug.

'And certainly *slow to quit.*' Giles brought both ends together and folded it into a neat square.

'Don't – patronise – me.' Peter kicked defiantly at a clump of weeds.

'Wouldn't dream of it.' Giles hefted up the hamper and we made our way back. 'And from now you're getting no help from me. Who knows, maybe Jimmy will emerge as a shiny hero, could be a died-in-the-wool villain. Or was he something in-between? Like the protagonists in so many of your modern novels, Helen. Which is something you and Peter must make up your own minds about.'

Chapter Twenty-Five

Tales Out of School

Giles insisted that Helen and I read the document on the premises under conditions of complete privacy. The contents might no longer be secret, if ever they had been, but it did contain information of a sensitive nature about individuals living in the area, and he had his father's reputation to consider. A quiet room off the library had been set aside for the purpose. I remembered disturbing the old Squire over his port and cigar in there one evening when we'd been given the run of the house to play hide-and-seek, discovering that the upper classes really did dress for dinner, just as I'd seen them do so often in films of the time.

'Hard to imagine him down in the funk hole,' I said, 'subsisting on war-time rations with only a chemical toilet between them.'

'Reliving the glory days,' Giles mused, 'snuckered down alongside his men, waiting for the signal to emerge, the sabotage and hand-to-hand combat to begin.' There was more than a touch of admiration in his voice.

'Whilst Jimmy was kept busy out there tracking down the enemy the way he had Grigorio. Keeping the woodlands free from the prying eyes of children.' Helen reminded him.

Painting *Mappa Mundi* as a childish form of revenge? Maybe. But double-dealing and treachery? Whatever Geraldine said or Helen suspected, I could never believe that of him.

The diary had been kept in a foolscap ledger, bound in a hard blue cover, the pages lined, with thin red columns running down the right-hand side for the keeping of accounts. The opening section had been ripped out, the final part left blank, the rest filled with a script I vaguely remembered. My mother treasured even the most perfunctory of Sir Desmond's notes, and the green ink, seeping through to the sheet beneath, was precisely the shade he'd favoured. Made to order by the barrel, according to Jimmy, and no mistaking it now. Line after line, some of the entries a sentence or two only, others occupying a page or more, with spaces left in between. Each of them had been dated; all heavily underscored. Nor had the Squire been consistent in keeping up with events. Beginning in the late forties, the text ran intermittently over the years, days sometimes recorded in sequence, leaving gaps of a week or more also. The writing became progressively less legible into the fifties, finally petering out in a series of scrawls, incoherent almost and undated, into what must have been following decade. We found ourselves consulting Giles as to the circumstances under which they'd been written. His continued presence had seemed an intrusion to begin with, but we were to be more than grateful for it by the time we'd finished.

Jimmy hardly appears in the early pages. There are glimpses of him casting a protective eye over the woodlands, disarming traps laid by poachers, upsetting some of the newer teachers over his assistance with our homework, and there he was creeping from the school via the back door prior to some gubernatorial visitation. He is mentioned more fully at the time of the ceremonial 'beating of the bounds', which took place every ten years. According to custom, the schoolmaster administered the traditional 'six-of-the-best' to his scholars' backsides at strategic points around the village, the time-honoured means of preserving territorial integrity from one generation to the next. Enid Quintock, though, could not be persuaded to participate, no matter how earnestly

Sir Desmond assured her no harm would come to the pupils; that it was a colourful spectacle only.

'Insisted she was no "schoolmaster",' Giles was telling us. 'And that being the case, the ceremony had to be cancelled.'

He was fresh home from public school as I remembered it, scoffing at such antiquated notions, coming to blows with Chunky over the issue.

Giles smiled ruefully. 'Grounded for six weeks when I arrived back with a black eye and bruises all over my face.' The source of still further derision when it became known.

'Ended with Jimmy volunteering to be "beater in chief",' I remembered.

Feather-like had been the Squire's verdict on his efforts, the diary recording Jimmy's own comment: that the sadists among them must now *restrain themselves for a decade for the next such performance.*

But Helen's attention had been caught by an entry on the opposite page. A few lines of verse:

Do not despair for Johnny Head in the air
He sleeps as sound as Johnny underground.

Copied out meticulously in the Squire's best hand.

'Strange affair that, and the diary's not much help.' Giles pushed it to one side. 'Believe it or not, my mother's choice for Vernon's memorial. Remember how keen she was on the movies, Peter? Well, this was a quote from one of the films she'd seen.'

I was about to remind Helen of our previous discussion regarding the topic, accompanied by some 'I told you so' comment, when… 'Of course.' She cuffed her forehead. 'The John Pudney poem! Quoted in *The Way to the Stars*!'

'Written during an air raid, on the back of an envelope, I believe.' She quickly recovered her poise. 'And used to great effect in the film. Celebrating war heroes. She can't have chosen more appropriate an epitaph.'

'Not to my father's way of thinking.' Giles was shaking his head. 'He was no great supporter of the church, had to be dragged there almost every Sunday. Didn't stop him regarding that poem as sacrilegious though. Don't know which annoyed him most, that or the rector's suggestion.'

Which had been some Biblical text featuring angels. Eventually it had been Jimmy who came up with the solution: the Brooke *some corner of a foreign field* inscription.

'Mother was delighted, sold on Jimmy's notion that the plaque stood for *all* the fallen, heroes or otherwise, especially those whose remains were never discovered – the "unknown warriors". He laid it on thick, even sketched in a St Christopher motif to make his point, along with that Latin tag that goes with it.'

'*Vade Mecum*,' I said, recalling the medallion he wore around his neck.

The Squire, though, had regarded this as even more irreligious, and the rector had agreed, with Dame Alice settling for the plaque in its current form. After which Jimmy vanished once more back into obscurity.

To reappear, some eighteen months later intermingled with the fortunes of Miss Quintock's successor. As chairman of the management committee, the Squire's decision had been influential in Eric Stapleton's appointment, thoroughly approving of the tighter discipline the ex-serviceman brought with him. The diary confirmed most of what Howard had told us of the man; a strict disciplinarian, determined to wrest the establishment from the disorder into which it had fallen since Miss Quintock's demise. The Squire had high regard for the approach he adopted, various entries noting improvements in the attendance rate and behaviour of the pupils both in and out of school. His suggestion for the formation of a cadet unit, consisting of the older boys together with any other teenager with time on their hands, was taken up immediately, the two men pooling their military experience, and before long they had twenty or so recruits, kitted out, marching back and forth across the recreation ground two evenings each week.

At which point Jimmy makes his next appearance in the diary, arriving at the hall in high dudgeon to complain that these were exercises in mindless obedience, more suited to the Hitler Youth movement. He'd not been taken seriously, *ranting like the Fuehrer himself* wrote the Squire. All Jimmy had achieved was the bringing of the two men more closely together.

But there were elements of the Stapleton regime even less to Jimmy's liking. Two entries in particular took my attention:

25th March

A few of the parents worried. Sensitive souls whingeing about Stapleton's use of his Korean experiences up at school. Asides during lessons, references to current situation – atomic warfare cf. Battle of Hastings, mushroom clouds cf nimbus formations, four-minute warnings cf the beacon in our woods, Eastern religion cf mind-bending techniques, etc, etc, etc. Told them I'll look into it.

27th March

At school this a.m. Morning assembly first class. Children well behaved & respectful. More highly strung ones a bit nervous. Probably upset by my visitation. S. denies allegations. Occasionally egged on by older boys, it seems. Promises to be more circumspect in future. No sooner home than Jimmy on doorstep. News travels fast! His version: children scared half to death; parents every right to complain. Exaggeration, Stapleton assures me. And children not the most reliable of witnesses. Must say I agree.

Told Jimmy so. In any case, teacher only doing his job; being wise before rather than after event. Unlike our leaders back in '39. Not that he listened – any more than they did! Write letter of assurance to those concerned. Afternoon – cadet inspection. Splendid turn-out; agreed to look into matter of badges & insignia. Final word in S's ear. 'Sapientia satis'. Go easy on the reminiscences.

No doubt as to where the Squire's sympathies lay, nor how seriously BadEgg took the warning.

Little more than a week later the proposed screening of two American documentaries – *Atomic Alert* and *Cities Must Fight* – warning of the dangers inherent in a third World War, were vetoed by the managing body. Then, within the month Jimmy was once more at Amberstone Hall, brandishing a copy of the Home Office *Manual of Basic Training* that Eric had dispatched to committee members. Pamphlet 6, *Atomic Warfare,* to be precise, containing details of heat flash, radioactivity and blast, estimates of casualties in a British City (50,000), with explicit photographs appended to make the point. There'd been a covering letter, outlining the *steps* implemented *to cover such eventualities.* Jimmy had witnessed one of these first-hand: the 'duck and cover' exercise masquerading as a PE lesson with six-year-olds running into the classroom and squatting beneath their desks at the toot of a whistle. Followed by another, four minutes later, at which those not making it were instructed to curl themselves into a ball or hide down behind hedge, wall or building.

I remembered the press and radio reports of hydrogen bomb tests in Bikini and Monte Bello; newsreel footage of the devastation at Hiroshima; doom-laden maps extrapolating how British cities would be targeted, along with photographic evidence of expected injuries, immediate and long-term. The staple fare of rumour and apocalyptic comic strips, banned in most households, yet freely available in backstreet or playground; infants and the unimaginative coping well enough, but the source of nightmares for 'sensitive souls' such as Howard. We'd attempted to shield him from the worst excesses of the media, but none of us realised just how close to home they'd come. Not till I read Sir Desmond's diary.

Helen was appalled. 'What about the parents?' she demanded. 'You mean they accepted what was going on? Just stood by passively and allowed the man to do what he liked?'

'It was the 50s,' I reminded her. 'With teachers acting *in loco parentis*, actually trusted to know what they were doing. Make problems at school and there was worse for you once you got home. With the Squire's backing, BadEgg would have been king of the castle.'

'Peter's right.' Giles shrugged apologetically. 'Parents deferred to Father's every wish. It was what they were brought up to expect – a way of life.' I remembered the obsequious 'thank you' letters I'd been forced to write following each of my visits to the Hall; part of the invisible barrier that stood between our two worlds, excluding me from entry into his just as it barred him full membership of ours.

'But not Jimmy,' he was saying. 'He always stood up for what he believed. My father respected him for it. Not that it cut much ice when it came to Stapleton's leadership style. Which was when Jimmy went on the attack, retaliated in the only way he knew how. Here, let me show you.'

He leant over and, flicking through the pages, indicated various entries, some complete in themselves, others no more than a single sentence or afterthought. Complaints had begun to be heard over Jimmy's stories, isolated but persistent, and dismissed by the Squire in a sentence or two.

- Stapleton upset regarding Jimmy's interference with the current-affairs homework he'd set – *thought that had died out with the Quintock regime.*
- Amusement at Major Grant's references to Jimmy's *bolshie ideas.*
- Danny Earl, worried over the content – unspecified in the diary – of Jimmy's latest offerings. *The man's got his wires crossed?*
- Then, in quick succession, Joe Wickbourne and Thomas Carter – had he heard Jimmy's latest and what did he intend to do about it? *Might help if I knew what they were talking about. Stop beating about the bush and come right out with it!*

Later, an enigmatic entry, singled out by Giles for our special attention:

> *1st October*
> *...beginning to add up once you hear the stories as a whole. Twisting history, religion even, to make his point. Threatening me – all of us – in this way. I can't believe it of him. The man must have taken leave of his senses.*

And, finally:

> *3rd October*
> *Jimmy refuses to come clean. Claims my information incorrect. Nothing more than adventure yarns. Same as he's always told. So why my sudden interest? I give no ground. Not the version taught at any school I know; so where his ideas coming from? Archaeological evidence according to J. And legend. None that I or the family heard before. Fantasy more like, I tell him. 'Fabricated to suit your own ends, so don't play the innocent.' Both of us aware what we're getting*

at; suggests he comes clean. Blank face. 'Or what?' he asks. And each of us knows what he means by that.

The Jutes, it must have been, or the stories Jimmy told about them. All that business of social equality, freedom of land-hold, pagan worship, used by him to get back at Stapleton for the way he ran the school. Suggesting there was a type of ancestral proto-communist blood coursing through our veins, the same as had inspired his captors. Encouraging us to follow suit. 'Stop putting the fear of God into the children, if you want the stories to stop. You're not the only one to twist history for their own ends. And if it's a competition, guess which one of us will win!' BadEgg must have hated it. Not so Tom, Joe, Alf and the rest of the bell-ringers; they'd never previously complained of Jimmy's tales, but here they were doing so. As was the Squire who, up to this point, had enjoyed them as much as the rest of us, despite their plot-lines. So why now?

'Fits in with everything else we've heard, though, doesn't it?' Helen glanced across at Giles for confirmation. 'Feeding the children disinformation the way your father encouraged him to in time of war, keeping them clear of the woods so that the unit's activities could remain secret. Except this time he used the same weapon for rather a different purpose: targeting the teacher for the way he conducted his lessons, before he won your father over completely with his anti-communist rituals.'

'Brought out the worst in both of them.' Giles pushed the diary aside. 'My father persuaded to Stapleton's way of thinking; Jimmy acting like a spoilt child, with BadEgg living up to the name we gave him. Took advantage of my father's military background, his interest in how warfare had changed. Acting for the good of the community, so he claimed, and perhaps he meant it – to begin with at least. After which…'

The Squire himself appears to have been unaware of the manipulation, so that it took us quite a bit of back-tracking before any sort of a pattern emerged. 'A gradual process,' Giles told us. 'A chance remark here, the answer to a question there, the old man led one innocent step after another. Idle curiosity in the early days I should imagine. Ex-soldiers comparing very different forms of warfare. Relief for my father that here at last was someone with whom to share his secrets.'

Yet BadEgg was persistent till there was little that Eric could not have known about the auxiliary units and their mission. And, once in possession of all the facts, had no scruples in using them for his own ends. Persuading, blackmailing even, the Squire to join his fantasy.

Everything became clear in an entry some nine months later. Here, for the first time Squire Desmond writes openly of such matters. Having taken the headteacher into his confidence, unwittingly at first, drawn in and, almost before he knew it, too deeply compromised to retract, he confides in his diary, sharing his secret with us also:

> *5th December*
>
> *Eric with his usual flattery about the units. Compares our times with those of wartime Bereden. Speaks of us as 'heroes'; wonders if current generation has it in them. Conventional weapons for the most part things of past. Claims McArthur up for atomic retaliation in Korea. The Russians also? And who knows about Chinese? But what about next time? Before and after the bomb falls. He's frustrated at my refusal to sanction cadet training in such matters. Reckons current methods as useless today as Home Guard in Hitler's. Suggests something more effective required, along lines of the Auxiliaries. Working locally, but underground against Soviet invasion/infiltration. Cites Burgess/McClean scandal. We agree. A sickening display of incompetence. Which I can vouch for, having known several of those involved.*

8th December

'Times' report on parliamentary debate. Preparedness of country for worst outcome nil. As Eric says, we've learnt nothing. Korea a dress rehearsal for Third World War, just as Spain and Sudetenland were for Second. Makes one think. Network established; we have experience, those that are left. Nothing illegal. Private citizens acting in own interest. Together with extension of cadet training. Eric a splendid 2nd i/c. Sounded the others out. Jimmy persisting in his nonsense. Will need to be short-circuited somehow, or God knows how it will end.

Nor did we.

Helen, storming at Giles: '"Nothing illegal"? "Private citizens" running their own army in time of peace? A kind of treason surely. Bound, as they probably were by the Official Secrets Act. In wartime a hanging offence.'

Myself unconvinced: 'The Jutish stories some form of "blackmail"? An egalitarian threat to topple "the Squirarchy and all it stood for"? Not his way at all. The Jimmy that I knew would have said what he meant and have done with it.'

And Giles, shaking his head in mock consternation: 'An academic and a librarian. The truth staring them in the face and all they do is bicker over the details.' Glancing from one of us to the other. 'And they still don't get it.' He sighed. 'Forget the ultra-democratic sentiments, Jimmy's tilts at the hierarchy and religion. Minor issues, small beer compared with what he was really doing. From the moment he started telling those stories about the Jutes. With those in the know realising what he was up to. Which is the reason he became so incredibly unpopular. And why, eventually, one way or another, he had to go.'

Chapter Twenty-Six

The Dangerous Edge

'You still don't get it, do you? An academic and a librarian.'

'And neither of us a mind-reader,' Peter growled back. 'So why not just tell us what you know?'

But Giles was not letting go that easily. 'It's all there in front of you. Forget any deeper purpose Jimmy might have had: the egalitarian, anti-authority overview. Concentrate on the broad outline, the characters especially, and those most upset by the stories. The first to complain for example. Remember who they were?'

'How should I know? There were so many of them.'

'Okay, let's take it a bit at a time. Go back to this morning. The route to the elephant trap. Stoyan showed us the way, right? From *Mappa Mundi* to its exact location. But he wasn't alone on that journey. There were his companions, each with a special talent, which came in handy at the crucial moment, just when the quest seemed doomed.' Giles had produced his sketch-map and was identifying the landmarks we had followed. 'Just like the super-heroes we read about in comics: *Batman*, the *Incredible Hulk, Spiderman* and the like. Puts you in mind of nothing closer to home? Queuing up to have our bikes mended or penknives sharpened? Along with those from miles around, bringing in their tools?'

'Joe Wickbourne?'

'A dab-hand at producing gadgets or labour-saving devices as well. Silencers, commando knives, garrotting wire would have been child's play. Quite something when combined with the man's strength. Remind you of someone? More of a blacksmith than a farrier?'

Peter, eloquent in his stubbornness, made no reply.

'Redwald?' I volunteered.

'Right! The "blacksmith from hell", transported from his real-life forge into the world of make-believe. Not the only one either. Remember Alfred Thomas, down at the Jugged Hare? Wonderful cook, could turn his hand to most ingredients; roots and grubs from the soil, cactus if needs be. Knew everyone in the village, everything that was going on as well, all of it discussed over his bar. Jimmy might have been the expert in disinformation, but when it came to the daily goings-on around Bereden, Alf was your man. A genuine bell-ringer, down at St Matthias with the rest of them, revelling in folk history but among the first to complain when it came to the Jutes. Then there was Thomas Carter, another of Jimmy's fans who kicked up a fuss according to the diary. Always fresh trout or bass at the Fish-Fry Delight on a Saturday night. Knew every inch of the Meon. No scruples about blowing his catch out of the water, either. As useful an addition to my father's unit as Tonbert was to Stoyan.'

So that was it: the truth about the auxiliary unit revealed through the *Jutish Chronicle.* Their Robin Hood existence in the woods – snipers in the tree-tops, secret caches of weapons, underground escape tunnels – identical to the guerrilla tactics the Squire's secret army had been trained to employ. No wonder they'd objected so strongly to Jimmy's reinterpretation of history.

'And Alric, the nobleman. Your father, presumably?' Peter, sarcastic, but all attention now he knew what Giles was driving at.

'Not so. Alric had a far more important part to play in the story. There was no compass or direction-finding device at the time of the Jutes, remember. Nor did the map they'd been given take them the whole way. Leaving them dependent on Saba up there above the trees whispering the way forward in her master's ear. Rather like the crystal-sets we bought in kit-form from Danny Earl down at Sound

Business, don't you think? Terrible reception, but signals of all sorts reaching us from miles away. More to the point, the ham radio he kept up in the attic, sending and receiving messages from all over the world. Making him another valuable member of the unit.'

'But they're archetypes: blacksmith, innkeeper, fisherman, nobleman – the lot of them. It's what Jimmy did all the time: taking characters or events from real life and weaving stories around them. Everyone knew that.'

'Then what was it got my father so worked-up about the *Jutish Chronicle* when he found the rest of Jimmy's stories so amusing?'

I'd always known there was something suspicious about those stories, but never anything like this. 'Think it through, Peter,' I said, ensuring I'd got it straight in my own mind. 'Day after day that so-called teacher putting the fear of God into the children. Your brother's breakdown might never have happened but for the Stapleton approach. To say nothing of his influence on Giles's father. The auxiliary unit top secret, not a word breathed about it. Till that man appeared on the scene, inciting him to treason almost. With Jimmy in the know – caught on the "dangerous edge", as friend Browning put it. Obliged to remain silent to save his companions' reputation, yet aware of the consequences if he didn't.'

'Creating a whole mythology, dreaming up legends, picturing it out.' Peter was distant, myopic almost, putting it together for himself. 'Just what Jimmy would have done.' He lapsed into silence.

'Stalemate,' Giles continued, 'a battle of wills. Each knowing the truth about the Jutish tales, knowing that the other knew, yet both of them denying that they knew what they knew. Comic if it had not been so serious. Hilarious on the stage or part of a comedy routine. Heaven knows how long they'd have kept it up, or which of them would have backed down first. Jimmy turning threat to reality, coming out into the open, telling all he knew. Or if my father had swallowed his pride and sent BadEgg packing. As it turned out, neither of the two outcomes was required.'

Reaching across, he opened the diary at a fresh page.

22nd March

S. at Hall again yesterday. Greatly excited. Recalls my mentioning Operations Base. Thinks it suitable for Fallout Shelter. Badgers me to show him. Agreed, if only to keep the man quiet. Up there this pm. S. with binoculars, measuring tape and book of words. Place just about inhabitable, but access dangerous. He prances around, making calculations, noting down figures. Pronounces it perfect. Concrete, bricks + earth all protect against gamma rays, so he says; whole thing below ground; entrance at right-angles (g. rays again!) but walls need strengthening (no longer blast-proof). Ventilation a problem. Filters and hand-cranked blower will suffice, he promises. Shows me diagram. The man's certainly done his homework.

25th March

Good to see Funk Hole again. Always intended restoring to wartime condition. Open to public once story can be told. A tangible reminder of what we went through. St. taken idea on board; two birds with one stone. Has sent me ground plan + costing according to latest USA figures. Let him get on with it, but stress secrecy. Auxiliary Units, ops centre included, still under official embargo. Imagine fuss if word got out about its new purpose! Employ only those can trust. Interview them personally myself. We concoct cover story also. Hide/underground hunting lodge, constructed on site of an old air raid shelter. Thin, I tell him. A hide for viewing earthworms? Reinforced walls to keep out moles? St. seems confident enough.

Despite his misgivings, the Squire continued to record happy memories of the funk hole, Stapleton to urge him on. The cadets were occupied with their march and counter-marching, their teacher pestering both pupils and parents concerning the dangers they were in. Steady progress was reported on the operation centre/fallout-shelter/hunting lodge front. Until the project was brought to a sudden and dramatic conclusion. Hardly surprising – the reconstruction was no simple matter. Several outsiders must have been brought in and sworn to secrecy but, sooner or later, the story was bound to have leaked. The wonder is they'd kept it under wraps that long.

Hints there'd been. Incidents. Trivial at the time and seemingly unconnected. Until one looked back and realised their significance as part of a larger pattern.

21st July

... telephone a.m.; questions regarding renovations up at Hall; to whom estimate sent? Wrong number, presumably.

25th July

Gerrard from local rag; calls himself 'Editor' these days. Wants to run story about bomb damage & repairs; to outhouses somewhere in grounds, he's heard. Ten years too late, even for 'Argos' I tell him, and then all raids other side Portsdown, not even near misses.

(undated entry)

... builder's van arrives, wanting measure up + cost. Sent away with flea in ear. Practical joke...?

28th July

...Rushton, out at Meonstock Cottage. Excavations in progress near his property. Worried over security of tenancy. Telephone company responsible? Gas, electricity? Promise him I'll check it out. Tell St. to be more circumspect.

30th July

Jimmy, pig-headed as ever, still playing the innocent, but guarded queries about Funk Hole. Fed him cover story; he accepts what I say – but you never can tell with him. Sly references to success of Jutish stories; but 'what's the use of a story without pictures'? Leaves without clarifying matters further. What's he up to this time?

2nd August

... estimates back from Kennedy's; S. signature insufficient for specialist materials... Those in know aware of Jimmy's game. He's fast becoming a pariah. Nothing new from him on Jutish front; can't get anything out of him. Said to be painting. In secret. Subject matter unknown!!!!

5th August

... Gerrard on phone again. Confirmation of story re hunting lodge required. Where? Open all season? What type of game? Available for public hire? Send photographer? Told him stay off Estate; dogs and mantraps. Rang off on him.

And, at that point, the entries cease. A few pages are left blank. All mention of funk hole, auxiliary units, 'duck and cover' or cadet corps forgotten. Fortunately Giles was on hand to supply the details.

'Must have been the next day, 6th August, or soon after. Reporters, columnists, photographers descend on the village. With Gerrard leading the pack. Not only editor of the *Argos* but stringer for a national daily as well. The "builder" father had dismissed with "a flea in the ear" one of his cronies. Some take themselves up to the Hall, others start banging on Jimmy's door, the rest swarm off into the forest. There's no stopping them till the old man gets on the 'phone, which is when the fleet of shiny cars arrive, as does PC Granger. Men in grey suits pile out, reporters are rounded up, photographs confiscated, the lot of them sent packing. Got it at last, Peter? That's the real reason they were there. The press I mean. Nothing to do with your having blown the gaff about Jimmy's prowess as an artist. If anyone's to blame it's my father, who doesn't emerge with much credit, I'm afraid – you can understand my holding back on it.' He paused, expecting some response – absolution, perhaps. Realised that Peter was not yet ready, or too far absorbed, and hurried on.

'Not so his bosses. The old man was summoned up to

Whitehall – that part I got out of him after the 1970 article had appeared – and to this day I don't know what story he spun them. Building a private-enterprise fallout shelter was bad enough. Using it as an operation centre – if that's what they really intended – worse. The auxiliary units were still hush-hush, remember, and running a private army in peacetime – if they got to hear about it – as Helen says must surely have been a treasonable offence. Fortunately, he still had friends in high places. And, of course, they were the people who not only recruited Burgess and McLean, but gave them access to our secrets, then let them slip through their fingers once they were discovered. Which my father was not going to let them forget, especially as he knew where quite a few of the bodies were buried!'

Peter fully exonerated; no longer the arch-betrayer he'd believed himself to be. 'With BadEgg showing his true colours. The "fourth man" in the spy ring even!' I could hear the relief in his voice.

'A KGB agent, leaking the secrets of our Eleven Plus papers to his Soviet masters? Using copybooks as ciphers? Hardly. Onwards and upwards in the educational hierarchy rather, an inspector no less.'

'And no credit for Jimmy,' Peter reminded us. 'Not even when the truth emerged? Think of how much trouble your father would have been in if he'd *not* dreamt up the *Jutish Chronicle*.'

'And you're quite sure that *was* his motive in telling them?' Important to be certain. I don't think either of us could have stood any further disappointment.

'Not the earlier stories. My guess is they were more about the erosion of the countryside, the disappearance of the old landmarks and the tales that went with them. He started inventing new ones to replace them, hit upon the Jutes as the perfect vehicle, then realised how perfect the match was – between them and the auxiliary units. It was Jimmy's way of bringing my father to his senses. Not wanting to endanger those who'd been inveigled into following him, yet an early warning before they went too far. As long as he continued telling them there was a chance people would cotton on. And, if they didn't, he could always make them more explicit, bring the whole project right out into the open if needs be. Might have worked as well, but for Bad Egg's duplicity. You've got to hand it to him.' Giles shook his head in mock admiration. 'Turning Jimmy's stories back against him. Claiming they were responsible for Howard's breakdown; persuading others that was the case. How Jimmy was a bad influence. Leading the children astray.'

'And your father really believed it?'

'I don't think Howard's little adventure made much of an impression on him. But threatening to betray the revamped auxiliary unit? Another matter entirely. All that was needed was for someone to hint that Jimmy had leaked the story to the press.'

'No prizes for guessing who that might have been.' Peter seemed fully to have regained his spirits.

'Spelling it out even more clearly with rumours about an illustrated version of the *Jutish Chronicle.* What else was the old man to think? You've seen from the diaries the kind of state he was in.'

'With *Mappa Mundi* putting in an appearance at the crucial moment?' I suggested.

'And Codpiece horrified by what he'd seen of the picture, desperate to discover what further blasphemies it contained. Both of them vying with the other to get their hands on it. Dreading what they might see, but for very different reasons.'

'And once your father got hold of it, what then? Destroy the picture and send the painter on his way before he created any more trouble?' That last meeting with Jimmy, the time he'd camped outside Third Class Cottage, still lay heavily on Peter's mind.

'Not at all. And if you don't believe me, it's all here in the diary. If you can make it out. He was getting on by then. Must have realised that Stapleton had taken advantage of him, and never quite the same once he returned from the grilling they gave him in London.'

Just a few pages remained. Seven or eight at the most. And we could see at a glance there was a marked difference between them and what had gone before. Beginning, clearly enough, with a stark entry that summarised the Squire's dilemma:

> *... not many in village left who J not upset: churchgoers who listen to Draper, teachers eager to get own back, worried parents, our new masters upset by his socialism, incomers who know no better, and now survivors of the unit themselves with this whole business of the Jutes. What's to be done with the fellow?*

Thereafter gaps between entries became more frequent; the writing progressively illegible. Whole pages were omitted. Little attention had been given to dates, so that we had the greatest difficulty in piecing together anything approaching a precise chronology. But, with Giles's help, we did our best.

Just when or how *Mappa Mundi* was discovered is uncertain. Not so the Squire's reaction:

> *J at his very best. One in eye for our sanctimonious rector; even tried to scuttle Vernon's memorial – the only worthwhile thing at St Matthias. Foolish letting the man have sight of it even. The picture's dangerous he tells me. How right he is; did he but know it. And I suppose it has to go. Wish now I'd kept more of Jimmy's work.*

The reference to the plaque that Jimmy had designed was significant. According to Giles, the older boy had been much on the old man's mind at the time, both Jimmy and Vernon being artists, the bond that had originally brought them together.

Maybe it was this that changed his mind regarding the picture's fate. Just as likely to have been the Rev. Theobald Draper's intransigence. We'd have missed the relevant entry if Giles had not pointed it out to us:

> *Another dreary Draper diatribe; heavily disguised attack on J's painting. Turns to Savonarola as role model. Congregation, those still awake, floored.*

Italian fellow, I believe, burnt books. 'Bonfire of the Vanities.' Ended up on the pyre himself if my memory serves.

'No more than an afterthought, not that I remember it all that clearly, being home on half-term and revising like mad for Oxbridge entry. Right at the end of the sermon it was. A throw-off remark so I thought, five minutes at the most, and the old man's right: passed right over the congregation's head.'

But not the Squire's. Giles had returned in all innocence to his studies leaving his father in turmoil. As evidenced in the diary. *Pity can't be Vicar himself on the bonfire,* he scribbled. *Doubt he'd give off much heat. Incense only!*

Then, halfway down the following page: *Protective custody. Out of harm's way. Must act quickly before they steal a march; otherwise it's the Savonarola scenario for certain.* Followed by further references to *Holy Joes,* the importance of secrecy, a life-and-death situation almost.

'It's not what I'd have wanted you to see,' Giles admitted. 'Nor the way I like to remember him. Obsessing over that picture, regret for the way Stapleton had fooled him, remorse at his treatment of Jimmy tied to memories of Vernon – all pushing him more or less over the top. But you were insistent, you'd put so much time into your "quest", and it seemed Peter had devils of his own that needed laying to rest.'

Both of us, had he but known it.

'Not content with which, he dragged in the rest of them to help him.' Giles had returned to the diary. 'Joe, Tom and the others. See, here and here, you can just make it out. And you can imagine how delighted they'd have been, hauled in to protect a picture that must have seemed worthless to them!' Stray references to *find the lady, Indian rope-trick* followed, then the final entry: *J. gone. Draper triumphant. Claims 'all for the best'. Maybe, but the man doesn't know the half of it. Pity about the cottage, though.*

Giles had closed the diary. 'Never figured out exactly why or where he went. Unlike Jimmy to give way under pressure and my father always maintained it was none of his doing. I suppose other members of the unit may have rounded on him, especially if they'd not been briefed as to his innocence – which seems highly likely judging from the old man's state of mind. It's the best I can do. I must have read his words a thousand times, without coming any closer to an explanation. So maybe there isn't one. Perhaps Jimmy just felt it was time to move on and did so. Precisely as he'd arrived in the first place.'

Which, we agreed, was about as far as we could take the matter. Peter, in his own mind, unsure as to whether – one way or the other – Sir Desmond hadn't been responsible for Jimmy's departure. Inadvertently tipping a wink to the unit: 'Who will rid me of this turbulent priest?' Or deliberately setting out to discredit him? I didn't see it that way. Jimmy, despite all I'd said about him, had proved himself no enemy. Just the opposite in fact, saving Sir Desmond from what could have been a very nasty situation. And he'd no motive for driving Jimmy away. 'Keep your friends close, but your enemies closer', isn't that what they say? Especially if there was some secret they might reveal once out of your sight.

By now the search had taken some eighteen months. We'd discovered as much as it seemed prudent to know about Jimmy; learnt even more about ourselves. Peter was finally absolved of the sense of betrayal he'd clung to since childhood; Geraldine's matrimonial experiences were helping me form a more dispassionate view of the duplicity that had overshadowed my own. And we spoke more freely now about such matters. Jimmy we'd left behind us; a thing of the past. He, though, had not quite finished with us.

Chapter Twenty-Seven

The Singular Saintley

Geraldine's death should have come as no surprise; it was a wonder she'd reached seventy, let alone eighty, smoking the way she did. She'd always taken an active interest in what was going on around her, though, and Mildred's company would certainly have kept her on her toes. Nor could her memory be faulted. We'd receive cards regularly each Christmas, carefully chosen. For me something of suitably sociological significance – a nativity scene featuring both kings and shepherds, the Holy Family's homeless flight to Egypt, Christ teaching the wise men in the temple; a more literary offering – Pickwick, Lords a Leaping or Wenceslas – for Helen.

The handwriting became increasingly unsteady as we entered the 1990s, but her greetings remained as cheerful as ever. She had, in fact, acknowledged a copy of my new book – one that I'd edited rather – just a month before the message came through. Mildred, pointedly wishing to speak to Helen rather than myself, quite calm, but giving the brief details of how it had happened – suddenly, in her sleep – and inviting us to the funeral.

This turned out to be quite a grand affair, conducted according to her own precise instructions and attended mainly by professional colleagues who'd made their way down from London. A eulogy took in the full range of her artistic and literary achievements, a handsome tribute being paid to 'the kind soul who'd watched over her declining years'; mention even of 'newly acquired friends from academe' – and here the vicar beamed over his spectacles at where we sat halfway down the aisle – but no mention of Derek from beginning to end. The introit hymn – *Dear Lord and Father of mankind, Forgive our foolish ways* – could well have been a parting shot in his direction, the Psalm, *Deliver me, O Lord, from evil men*, smacked of more of her companion, but the reading she'd selected from *Corinthians* stirred up old memories:

> *Love is patient and kind; not arrogant and rude. It does not insist on its own way; is not irritable or resentful. Love does not rejoice at wrong, but applauds the right. It bears all things, believes all things, hopes all things, endures all things.*

Her true feelings? Mildred certainly felt so. 'Came looking for inspiration for the embroidery, found the husband who'd deserted her,' she reflected later at the wake held at the Spurs and Stirrup, again exactly as Geraldine had planned it. 'Derek, alive and well after all those years, just when she'd managed to settle down, to make her own way in the world.' She sniffed disconsolately into what must have been her fifth sherry. 'Together with a schoolboy only too eager to help. Think you were hard done by, Peter? Never got over your supposed "betrayal"? Well, neither did she, and with far greater cause. Forever wondering if she'd done the right thing. Whether she should go back to him. Only to see reason at the last moment.'

I ordered up a further schooner. Let her get it out of her system; with any luck she'd remember little of this in the morning, by which time we need never meet again. So I thought, but hardly a week had gone by before the letter arrived. Formal, professionally typed on cream vellum, signed with a flourish by Anthony J. Underwood of Messrs Townsend, Bright and Underwood, Solicitors, acquainting us with the last will and testament of one Geraldine Leapman, deceased. Mildred, it appeared, had inherited the house, together with a small annuity and a few paltry investments. Well deserved; it can't have been easy looking after the old lady all those years. Helen was to have first choice of the needlework collection, the rest to be dispersed according to arrangements discussed with her agent, together with the mahogany tea box – a kind touch this and least expected. Till we reached the final paragraph. Funding had been set aside for an exhibition of Jimmy's work, all save *Fiddlers Three*, which was to be mine, on permanent loan as administrator – three readings before I took it in – yes, administrator, of *The Saintley Collection,* if this could be fitted round my other responsibilities.

I was hesitant. Not Helen, who relished the prospect of our co-operating together on further research, nor the University, which was more than content to have their name associated with such a venture. What finally clinched the matter was Giles's plans for the future of the operations centre. Information regarding the auxiliary units was by now emerging right across the south coast so that, given the funding and fitted out with its wartime accoutrements, his father's dream of restoring the funk hole as a permanent memorial would be realised.

Bereden, where most of Jimmy's artwork had been conceived and painted, seemed the obvious location for the proposed Saintley collection, and it did not take a massive leap of the imagination to put both of these ideas together. The paintings and the shelter had been created at the same time, complementing one another. As had the historic furniture, portraits of ancestral admirals and generals, bric-a-brac looted from defeated foes scattered about the Hall and the effigies of these self-same heroes languishing down at St Matthias. Add the yet-to-be-discovered underground tunnels, the stories and legends concerning them that Jimmy himself had perpetrated, throw in a replica of Third Class Cottage, and you had an almost unique record of one family's day-to-day existence over the last couple of hundred years. Rather a belligerent one, it's true.

'*The Armigerous Amberstones,* the perfect title,' Helen joked. 'The kind of hands-on experience that museums would give their eye-teeth to possess.'

'Or those stored away in their vaults,' I replied.

We settled on *The Singular Saintley.*

Giles and the centre's management had little difficulty in obtaining a grant. Mildred – probably only too pleased to have 52 Willow Drive shot of Jimmy's artwork – approved of the idea, and the two of us – Helen and I – decided to operate as a team on the project. She would return to Bereden to work with Giles on sorting out those parts of the Squire's diary that might be included in the exhibition, whilst it was back to the Spurs and Stirrup for me, getting the pictures ready for transport and helping Mildred with whatever documentation Geraldine had left behind. I was not looking forward to this part of it. Neither of us had been at our best on previous occasions and I seemed to have inherited most of the resentment she felt towards Jimmy. This dissipated over the week as we worked together removing paintings that hung on the walls and retrieving those we found stored away in cupboards. Nothing of great interest emerged: a few ineffectual first drafts of the *Postbag* series, a poor copy of *Shakesphere V – Winter of Discontent,* a rather charming *Nervous Wreck* I'd not seen.

Till, crammed into a small shoebox, we discovered what might have turned out to be a goldmine: the letters that Jimmy – or should that be Derek – had written to Geraldine – Veronica as she then was – from Pendarrell. Maybe she'd intended to destroy them or have them buried with her – further evidence, much to Mildred's irritation, of how much she'd cared for him. Interesting enough, confirming everything she'd told us, but of a very personal nature. Once read, I gave them to Helen to dispose of as she felt fit, no questions asked. Of far greater significance, tucked in beside them, were a few notes in Jimmy's own hand of the three years he'd spent at the college, some of them verbatim records of conversations that had taken place. Almost as indecipherable as Squire Desmond's had been, it took several years, off and on, before we made sense of them, providing an invaluable supplement to Geraldine's own account of the time he'd spent with the 'brethren'.

For the moment, I had other things to think about. We packed the artwork carefully into the car and I spent the long journey south mentally setting them out to best advantage in the various rooms that had been placed at our disposal. Everything was coming together splendidly for the grand opening later in the year.

'Apart from *Mappa Mundi*,' Helen informed me on arrival. Damaged in transit from one part of the building to another, the painting itself unharmed, but one corner of the frame smashed and a horizontal gash running along the top. Nothing to worry about, but: 'Thirty years hidden safely away, unblemished. Yet once the "professionals" get their hands on it…' Giles paused as a group of rowdy sixth-formers pushed past us up the stairs. 'Given my way, I'd lock them up for five years in a cell with that lot and throw away the key.'

He'd brought a specialist in to deal with the repairs. A Swedish lady of impeccable reputation but few words, who spent an expensive afternoon striding about the building in search of a suitable location to use as a workshop. Having finally selected the Mauve Attic, part of the old servants' quarters with a large skylight running the full length of the ceiling, she supervised our heaving of the *Mappa Mundi* up two flights of stair, ensuring it was positioned precisely to her taste, before ushering the three of us from the room and settling down to work.

Some three-quarters of an hour later, she came looking for us.

'Not more problems?' sighed Giles.

'No, more picture.'

She led us back to the attic and we squeezed in behind her. The floor was now covered with what that morning had been a white sheet, and the tools of her trade – chisels, hammers of various sizes, a set of intricately shaped knives – had been arranged purposefully on a small table. An angle-poise lamp was set up bedside them whilst, somewhere in the background, a radio promised us fair weather for the coming week. *Mappa Mundi's* frame, reduced now to splinters, lay scattered about the room, the picture itself propped drunkenly against one of the walls.

'Two for the price of one.' Kicking the debris aside the restorer hefted it up, turning it round as she did so. 'Same artist. Less colourful. Modern art, yes?' And she was right, there was a second painting on the reverse.

A picture of sorts. Two green brushstrokes, slashed diagonally corner to corner, all but obscuring figures – joking, plotting, gambling? – an old man, Harlequin, a dog – or was it a rabbit? – clustered around the periphery. With the centre left empty.

A daub, I'd called it. Something he'd given up on, had difficulty with, or hadn't the heart to finish. And there it was again: rough-edged, released from its frame, just as I'd first seen it. With the furniture stacked up around us, precisely as it was now, complete with radio broadcast.

'It was the way he worked,' I heard Giles explain. 'Grabbing the nearest object to hand: canvas, wood, paper, tin trays, old pictures even. Palimpsest, isn't that what they call it?'

I heard, yet was barely aware of, what he said, back as I now was with Jimmy, meeting him that last time, at Third Class Cottage...

... dimly lit. The radio playing, tuned on this occasion to the Home Service. A weather forecast: dry, overcast, rain expected.

There'd been a scrambling before he let me in, reversing the picture on its easel.

'By no means uncommon.' The Swedish lady, unimpressed, was reeling off numerous examples.

He attempts to assuage my guilt. "Conned by the power of the press… happens to the best of us, Peter… a lesson well learnt." Relief; he knows nothing of my disloyalty.

'Not "boxed in"… "preserving the immediacy"… "the unity of experience and expression". Giles quoting Jimmy directly now, his voice reaching me from afar.

I'm unable to make out the details. 'My Last Duchess', he calls it. Not a portrait, though. I crane forward to get a better look. A Shakesphere? King Lear? Othello? Twelfth Night?

'… only natural boundaries permitted.' He was always sounding off about it…

"time I was moving on"… "no need to worry". He brandishes the medallion. "A talisman as looks after me". "Constant Companion", where I go she goes…

They'd stopped talking, were staring at me.

Was it then or later he hushes me, eager to catch the news broadcast, gives it his full attention. Very un-Jimmylike. Unemployment at all-time low; ramifications of the General Election; theatregoers upset by 'Waiting for Godot'; Ruth Ellis executed…

…'Peter!…'

…the body of Julius Soroyan, an American academic, missing for several weeks, discovered. Murdered along with his disciples. Those who'd not fled. The police seeking to contact those that had. The closer they'd been, the greater the danger, the more urgent the appeal. Jimmy switching off the radio. Ushering me out, returning to his packing with renewed vigour.

Soroyan! The name mentioned by Geraldine the last time we'd met. Which I'd been struggling with ever since. Benefactor of Pendarrell House, Jimmy's mentor whose influence had been so crucial in his early days, who'd taught him the value of solitude, to 'embrace the emptiness'. From whom he'd caught a penchant for reticence, his self-reliance, a belated love of Browning. The American whose scholarship he respected and whose privacy he'd guarded. From religious fanatics whose vindictiveness was equalled only by the extent of their tenacity. And from whom he'd escaped so narrowly with his life.

I was back at Amberstone Hall once more. BERCEN rather. *Mappa Mundi* returned to its easel, the gilt frame in shreds about the floor, struggling to explain the significance of that broadcast.

'And you're sure that's the reason for his leaving?' Giles kicked idly at a piece of debris.

'Would explain why he got out in such a hurry, without telling anyone.' The perfect fit? Two opposites coming together: what I knew of Jimmy and Geraldine's revelations about his early days – the 'dark side of his moon'?

'And Peter's right about one thing.' Helen had taken the torch and was examining the picture. 'It's the *Duchess'* backside, if you'll excuse the expression.' A crudity by which *Mappa Mundi* came to be known by all three of us – probably the Swedish lady also, who, for the moment, stood dumbfounded.

'An English joke, my dear, nothing to worry about.' Taking her by the arm Giles ushered her from the room.

'Which leaves Jimmy on the loose somewhere out there.' Helen had begun gathering up the remains of *Mappa Mundi's* frame. 'If he's alive, that is.'

'You'd have thought he'd have made contact if that was the case.' Giles moved the easel and began folding the sheet.

'Must be into his eighties now,' I said.

'But intending to return, surely, once it was safe to do so?' Helen seemed to have come to a more equitable view of Jimmy's motivation.

'With bookcase empty, chairs on table, every stitch of clothing packed? *The Night Watch* removed from the wall, talk of "outstaying his welcome", "pastures new"?' Jimmy was off for good, and he knew it. Entrusting Miss Quintock's book, her *Songs of Innocence and Experience*, to my safe keeping. And, as far as Jimmy was concerned, you couldn't get more final than that.

Chapter Twenty-Eight

Catch 22

At last, a plausible explanation for Jimmy's sudden departure. Peter, though, was assailed with doubts. A coincident. He'd confused Soroyan with Stoyan; misheard the radio broadcast; jumped to conclusions. That part, at least, was easy to check. We had the man's name, a rough idea as to the date and the whereabouts of his death. Patience, a little ingenuity and access to the combined resources of the county library service were all that was needed. Ten minutes to be precise, cross-checking the records, followed by quarter of an hour's crash-course on operating the somewhat dilapidated microfiche. And there was the information, spooled up before us in all its grainy detail.

The discovery of the body had been a national sensation, the tabloids revelling endlessly in the gruesome details, the more sober of the dailies searching endlessly for a motive. All of them linked his murder with the Ruth Ellis case, their letter pages fulminating with the pros and cons of capital punishment. Agency photographs, blurred and indistinct, showed the man as he had been in the States, some fifteen years previously. On his own two feet, before an explosion confined him permanently to a wheelchair. Deliberate according to one source; accidental claimed another. Both limbs blown off stated the former; amputated according to the latter. Aged anywhere between fifty-five or seventy-six depending on which of the papers you read. An agnostic; no, an atheist. Wealth acquired or built upon his father's/grandfather's tobacco/sugar/oil empire.

Millionaire/billionaire. Pay your money, take your choice – the press barons' rather.

The local press proved rather more fruitful. Pendarrell House had been a religious retreat bankrolled by the man himself. Quite a bit of damage had been done on the night in question, but nothing of note stolen. The gang, about a dozen in number, had broken in and ransacked the American's apartment. They'd burnt his manuscripts, dumped all the books they could find into the sea and murdered two of his closest 'disciples'. All that remained of Soroyan was the wheelchair. Till his mutilated corpse was recovered a few hours later. Mystic rites, hinted one of the papers. At high tide added another; by moonlight, with Saturn in the ascendency.

Not much else had been discovered about the man himself. Nor could journalists – whether based in London or North Wales – shed much light on the eccentric semi-religious group that he'd founded. We discovered little trace of them in the records. Pendarrell House had become the Penreath Holistic Health Centre – affluent, expensive, access by appointment only, letters of reference also required. Unlikely that either of us would gain admittance, let alone afford one of their exorbitant cures. No point in following up the Liverpool connection either. The churchyard where Derek had been buried was long gone. Grassed over, its tombstones removed; the paperwork untraceable in the county archives. Little to show for our efforts, but all of it adding to what we already knew about the 'dark side' of Jimmy's moon.

Developments on the home front were by now occupying a lot of our time. The library was in the process of moving to new premises and threats of internal reorganisation hung over all our heads. Much the same thing was happening down at the University. For some time now it had depended upon government grants, hand-outs from a decreasing circle of benefactors – most recently the largesse of industry. New faculties were being established, older ones encouraged to develop programmes of a more vocational nature:

sandwich courses, technological transfer, industrial placements and the like. *Liaisons dangereuses* according to Peter, but he need not have worried. Quite the opposite in fact. This 'entrepreneurial' venture in which he was involved, just the kind of forward-looking 'go-out-and-get' initiative those in high places were looking for. 'Networking, not grandstanding' – most commendable. Peter had stalled, not knowing just what it was he'd gone-out-and-got. Nor the language with which they spoke. His hesitation was taken as a ploy for greater remuneration. A research assistant or more office space? Neither of them available. They admired his strategy, though. Just what they'd have done under the circumstances. Worthy of a Chair? And why not make it a personal one? After which…

'It wasn't till then I realised it was the exhibition they were talking about,' he told me later. 'Professor Emeritus. How am I going to explain it to the others? All of them just as qualified and far more deserving.' True, Peter was not among the most eligible or pushy within the faculty. 'And what did they mean by that last bit. After which – what?'

'You poor innocent,' I said, kissing him lightly on the forehead. 'Don't you know, it's a truth universally acknowledged, that a University man in possession of a Chair must be in want of a seat on Council?'

The aftermath was to prove just as rewarding. But for the new spirit of enterprise we might never have met Professor Brady Alegandro. As *Numero Uno* guru of the new management techniques his lecture was obligatory for all members of the academic staff. Peter sat backstage, decked out in full regalia amid a phalanx of departmental Chairs. I'd been placed in the front row, the Vice Chancellor to my right, with an ageing Uncle Henry snoozing a little further down the line. Alongside him a gaggle of University wives. And there was the man himself, up there no fewer than ten feet before us. Shorter than I'd expected, about Peter's age, a scholarly pair of frameless glasses perched between defiantly non-academic sideburns, his dark suit and pale features contrasting with the multi-coloured hoods and gowns arrayed behind him. Ostentatiously detaching the microphone from its stand, he advanced to the edge of the stage, and declared how delighted he was to be with us.

He'd taken *Five Protocols of Progress* as his title, the transatlantic accent – 'Sir Winston Choichall', 'absoid notions', 'take my woid for it' – holding my attention for a while. But: there were preparations for the exhibition to consider… the booking of next year's holiday… what to wear at the graduation ceremony. I made it through to Protocol Three before drifting off.

'Goid's Intent being a prime example…

I was wrenched back suddenly to the present, straining desperately to recall what the man had said. Something about the influence of dynamic individuals on the companies they ran? The force of their moral principle driving the enterprise forward, religion often having a key part to play. Lord Reith, Cadbury, Rowntree for example.

Not to worry; there it was, set out neatly on the screen behind him. With the professor still in full flow: 'O.E.I' – 'Omnipresent Enterprises Incorporated', providing one of the best, but a very rare example: 'that of a woild-wide oiganisation emoiging from the narrowest, most rigid of religious precepts. Those of Goid's Intent. Their founder, christened – I kid you not – Praise the Lord, spent a foitune expunging what he took to be wickedness from the face of the oith but went to the chair for foist-degree moider. Not an oispicious beginning you'd have thoit, considering what Omnipresent has achieved since then. It's success in no way hindered – and here's da poynt – despite retaining those self-same restricted values. Or could it be the ruthlessness with which they've carried them through? Remember the Finnish Markka Conspiracy. The run on the Mexican silver market. The so-called "Outback Shoires Swindle".

'And there was that problem you had with them this side of the pond a few years back. Nothing like it since the dissoilution of the monasteries, but coisting one of my compatriots his life. Pure fabrication accoiding to O.E.I's spokesman; stories put about by their rivals, the kind of thing so many top-noitch oiganisations endoir these days. And I'll go along with it.' His body language told us it was the last thing he'd do. 'Guess I have to considering the moinumental sums they receive in damages.' There was sympathetic laughter from the audience, amid which Brady passed quickly on to Protocol Four.

The man knew more than he was saying, but no point pressing him in the question-and-answer session. He'd only have clammed up. We missed out at the reception as well, the distinguished visitor led from group to group with never a moment to himself. No chance in the toilet either, where Peter spent a good ten minutes discreetly scrubbing his hands. He'd checked out of the hotel by the time we reached it and there was no chance of waylaying his taxi. But we cornered him in the VIP lounge at the airport, his retinue departing and only thirty minutes to spare. Peter relieved him of his hand luggage as I commended the quality of the presentation and together we steered him to a quiet table in the corner. The professor, however, proved as wary as ever. Till a bottle of whisky was purchased; several drams downed.

'All seems far-fetched to me,' I challenged him. 'A leading company, listed on the stock market, controlled by a bunch of maniacs. More like a novel.' I refilled his glass. 'And not a very good one at that.'

'Which is moist people's reaction. Like I say, part of the reason for their success.' Which seemed all we'd get out of him.

Till Peter took a hand. 'A chance of a lifetime, meeting you like this. It would help my career enormously to know more. Some ice perhaps?'

'Best stay well clear of them is my advice. Surprised you've not coight up with them already.' The cubes cracked as the American dropped them in his drink. 'Happy to tell you all I know, but we haven't got much time and moist of it covered in the lecture. Goid's Intent hiding all these years behind a larger, respectable oiganisation. Tiny, anonymous, yet controiling all O.E.I's activities. Thanks to the old man's successor. The son, every bit as bigoted as his father, but a genuine businessman, with a real flair for commoinication. Built himself a woildwide netwoik of contacts; access to market trends, insight into commoicial ventures in all continents. All adding to the wealth he'd inherited.'

Rather more sensational than we'd expected, but not much here we didn't already know. Still, there could be more to come. 'Sounds like the son's a real go-getter.' I replenished Brady's drink. 'Could teach my husband a trick or two by the sound of it – both of us for that matter.'

'Go-getter? That's soitenly one way of putting it.' The American smiled ruefully. 'Driven, more like. Set on cleansing the woild of evil, just like his daddy toit him.' He swirled the dregs of his whisky grudgingly around the glass. 'Clever though, I'll give him that. Ninety-eight percent of Omnipresent's operations legitimate. Raking in the cash, keeping the investors happy. Looking the other way whilst he uses infoimants the woild over to fund the remaining two percent. Which don't bear scrutiny in any language. Finland, Australia, Mexico, like I said in the lecture. To say nothing of his dealings over here. But you'd know about that.'

'Only what we've read in the papers and way before my time. The murdered man an American, you said. Commercial rival was he? Here, let me top you up.'

'The hell he was!' A complete change of tone. 'Goid's Intent hitting pay-doit more like.' Brady scowled into his whisky. 'Discovered their noimber one enemy – the *Antichrist* would you believe it – not fifty miles from where we're now sitting. Tracked down and moidered in cold blood, along with those who'd protected him. Rumoirs, of course. An oiban myth. Same as alligators in the drains, the angels of Mons.' There was real bitterness in his voice. 'What else could it have been with Omnipresent's lawyers having such deep pockets, Goid's Intent so far out of reach? No mention, either, of what was going on behind the scenes. Resignations and demoitions. Police, hoim office, coist guard, the armed soivices – all of them blaming one anoither. With everyone from the toip – and I mean the very toip – down detoimend it should never happen again. Except that it did.'

Now we were getting somewhere. 'You mean there's more?' I asked, replenishing his glass.

'Always is as far as O.E.I's concoined.' There was a tannoy announcement; Brady's flight was called. 'But I've a plane to catch.'

'Best make it quick, then.' I planted my feet on his luggage. We'd come too far to be stymied at the last moment.

Brady glanced desperately from the luggage to the departure board, to Peter, myself, then back to his luggage, obviously weighing the merits of a public tug-of-war, before: 'Hardly woith repeating.' He shrugged a slurred surrender. 'One week Goid's Intent causes mayhem up here in the noith. Public woinings, radio broadcasts, shipping checked, twenty-foir hour watch on airpoits – all the stops pulled ouit. Then, just a few days later, a secoind strike – the one no one's hoid about – down in the south this time. Foices of law and oider left completely in the dark. Some outhouse boint down, that's all that was repoited, and no telling why they were there, what they were after. All rumoirs, like I say, and best forgotten. Now give me my Goddamned luggage and get me out of here.'

Together we made our way across the lounge, Peter in possession of the hand luggage, Brady unsteady on his feet. 'Praise the Lord', 'Goid's Intent', Antichrists – you couldn't make it up,' he muttered. We joined the queue at the boarding gate. 'One day someone will write a Goddamned book about it. Make themsoilves a foitune!'

With which he was gone. Leaving Peter clutching the empty whisky bottle and a scenario, if the rumours were true, that neither of us had considered. Third Class Cottage trashed neither by louts out on a spree, nor the secret army on the rampage but God's Intent. Fitting perfectly with the facts as we knew them; just a few more days, hours even, and it'd have been curtains for Jimmy.

Sending me right back to the diary. I'd spent hours with it over the last few weeks, deciphering just what it was the Squire had written, selecting extracts suitable for inclusion within the exhibition, deciding how best to fit them in with the rest of the material. Left to my own devices this time, with no one to guide me; turning the pages, providing a running commentary, suggesting where I should, and should not look. And I'd come to rather a different conclusion. True, it had rambled, was unintelligible in places. So, too, had a score or so others that I'd read, both published and unpublished, with celebrated authors and playwrights among the worst offenders. The writing grew progressively more difficult to read, but tell me whose doesn't as they grow older. Even so, there was a rough overall coherence to the narrative and, no matter what Giles said, Sir Desmond did seem to have had his wits about him. Those references to Savonarola, for instance; the *auto da fee,* that *satis sapientia.* The way he'd dealt with the MI5 contingent in their shiny black cars with the swept-back mudguards. Capable enough to spot the danger presented by *Mappa Mundi,* of whisking it away into *protective custody.* And sound enough to remember 'where the bodies were buried' when challenged by his superiors.

The rector, though, had acted right out of character. *Codpiece* they'd called him; *doubt if he'd give off much heat* had been Sir Desmond's assessment. Yet here he was *stealing a march;* plotting with others to *get his hands on it with no holds barred;* whilst the Squire must *act quickly* and bring in an ex-commando-like unit to protect it. Unless it was not the picture but the artist who was in danger; not the rector – who *didn't know the half of it* – but a far more sinister gang of *Holy Joes* from whom they were shielding him. I recalled the press coverage of the Pendarrell murders. Those photos of the American academic, wheelchair-bound and tortured. The *Savonarola scenario* was the least Jimmy could expect if ever God's Intent caught up with him. And who might he have turned to if this had been the case? Sir Desmond, whose authority might have been diminished, but who was already deeply in Jimmy's debt; the Squire who, but for his intervention, would have been in even deeper trouble with the authorities. And the diary's last entry: *Pity about the cottage* – regret that its destruction had served as an alibi for the picture's disappearance? Or merely his inability to save Jimmy's home as well as the fugitive himself?

Giles, though, stuck with his original interpretation. The old man had been too frail and vulnerable to take part in such adventures, "going the way of Enid Quintock" to quote him directly. Far more likely, he'd known nothing of it; Jimmy had gone of his own accord.

'He might at least have shown some gratitude,' I complained to Peter later. 'You'd have thought he'd have jumped at the chance to restore something of his father's reputation.'

'Not if you look at it from Giles' point of view.' They'd spent some time together recently, planning the exhibition. 'Our arrival put him in quite a quandary. Wanting to see Jimmy exonerated but anxious to preserve his father's reputation. Affable enough and holding nothing back, but suspicious of us from the outset, thrown by our continually changing stories; playing along to find out just how much we knew. Quite a shock, realizing we were aware of *Mappa Mundi's* existence, that our friend, the embroiderer, already suspected it held wartime secrets. What more might she have said? The picture, though, presented him with a golden opportunity. Take us through events as Jimmy portrayed them, as and where they'd happened, leading directly to the operation centre; diverting attention away from the Squire's peacetime activities. A good deal of one-upmanship involved, as he now admits, deciphering a puzzle that had foxed us, leading us along a route that only he could follow, but I suppose links between *Mappa Mundi* and the auxiliary units were fairly obvious.'

'To the bastions of academe and literature especially,' I recalled, 'as he was at pains to tell us'.

Peter shook his head. 'And he might have succeeded, suggesting Jimmy really *had* been what was it: a "stool pigeon", that he'd betrayed the unit, done "a runner".'

With Giles unaware of the guilt that had hung over Peter all those years. Not till I let it slip. 'A bravura performance,' I said, 'storming off like that,'

'Genuine enough. I don't think I've ever been as angry in my life.'

Bringing Giles to his senses, realizing just how much this meant to Peter. Unable to go through with it and allowing us to read the diary.

'With all that fuss about being there when we did so,' Peter was saying. 'Taking us through it line-by-line; his insistence that the old man was into his dotage almost. Your building him up as a hero undercuts all notions that the Squire was not fully aware of what he was doing. If he'd been that far gone, he'd never have masterminded Jimmy's escape. But, if this really is what happened, then...'

'...he'd have been savvy enough to know precisely what Stapleton was up to.'

'*Catch* 22, isn't that what you call it?'

'Or, as Brady put it...'

'Just another oiban myth.'

But, with the exhibition well-nigh upon us, we had little time to discuss it further.

Chapter Twenty-Nine

Threads

'Here's to her memory. Geraldine always knew there was such a picture. Right from the beginning.' Mildred clinked her glass against Helen's and Giles glanced anxiously about him. It had not been easy persuading him to feature *Mappa Mundi* as a focal point of the exhibition, nor to invite feature writers and art critics from across the cultural spectrum to attend the opening ceremony. He need not have worried; few of them replied, still less had availed themselves of the opportunity.

'Such a shame she couldn't be here to see it.' We'd taken Mildred on a conducted tour of the grounds that afternoon and she stood in front of the picture now, making a great show of scrutinising it, top to bottom.

'Checking it out for clues she might have missed?' I enquired.

'Just searching for that elusive Duchess, my dear. Oops! There I go forgetting myself again! We're going to have to treat him more respectfully, you and I, now he's come up in the world.' She'd turned to Helen. 'No more tales out of school. Glamorous redheads, adolescent crushes – all forgotten. I promise.'

Unlikely. Mildred was not going to forget my youthful indiscretions, never in a hundred years; not if I became Chancellor of the most prestigious university in the land.

'Beats me how you and Geraldine could have known about the picture,' I came in quickly, forestalling any further comments, 'when all you had to go on were deductions from a newspaper article. The name even: *Mappa Mundi*.'

Mildred accepted my flattery as nothing less than her due: 'We made a good team, that's for certain. If there was anything to be known about the man, she'd be bound to hear about it. Depended on me for most of the actual research, of course, not wishing to be recognised around these parts. A natural journalist, though, Geraldine. Talking of which…'

We were being signalled from across the room. The press had arrived and a photographic record was required: Giles for the board of management; myself as executive director; Helen the distaff side of the partnership; chairmen of the parish, district and county councils – all of us gathered before a portrait of Sir Desmond Amberstone, moved from Hall to exhibition centre. By the time we returned, Mildred had disappeared.

'Guesswork, more like,' I said, returning to the previous topic. 'Picking up rumours about *Mappa Mundi* and how it came to be painted, then convincing themselves it must have been destroyed.' We made our way out of the dining room, where a band was getting ready to play. 'And with Geraldine gone I don't suppose we'll ever discover how much she actually knew about it.'

'Maybe Jimmy will show up, let all of us in on the secret.' Something that had been on Helen's mind since our conversation with Brady. 'Could be he's out there watching us right now.'

'Shacked up in the forest, you mean – at eighty plus? Not that we ever got to know just how old he was, nor even the date of his birthday, no matter how much we pestered.'

'What's that got to do with it? Didn't you tell me that out there time stood still?'

Yterdene, she meant. A settlement deep in the forest to which the Jutes had fled following the final Saxon invasion. Living there to this day in a type of perpetual time-warp according to the stories I'd been told as a child. How else had ramblers sometimes caught a glimpse of strangers in old-fashioned attire disappearing into the trees? Or toddlers lost in the forest tell of waking blindfold; being comforted by unfamiliar voices, tended and gently led to safety by unseen hands? How was it that, long into the age of musketry and gunpowder, brand new axes, sharpened to perfection, were discovered embedded in oak or ash; freshly wrought swords of antique design found along its most distant pathways. And why, with the forest all but destroyed, was the sound of metal being beaten into shape sometimes heard echoing across its empty valleys; at sunset, plumes of smoke seen rising skywards, and yet no trace as to their source?

'Along with the screech owls and cockatrices.' Helen shielded her eyes and gazed theatrically mid-distance into the woodland. 'Except Jimmy, of course, had that St Christopher talisman to ward off evil spirits.'

It was at that moment, I swear it, we heard the bell, a steady regular chime. 'Nice touch,' I said, 'ringing *Saint* to mark the opening.'

But here was an anxious Giles hurrying towards us. 'None of my doing, they've been out of commission, waiting for renovation, these last six months. Someone will do themselves an injury if they're monkeying around in there.' And, as he spoke, Jimmy's bell continued to toll.

Down at St Matthias, the constable was equally perplexed. 'Stopped the moment we arrived,' he was telling the rector. 'Door wide open, rope still swinging, but the place deserted and not a soul in sight.'

'The choirboys up to their usual tricks,' intoned the rector.

'Could have been anyone, keeping the church unlocked as the reverend does. Those scoundrels from the youth centre, most like. Knew how to deal with them in my day.' The constable adjusted his helmet. 'And nothing suspicious up at the Hall?'

Giles shook his head and the three of us returned to the festivities.

The rector had been right. Quite obviously a practical joke and anyone could have been responsible, just as the constable suggested. But I had my suspicions. Strange how *Saint* came in on cue, just when Helen led me into a discussion on Yterdene, at the mention of screech owls – the moment she'd shielded her eyes. A signal, it must have been, with Gerundive lurking not too far away. Both of them in it together.

They denied it, of course; have continued to do so. 'Ask not for whom the bell tolls,' was all Helen would say at the time, insisting we double-check all the 'Saintley' haunts that evening.

'A theme park in the making,' I grumbled, as we ducked under the *Parkland Closed* barrier and made our way up Stoyan's Hidden Pathway. Neatly sign-posted, with further directions to *Morgana's Mystic Grotto* and *Bereden's Secret Bunker.* 'And "tricks of the light" to go with them.' A series of multi-coloured mini-lanterns had come suddenly to life, snaking their way along the route we should follow. 'Geraldine must have had a hand in the planning.'

'Solves Jimmy's problem, though, doesn't it? What happens after the folk are dispersed, when their landmarks are uprooted?' Helen had pressed on ahead and stood waiting alongside a *This Way to Tonbert's Stepping-Stones* sign-post. 'The answer's simple: we create new ones.'

I struggled up the hill to join her, wondering what new stunt she'd planned this time.

'But still the same old stories.' Helen chattered away, to herself almost, as I did so. 'The ingredients rather. Love, hate. Hope and despair. Loyalty, betrayal, deceit. The sort of thing you read about in Homer or Dante. Boccaccio. Scheherazade. Grimm. Hans Christian Andersen. My daddy; your Jimmy.' She took both my hands in hers. 'Though I doubt we're ever going to agree about either of them.'

'Nor the music,' I said. Below us the band had struck up,

catches of some rhythmic refrain, straight from the charts, reaching us faintly on a quickening breeze. Miniscule couples had emerged onto the terrace, floodlit for the occasion, and were gyrating like so many puppets. 'And certainly not the dancing.'

'Well, we've always seen things differently, haven't we? Part of the attraction, I suppose.' Helen was snapping her fingers to the beat now. 'The knack you have of separating out everything that happens to you. Schooldays with Miss Quintock, the meeting with Veronica in your youth, then later as Geraldine; Jimmy's stories, his pictures, Squire Desmond's secret army, *Mappa Mundi,* Brady's revelations. Each stored away in a different compartment of your mind. A file-card index almost.' Her arm snaked round my waist. 'Whilst to me they're all of a piece. Like Geraldine's embroidery. I've been thinking a lot about it since her death: individual threads, contrasting colours, different textures. Each one important in itself, adding to the overall effect, but it's not till the end that we realise how each fits in, contributes to the picture as a whole. Like the man says – Kierkegaard, not Jimmy! – we live life forward, understand it backwards.'

Fine, I think, as long as you know when the whole thing's finished; if you're lucky, and the colours don't fade. Or, sticking to her previous analogy, the file-cards aren't shuffled. Even then we find what we want to find, hear what we're accustomed to hear, see what we're used to see, read what we expect to find on the page.

'Each time feeling sure of our facts,' I tell her, 'certain we'd reached the end of the road, confident in our suppositions. When suddenly, out of the blue – an inscription in a book, a meeting with an old flame, a newspaper article long forgotten, the framing of a picture, the backside of a canvas, an American academic – fate, chance, kismet, providence, call it what you like, was on hand, suggesting another route; pointing us in a different, more profitable, direction. "*Just when we were safest,*" in fact.'

Helen comes in on cue:

'... there's a sunset touch,
A fancy from a flower-bell, someone's death,
A chorus-ending from Euripides,
And that's enough for fifty hopes and fears, –
The grand Perhaps'

– the few lines of Browning she could tolerate.

'And not a bad epitaph for Jimmy,' I say.